SEAWEED
RISING

Also by Rob Magnuson Smith

The Gravedigger

Scorper

SEAWEED RISING

RISING

ROB MAGNUSON SMITH

SANDSTONE PRESS

First published in Great Britain in 2023 by
Sandstone Press Ltd
PO Box 41
Muir of Ord
IV6 7YX
Scotland

www.sandstonepress.com

ISBN: 978-1-914518-28-7
ISBNe: 978-1-914518-29-4

Sandstone Press is committed to a sustainable future.
This book is made from Forest Stewardship Council® certified paper.

Cover design by Heike Schüssler
Typeset by Biblichor Ltd, Scotland
Printed and bound in Great Britain
by TJ Books Limited, Padstow, Cornwall

For Leslie

'We feel the floods surging over us, we sound with him to the kelpy bottom of the waters; seaweed and all the slime of the sea is about us!'

Herman Melville

MANFRED

The village lay on the south coast of Cornwall. Every day the fog came over the ploughed fields and sucked at what lived beneath. Gweek would have been called a fishing village, if there were any fish or fishermen left.

The college had offered Manfred a teaching position in remedial English. He'd done this work in the past. He had no children to look after and no partner to accompany him to the restaurants he no longer liked. It seemed the last stage had arrived, the time for checking out. Others in Cornwall had made similar decisions. A few weeks' holiday had turned into retirement and death. He saw them in Falmouth and in Penzance. He saw them in St Austell and in Truro. They roamed the cobbled alleyways, pubs and waterfronts – aging alcoholic surfers, drug-addled Londoners and terminal cancer patients.

Manfred still considered himself different. Yes, his eyes had developed dark tunnels where the flecks of blue had been. Yes, he was past fifty, but he wasn't yet dead.

He found a stone cottage overlooking the Helford River. It was technically a holiday let, but the cottage hadn't been occupied in years. There was no central heating and the tile roof leaked. Inside, there was a strange creeping mist intent on crushing what was left of his soul. The place did have its attractions – and a view, over the back garden, of an abandoned fish factory. The garden itself was pleasantly overgrown. A pine tree attracted birds, which in turn attracted the neighbour's cat. An old bathtub sat in the middle of the grass, with weeds and wildflowers growing inside.

Gweek lay in an inter-tidal zone, where many lived on houseboats. The smell of burning wood mingled with the smell of kelp. When the mist cleared, you could see upriver past a network of rickety wooden walkways. Some just ended over the water, like gangplanks. Plenty of ship carcasses lay about. When the tide came in, their rotting hulls rose high out of the mud. From his bedroom upstairs, Manfred stared straight through the missing planks. At low tide, tiny fish surfaced in the rock pools and sandflats, flopped in the beds of eelgrass and calcified maerl. The lucky ones spawned quickly in the dark. The unlucky were eaten by the kingfishers, egrets and oystercatchers.

A few farms surrounded the village. They seemed to be entirely comprised of collapsed trees and sunken wet fields. Behind the cottage, in the surrounding wood, the oak grew gnarled and twisted. These trees were ancient. They ranged from light grey to dark, almost black, even in sunshine.

Manfred went on walks to tiny damp hamlets with names like Goonhallow and Ponsharden. Hedgerows rose high along the footpaths. Empty shells of barns listed in the mud. Meadows of daffodils, come January, were picked by Eastern European workers. They lived in temporary trailer camps in the fields, surrounded by more fields, with no designated roads leading to them. What roads there were curved and climbed, then suddenly dropped. Men with beards pushed prams behind tall iron gates that concealed private drives. Manfred noticed seaweeds lurking in the grass, and more heaped under hedges. Overhead, ancient oak and pine grew along the streams and creeks leading down to the Helford. After a heavy rain, these trees looked like inverted kelp beds swaying in waves of wind. All the skies over Cornwall looked like former oceans.

Gweek's only tourist attraction was a seal sanctuary. For something to do, Manfred joined the locals on their regular beach clean. He caught a bit of local gossip. Someone mentioned that a start-up was moving into the old fish factory. A younger man, after noticing Manfred catch his breath, pointed out the red phone box with the village defibrillator.

There was plenty to be thankful for. What kind of person didn't acknowledge it? In the city where Manfred last lived, he had a bus and two trains to catch, and if each of these ran on time, he made it to his first class in an hour and a half. Commuting to Gweek College meant opening his back garden gate for a short walk down the beach.

The campus consisted of four single-floor office buildings and a communal patch of grass. Students could take anything from hairdressing to animal handling. The staff were roughly half his age. Hardly any of them lived in Gweek.

On the first day, he met Simon. He was on the shorter side, with a small round head and wispy hair that wafted back and forth like grass in the wind. Simon also taught remedial English. They ran into each other in the corridor, heading into adjacent classrooms.

'Manfred's an interesting name,' Simon said. 'Not often you hear that.'

Each time he had to introduce himself, Manfred heard the same thing. Simon was still waiting under the fluorescent lights, as if for an explanation.

'It's a poem by Byron. My parents thought it would inspire me, I suppose.'

'Ah.' Over the top of Simon's floating hair, a gust of wind and rain came through an open window. 'If you wanted,' he went on, 'you could just go by Fred?'

Manfred went over to close the window. What a piece of magic it would be, if all his problems could be sorted by changing his name. Out in the courtyard some seaweeds had washed up from the last storm. He shuddered at the way they lay there, gathered in the wet. There would be more soon – he could smell them coming.

Maybe, he decided, he *would* go by Fred. It would be a rebrand that took away the curses. By the time he'd turned around, Simon had gone.

Falmouth was the nearest town. He took a bus, wandered the high street, made the obligatory effort.

Instead of sandwiches for sale, there were pasties. Instead of plain shirts, there were ones with blue horizontal stripes. The

4

art galleries sold pictures of boats and seagulls. Noticing these things, while falling in step with the other tourists, gave Manfred a dry and hollow sensation in his stomach.

At least Falmouth had fresh air. Gweek lay near the mouth of the Helford's brackish waters, but Falmouth had sandy beaches and blue water. Cliffs and coastal paths overlooked the sea. The docks were busy with workers. Cafés, restaurants and pubs dotted the waterfront. In the near distance, the metallic blue hull of HMS *Echo* stretched along the harbour. He'd read about this vessel in the *Falmouth Packet*. She had returned from the Indian Ocean on her search for the famous disappearing passenger plane, MH370.

He ducked into the nearest pub. He ordered a pint and overheard the ship's crew unburdening themselves at the bar. They had spent twelve weeks in four-hour rotations, pointing their binoculars at the empty waves. Their ship apparently had the world's most advanced sonar equipment, and they'd failed. He waited for a lull in their conversation.

'That pilot must have been a professional suicide,' he suggested. 'The best ones, they simply disappear.'

The crew looked up. Their eyes quickly discovered the depths of his tunnels. 'That's just a theory,' an officer said. His tongue plunged into his pint glass. He carried that particular arrogance of being in command of something small.

'Who are you?' another asked. His own eyes reflected the grey-black surface of the ocean.

'Fred.' He watched the man closely for a reaction. 'Short for Manfred.'

'Why don't you just go by Manfred, then? Much nicer than plain old Fred.'

The others laughed. They were still laughing as he took his pint outside to the pier. There were families sitting at picnic tables with fish and chips. Other benches were occupied by men, all of them alone. Some had brought their pints. Still others were sitting under the railings, smoking and staring out at the water.

Cornwall had long been a magnet for invasive species. It was a promontory, a catch-basin at the confluence of waterways. Manfred had been drawn there for the same reason. Into its harbours came the desperate and the mercenary, the dissolute sex tourists and mackerel fishermen, the shipping industrialists and legless military veterans, the university students and unemployed graduates, all of them clinging desperately to these seafront bars like barnacles. Now he was among them.

There was no special shame in it. The country had eroded over the centuries, a nation rotting from the inside while its cliffs tumbled into the sea. He was at the edge of the pavement before the final brush of the broom. Men with cigarettes, men with pints. He'd seen them on the coastal paths, standing under trees or staring down at waves that urged them to jump.

At the end of the pier he stopped. A young family was regarding him from a distance. The parents were keeping their infant safe. Boy or girl it was impossible to tell, enclosed in its pretty red carriage. Manfred raised his glass as they pushed the child away. He couldn't fault their caution. It was as if they saw his seaweedy ancestors alongside him in ghostly superimposition. There were always seaweeds at the turnings and seaweeds at the crossroads, their tangled shapes a mirror of his thoughts.

He went to the railing and stared down at the water. He could hear the crew of the *Echo* spilling out of the pub. Across the harbour, boats of all sizes were creating eddies in the water. The seaweeds were coming closer, into the regions between his ears. Soon they would cling to the underside of his chin. Plant holdfasts between his teeth.

The next time Manfred ran into Simon, he suggested a pint after work. He had been in Gweek over a month. At night, it got lonely in the cottage.

'Can't. I've a long drive,' Simon said.

Manfred nodded. The car culture had caught up with him, even in Cornwall. 'Where's home?'

'Bristol.'

'You drive from Bristol – every day? It has to be three hours.'

'Easy teaching jobs aren't easy to come by.' Simon was already jangling the keys in his pocket. 'And I wouldn't want to live in this crap town, would I?'

As Simon continued down the corridor, Manfred went to the window to check. There were more, just as he'd predicted.

He heard a cough and turned. It was Richard, the department head. He had on a big brown hat with a wide brim, as if he was ready for the Australian outback. He wore a waistcoat and his long black hair was in a ponytail.

'Hello. Cup of tea?'

'All right,' Manfred said.

They went together to the staff cafeteria. Manfred had first met Richard at his interview. They had since chatted once or twice. Maybe one day, he thought, Richard would invite *him* for a pint.

The staff cafeteria was a cramped little room with white plastic tables and chairs. There was a small, sauce-stained fridge and a microwave continually reheating Chinese. Over the sink someone had hung a sign: WASH UP AFTER YOURSELF!

'Settling in okay?' Richard asked, as they sat down.

'Everyone's been really nice,' Manfred lied.

'We pride ourselves in maintaining a good work environment.'

They sat in silence as other teachers and administrators came and went. Richard took off his hat. While they had their tea, he re-tied his hair so the little tendrils above his forehead were free to move around. Manfred decided that he didn't want a pint with Richard, even if he asked.

'We really hope that you'll make yourself available for open days.' Richard pushed a printed schedule across the table. 'Here are the next ones.'

Manfred looked at them. 'All Saturdays?'

'You weren't at the others. Still settling in, I expect. Staff are *encouraged* to attend. The college plays a vital role in this community.'

Manfred nodded. Behind him, the microwave door opened and closed, the beeps began and the rumbling heat penetrated the leftovers. He didn't know exactly when it happened, but after a while he found himself alone again. This time Simon was standing at the microwave.

Manfred got up. 'Hey. Do you go to those open days?'

'God, no. Waste of time.'

'Richard hasn't asked you?'

'I commute from Bristol, mate.' Simon was staring at his kung pao shrimp, rotating in plastic. 'Last place I'm going to spend my Saturdays is bloody Gweek. Dick knows that.'

'You call him Dick?'

'Keep calling him Richard, if I were you. He's got you going, has he? The only reason is you're local.' Simon leaned closer and lowered his voice. 'Dick's *very* local.'

'I don't understand.'

Simon made a face. 'He went to Oxford so he could come down here and tell everyone what it *means* to be local. He's about as middle-class as it comes.'

That afternoon, walking home along the sand, Manfred stopped under the lights of the fish factory. It was a hulking cement building with downspouts over the rocks, like gargoyles venting rain from their mouths. He decided he would work as hard as could be expected. He would shop at the weekend market and attend open days. And at nights, from his bedroom window, he would learn to relish his factory view against the darkening outline of the sea.

Each morning, as the neighbour's cat watched from a distance, more birds flew into his pine tree. He never saw them leave – as if they'd been permanently trapped. The branches filled and sagged under the weight of their bodies.

These birds had been lured into his garden by the sound of the wind thrumming across the sea. It was a sound both relaxing and frightening, like the sleep-inducing cacophony of a pumping heart. Manfred realised he had been lured by it as well. All his life he had been made almost deaf by the din of cars, appliances and commerce. In Cornwall there was a silence that trained him to be alert to nature. He jumped at the sound of an automobile. Whenever his neighbours came and went, he knew it.

Maybe it was boredom that made him start collecting on the shore. Later, when the worst arrived, he realised this explanation was not sufficient.

There were lots of things to collect – driftwood, old fishing nets, rusted bottle caps. He'd heard of a refuse island the size of Texas floating in a gyre of the north Atlantic. It was conceivable some of that had found its way to Gweek. Seemingly inanimate objects were teeming with life. Tiny sand flies had found a home in the driftwood. The fishing nets were draped with mussels. Even bottle caps carried plankton.

As a boy, on a family holiday to the seaside, he'd been mesmerised by washed-up seaweeds after a storm. He remembered that first smell, and the repulsion. Flies hovered. Seagulls fought to get nearer. It seemed the seaweeds were both alive and dead. Soon, others came trudging out of the mist, carrying metal detectors like outstretched swords, and waved them over the sea's deposits. They wore headphones and waited for the beep.

With their bare hands they separated the thick vegetal masses for buried fish hooks, tin cans, corroded motherboards. How lonely, he'd thought at the time, these people were. Now it was him.

Manfred carried his finds to his back garden. He made a little menagerie out of the driftwood and bottle caps. On the back of a metal chair he draped the mussel-laden fishing net. From a distance it looked like his grandfather's cardigan. One morning he found the right half of a pair of sneakers, and by the afternoon the sea had given him a left one. He put both shoes under the chair and pretended he had company.

The bathtub looked ready for an occupant. He cleared out the weeds and wildflowers and gave the surface a good scrub. Up in the pine tree, the birds watched him work.

It wasn't long after when he found his kelp. Walking along the sand, he spotted a long, rubbery Bullwhip. The specimen was fully intact, bobbing in the shallows like a beached seal. The big round bladder looked like a head. He waded into the water and got his hands on the thing. It was unusual to find a Bullwhip in Cornish waters, let alone one of this size. It was heavy, but he managed to hold it out by the shoulders as if to prove he was the boss.

Manfred had seen a photo of himself as an infant, staring up at a carousel of algae over his crib. Later his parents gave him a picture book on the various plants of the sea. He'd liked one story of an injured gull that had survived for weeks on a floating seaweed nest. The bird had drifted the Mediterranean, across

11

the Strait of Gibraltar, around Britain to the north Atlantic, all the way to the Arctic Ocean, where it was last witnessed leaping toward the glaciers. Now as he stood in the shallows with the Bullwhip, Manfred wondered what combination of forces brought it to Cornwall.

He dragged the Bullwhip back home along the sand. In his back garden he lay it flat inside the tub. The neighbour's cat came over to watch. Manfred filled the tub with water from the garden hose, and slowly the kelp bobbed to the surface. It lifted its round head and seemed to look about.

As Manfred continued to collect, he expanded his operation to the front garden. From the window of his sitting room, after adding something new, he watched the passers-by as they stopped to see what he'd added. If they noticed him watching, they moved on. It became necessary to hide upstairs in the empty second bedroom, behind the half-drawn curtain. Other-wise, how would he know what they made of the bright blue swimming goggles he'd placed around the plastic pumpkin? Not to mention his growing arrangement of carrier bags, flat-tened and tacked to the fencing?

Most people didn't bother to say anything. Then one morn-ing, hiding behind the curtain, he overheard a man say to his wife, 'What a load of old junk.' He spoke loudly, as if to make sure Manfred could hear. 'I hope he comes to his senses and clears it away.'

Not long after, Richard invited him for a chat in his office. 'One of our parents has mentioned your garden,' he said, settling back in his chair. Under his waistcoat, the dark hairs on his pot belly were visible between the buttons of his white shirt.

'Oh?'

'Normally – well, we'd just get on with it. Eccentricities of teachers, that sort of thing. But things have changed. We are public figures, after all.'

'What did they say?'

Richard shrugged and tucked his fingers into his waistcoat pockets. 'These days, we do have to consider the college a business. Customers can go elsewhere.'

'My garden isn't good for business.' Manfred glanced around Richard's office. The expedition hat hung on the back of his door, near a framed photo on the wall. It showed Richard dressed as a knight for a Renaissance fayre. 'Is that what you're saying?'

'Don't take it personally. Sometimes, we have to placate people.'

'Of course.' Sitting there, Manfred started to feel flushed. 'I'll be happy to take that junk away – getting to be a nuisance anyway.'

That weekend, he hired a removal van. He divided everything in the garden into its proper container. The driftwood went with the fencing, the tin cans with the crusty bottle caps, the fish net with the sneakers and other textiles, the goggles with the plastic bags. Everything he'd collected once had a life, and now that they were all certifiably dead, it was time for burial. After he'd taken everything to the recycling centre, his garden looked barren.

There was only one thing that didn't fit into a category, one keepsake from the beach he didn't return. The kelp had never *really* seemed dead. It moved in its tub almost independently, especially in heavy rain.

That night, Manfred sat at his bedroom window. Outside there was the thick slanting mist the locals called mizzle. The white tub gleamed in his garden. Now that it was alone, the kelp was free to wriggle about and splash its blades in the water. When the wind from the direction of the sea howled over the gate, the kelp seemed to rise out of the tub and listen.

Whenever he watered the plants, he watered the kelp as well. It was a big beast. He counted ninety-six little suckers on each of its eighteen appendages. The Bullwhip didn't appear to be dying – though it clearly had *been* dead, or close to it, when he'd retrieved it from the shallow waters. It needed saltwater for its nutrients, not fresh water from the hose. Early each morning he took two buckets down to the sea and brought them back full. When he poured the buckets in, the kelp bobbed its head with gratitude under the cascading water.

He looked up his specimen in the most definitive field guide, *The Future of British Seaweeds*. It had been years since he'd browsed through his copy, and he re-read the opening to the Introduction:

The number of known seaweeds expands each year, making each guide obsolete. This is why our title has an eye to the future. Even the first phycologist William Henry Harvey would be astounded at the hundreds if not thousands of new species discovered since his death in 1866. Naturalists have long depended on the assistance of amateur collectors for classification and analysis. This book would not have been possible without the many volunteers collecting specimens in our own waters and abroad. Indeed native seaweeds have recently been found roaming as far afield as the Arctic! The consequences of these findings are still being understood, and the future of British seaweeds in many ways reflects those brave souls determined to find them.

Manfred thumbed through the pages divided into greens and browns and reds. The reds were the oldest. Greens were found everywhere – in the soil, travelling in the air, embedded in the rocks and snow, even matted in polar bear hair. He stopped at his favourite brown, the Oyster Thief. This seaweed was named for its ability to float a young oyster out to sea by attaching itself to the bottom of its shell, retaining gas and releasing it all at once to launch into the waves.

His other favourite green was the *Volvox*, which formed hollow balls and moved through water by rolling. Most of its cells were for feeding, swimming and beating the water with their flagella to make the colony spin. Because this algae reproduced asexually, the mating cells did so only as an insurance policy. As Manfred studied the enlarged photo, with its bright green balls rolling inside its luminous circular membrane, he wondered if certain seaweeds had affected his own life decisions.

He used to be convinced of this. At university he'd studied botany and developed an unnatural fixation – a crippling, visceral compulsion – for handling seaweeds. Every morning he would drive to the seaside and wade the tide pools. He ran his fingers through the Dabberlocks and wireweed. Sometimes he chose remote coves to avoid being seen. He couldn't stop thinking about them arriving in wave after wave. These thoughts, over time, interfered with his relationships. Only later, after he'd successfully weaned himself from his worst seaweed compulsions, did he understand the cause of it all. It was the dark and deadly space. Between plants and animals there loomed alien regions, unspeakable and inchoate, drifting in the gulf between the known and the unknown. This territory stretched over a billion years. And within the gulf, as if waiting to pounce, lay seaweeds.

He had been right about the Bullwhip he'd found. The field guide indicated that he'd acquired something very rare for British waters. The official name of the kelp was *Nereocystis luetkeana* – mermaid's bladder.

The Future of British Seaweeds had been compiled by Mary-Margaret Dennison, the country's leading phycologist. She claimed the species in his bathtub was mostly found in the Pacific Northwest of the United States. More recently it had been spotted out of its range in the southern Atlantic and Mediterranean, off the coast of Africa. These specimens could grow over forty metres long. Past civilisations had used it as a trumpet.

Glancing out the window, Manfred thought of the journey his kelp made across the Strait of Gibraltar, where the powerful levant could have blown it west against the rocks. It could have washed ashore and turned into a crusty brittle thing, properly dead. Only this one hadn't washed ashore. It had sailed by its moveable blades, leaving African waters to the south coast of Portugal and Spain, then the western shores of France, before continuing north from Brittany to Cornwall. The journey would have been hazardous, the chances of survival slim. Any number of creatures could have eaten it. So many vessels plying the crowded waterways could have sucked the seaweed into its engines. In his wonderment Manfred clutched the pages of his book and studied the damp plaster under his leaking roof. His Bullwhip had found a way to survive, to keep on going despite the odds, as if on a mission to find him.

'I've got an early meeting with Dick tomorrow,' Simon said, in the cafeteria. 'I'm not driving back and forth to Bristol twice. So I found a hotel.'

'Oh? What are you going to do in Gweek?'

'There's a pub here, isn't there?'

'There is one, I think. I don't know how good it is.'

'You don't? What the hell have you been *doing* for the past eight weeks?'

Manfred wasn't about to tell him. He'd avoided his village pub because he couldn't bear the idea of walking in alone, and getting marked as desperate.

'Yeah, there's *one*.' Simon was already checking his phone. 'The Ship? Fuck me. Imaginative name, Cornish pub.'

They met that evening. The pub was packed for folk-music night – all the tables were full. 'The last thing I want tonight is local colour,' Simon said, as they took their pints to the corner. The walls were decorated with nautical instruments, anatomical sketches of fish, photos of wrecks. Across the room, a large group of younger people were impromptu dancing in front of the musicians.

'I'll just stay for the one,' Simon said.

Manfred nodded. The new faces, the smell of the roaring fire, the moving bodies and exposed skin – as the ale took hold, he started to separate from his anxieties. 'We could manage a bit longer.'

'I can't stand folk music,' Simon said. He'd changed from his work outfit to an open-necked silk shirt and a gold chain.

'You have a girlfriend back in Bristol?'

'God, no.' Simon scowled. 'What would I want with that?' He stood with his legs wide and his pointy shoes aimed at the door. 'The last thing *I* want, mate, is to be manacled. No matter how relaxed they might seem, the next thing you know they're moving in. Then, kids – always the hidden threat.'

'You're not interested?'

'What?' Simon stuck out his chest. His gold chain gleamed. 'A shedload of brats?'

They stood there a while, Manfred wanting to stay, Simon gulping his pint. The musicians announced a break between songs. Manfred noticed a woman near the fire looking over at them. She was pretty. Plus she was making her way over, chatting to people she knew. She had a floral dress and auburn hair.

'Sorry,' she said, twirling suddenly toward them. 'Aren't you the one who had that art installation in your garden?'

18

Manfred's mouth rose at the corners. 'You saw it?'

'Ruth,' she said, holding out her hand. 'That garden was quite something. What happened to it?'

'I took it down. Recycled the thing.'

'What's this?' Simon edged closer. Ruth smiled at him, and his eyes jumped away.

'My friend Simon,' Manfred said. 'He was eager to leave . . .'

'I'm not a fan of mandolins and harmonicas.'

Ruth laughed. 'That's the warm-up.' She put her hand on his arm. 'Maybe you have to test it out, stay for the next group.'

Simon headed to the bar to buy a round. When he came back, they all found a table. There began the shift in his attention. Ruth had been an art student at Falmouth University. She was from Buckinghamshire, not far from where Simon had grown up. Weirdly, they actually knew people in common. Ruth was doing what Falmouth graduates seemed good at – working odd jobs, sacrificing what she'd thought were career ambitions to stay in Cornwall. This place, she said with confidence, trapped people. Especially if they were lucky enough to make proper long-term decisions. Simon kept moving his stool closer.

The next musicians gathered. They played with authority, and much louder. Manfred became uncomfortably aware of himself. When Simon or Ruth addressed him, he couldn't quite hear – it was the music, it was the scraping of his nerves. Then, when he was getting the next round, he came back to an empty table. Simon and Ruth had moved over to the fire to dance. She was slightly taller than he was, and his arms fit exactly around her waist.

Manfred sat alone a bit longer. He drank his beer and felt himself getting drunk. Faces turned in his direction, and he needed to retreat. He stood up and wound his way through the narrow passageways between all the dancers.

Outside The Ship, the damp had set in. He had returned to the mizzle. He walked back along the sand as the guitars and mandolins faded behind him. The former fish factory caught the light along the water. It stood in the distance, compressing the stars and moonlight into its dingy metal roof. This was it, Manfred told himself. He was done going out. The nightmare of meeting people, and placing his desires at their disposal, was officially over. He came through the back garden. He avoided eye contact with the kelp and went straight to bed.

The music was still in his ears. He could picture Simon dancing, shirt unbuttoned and gold chain flashing. Perhaps he would invite Ruth back to his hotel. All night Manfred would have to think of this – the younger man getting the prize.

His thoughts abused him as he lay on his side with his face hidden in the darkness. The two of them, kelp and man, had been delivered to each other. It was why he'd sensed a connection each time he brought the Bullwhip seawater, or sat beside it in the garden. This kelp was the creature *he* would have been, had his ancestors stayed in the ocean. And the Bullwhip, looking at him, seemed to imagine what it might have been, had its ancestors moved ashore.

The night grew darker, the view from his bedroom window more obscure. It was the sea fret. It was the mizzle and sheets of mist. Finally he got out of bed and went to the window. In the distance, the foghorn sounded. The back garden gathered under the thickening mist. He could hear something calling inside the waves.

He put on his clothes. He went downstairs and trudged outside, across the grass. The mist had turned heavy – soon his shirt and trousers were soaking wet. It didn't matter. It was pleasant to surrender himself to the elements. He went to the tub and sat on the edge. For a long time he studied the water and waited for the kelp to surface.

The next morning he couldn't look at himself in the mirror. He was too ill even to think of breakfast. He delayed the inevitable until the last minute, when he crept into the back garden as if an intruder.

It was a clear morning. The tide was out. In his coat and hat, he came tentatively toward the tub. The grass bore evidence of a struggle – footprints, torn soil, mud. He kept walking. He headed for the gate and pushed out any memories that lingered.

At work, in the cafeteria, Simon was bleary-eyed, ebullient, still slightly drunk. 'Who knew,' he asked Manfred, 'there'd be a woman like that here? I mean, Gweek? Mate, I'm going to need a lot of coffee today.'

'You get back to your hotel late, then?'

'Never checked in. Went straight to hers.'

Manfred looked quickly around at the empty tables and chairs. 'But this is a small village. You'll have to dodge her now.'

'Why would I want to do that?'

'You mean, you want to see her *again*?'

'We've already planned it.'

Manfred moved over to the microwave. He stared into it, though there was nothing inside. 'Good for you,' he managed.

'What happened to *you* last night?' Simon joined him near the sink, fumbling with the kettle and instant coffee. 'Ruth had friends there, you know. She might have hooked you up . . .'

Manfred dragged himself to his classroom. His students were all waiting. Their rucksacks beside their chairs, they sat behind open laptops and the glow of phones.

'Good morning,' Manfred said. He switched on the overhead lights, and as the fluorescents flickered across the ceiling, his students sat up. They almost looked like dormant seaweeds. A few greens, even – there were roughly a hundred in the British Isles. They would be primarily freshwater, and some from subtidal brackish zones.

'Today,' he said, 'we'll be going over your last essays.'

He reached into his briefcase. He'd marked them up and planned to read the best aloud as a sort of encouragement.

'Nicely done,' he told the green mossy algae whose work he'd most admired. She sat patiently under his gaze like the interwoven mat of an Irish saltmarsh.

He took out her essay, but the print seemed to separate on the page. It was difficult to distinguish the words. When he looked up, more seaweeds lay in front of him. The big brown kelps were clumped at the back, their web-like holdfasts anchoring them.

'A slight headache . . .' He squeezed the bridge of his nose. Slowly, the printed words on the page returned.

'Sir?'

Manfred looked up. Toward the front, one of them had its hand up. This thing was definitely of the red variety. Wet ribs and veins glistened along its arm.

'Yes?'

'Will we be getting the essays back, then?'

He smiled. It was probably a red sea leaf, with its narrow blades and conspicuous ribs. The reds were the oldest, first to live and first to die. It was hard to know, exactly, if life was the progenitor of seaweeds or the other way around.

'Yes, you've done good work.' The students shifted in their seats as he passed among them, bobbing as if buffeted by the waves.

His life consisted of work and coming home to the kelp. In the evenings, he shared with it the anecdotes of his day – students who had been particularly difficult, run-ins with Richard and the bureaucratic nonsense of a teacher's life. The Bullwhip never interrupted. It maintained a lovely silence, broken only by the occasional ripple of its unfolding blades.

At last a Saturday arrived that wasn't an open day. He was free, as they said, to *kill time*. It was a phrase that always came into his head when he most dreaded it.

Clouds passed over the window. For over an hour he stayed in bed and stared at the sky, gripped by old fears. His dark urges at times became indomitable. Two things became increasingly clear: nobody would care if he was dead, and the natural world would only prosper if humans were gone.

The sun climbed over the roof. Manfred remembered that he was out of food. He didn't *have* to eat. If he stayed in bed, if he didn't eat or drink or do anything – he would, eventually, expire.

For another full hour, he lay there, doing his best to stay still. He could sense the Bullwhip out in the tub, watching him, challenging him to stay put and make good on his intentions. Finally he couldn't take it any longer. He got dressed and left by the front door so the kelp wouldn't see him.

In the past, all it took to get over his fears was leaving bed. Getting outside, walking amongst society as if he had big plans.

The farmers' market took place in the car park of the Village Hall. As he came through the crowds with his basket, new sensations fired like pinpricks across his skin. There was the fisherman selling Styrofoam tubs of cockles and whelks. There was the bearded man in his tweed jacket selling oysters. And best of all, there was the pretty cheese vendor. She had her arms exposed to the sun and stood behind a row of paper plates with cheese samples on toothpicks. Manfred visited her stall twice. He kept the toothpicks behind his ears after he'd used them.

He purchased his lettuce greens, his potatoes and onions, his mackerel. These were his staples, and he shopped for them with his eyes averted to avoid the embarrassment of recognising anyone. He visited the cheese lady a third time and splurged on the most expensive kind. Then, without anything further to buy, he did something unusual, something he hadn't bothered to do in quite a while. He lingered.

At the edge of the market, a woman was sitting on a wall playing a guitar. Beyond the market, boats bobbed at high tide on their moorings. It was a surprisingly warm day. He realised he hadn't once thought of the kelp. Not far away, a small crowd had formed in front of a new stall. It was next to the one for sea salt. A sign said, *Cornish Seaweeds*. He came closer. A woman was handing out free samples. There were lots of colours and kinds. People were trying the dried samples. As he stood in the queue the woman looked up and stared at him with her mouth parted. She had flat, almost fatally flat blue eyes and long straight blonde hair tucked behind her ears.

'Like to try some?' With her hand she made a sweeping motion over the little tubs.

'Thanks.' What's happening to me, Manfred thought, each second I spend looking at her, I want more than ever to live. 'Thanks, but I shouldn't.'

'Why not? On a diet?' She picked up one of the sealed tubs and shook it like a Spanish maraca. 'The bladderwrack's yummy. Plenty of health benefits.'

'Oh?'

'Loads of iodine. It'll go well with that lettuce in your basket. Everyone likes the purple dulse. And the nori, of course.'

'What's your favourite?'

'Plain brown kelp suits me. Good for muscle tone.' She poured some into her hand. She ate it while her eyes travelled over him. 'I'll be honest with you. I notice people who age well.'

'You're quite the salesperson.'

Manfred could feel it happening. He was being pulled in, drawn into the maelstrom. She was wearing shorts, he noticed, and despite himself he glanced at the shape of her legs.

The old urge – for life, for happiness – was too much. He started to leave. Someone was behind him, waiting to get at the samples.

'I can't be that good,' she said, 'if you're making off without a purchase.'

He turned. 'Let me ask you something. What are you doing in Gweek?'

'I could ask you the same question.'

She was flirting with him. It was the way she looked aside as she waited, as if she knew the answer. 'I'm a teacher at the college.'

'You like it?'

'The teaching part of being a teacher is good.'

She looked calmly around the market with her flat blue eyes. 'It's pretty quiet here, isn't it?'

'I've never liked a city. I prefer it rural.'

'That explains the toothpicks behind your ears.'

An elderly man with a little white dog came over. He nudged Manfred as he leaned over the samples. 'You with that start-up in the fish factory? What have you got here, seaweeds?'

'The future of British seaweeds,' Manfred said. Both man and dog looked up at him.

'Cornish seaweeds,' she corrected, as the man tried one of the samples. 'That one's sea spaghetti. Good for your joints. And this kombu's a good mixing seaweed . . .'

'This purple one's tasty,' the man said, picking at his teeth. 'Nice and chewy. What's it called?'

'Dulse.' She glanced at Manfred and made her eyes large. 'Helps virility.'

26

At that, the man moved along. Manfred stayed, unable to leave the booth.

'Here.' She sprinkled dulse into her hand and held it out.

Then he did it, he ate the dulse right out of her palm. It carried a strong flavour, almost like he was eating himself.

'What do you think?'

'Not bad.' He reached into his pocket and paid. 'You *are* good at sales.'

'Oh, yeah. I make a lot of money for other people.'

She put his dulse into a paper bag stamped with a bladderwrack logo. She wrote on the back of a card and slipped it inside.

'Watch out for any unexpected boosts in virility. If so, make sure you ring that number straight away.'

NORA

She hadn't been completely honest with Manfred – she'd known about him for some time. She'd just been waiting for the opportunity to say hello.

A couple of weeks back, cycling to work, Nora had stopped on the road above the beach. Down on the shore, a man fully dressed was wading straight into the shallow water. Tall and broad-shouldered, stooped like a professor examining the sea's offerings, he seemed unbothered by the surf. His coat hung open despite the weather. Nora didn't mind a bit of the cold herself. She liked to feel directly the wind on her thighs, the sting of the sun and wet of the rain. Strange – looking at this man on the beach, she felt an immediate desire. It was his rangy movements, the way he seemed to abandon himself to the sea. She squinted. The mist carried a glare. Every morning brought the same whiteness, the same blank expanse of sky. The metal roof of the old fish factory where she worked, glinted under a sun you couldn't quite see.

'Caught you staring at him.'

Pete waved as he came up the road toward her. He had on a thick coat and stocking cap. He was technically her boss.

Her bike between her legs, she moved sideways so that he could get by. Pete stopped and followed her gaze. 'It's that nutter. The one who collects rubbish for his garden.'

Nora plunged her hands into her coat pockets. And then she'd done it, before she could stop herself – linked the man in her mind with the last one she'd loved, along with the smell of the sea and white gulls. These days seagulls were like vultures and preferred anything dead.

Pete had come closer. 'I heard they hired him at the college and can't seem to get rid of him. God, what's he got now?'

Nora laughed. With both hands, the man was dragging a piece of kelp out of the sea. Then she saw what kind it was. The stipe was long and rubbery. It must have been fifteen metres long. 'How odd. Looks like a piece of Bullwhip.' She shielded her eyes from the glare.

'Where in the world's he going with it?'

The man looked up from a distance, as if overhearing them. His eyes flashed and darkened, like a lighthouse. Then he continued dragging the kelp down the beach.

Nora's memories stirred. She was back in southern Spain, in Caños de Meca where the sun made the pine trees shimmer and eviscerated the dust from the roads.

That year, the *migrantes* had started crossing the Strait of Gibraltar on the inflatables. Most died in the waves and drifted to the bottom of the sea. Others washed ashore for the living to collect. They were building new graveyards to accommodate them in Tarifa. The so-called lucky ones who approached the

29

coast alive were herded, while still in the water, to points south by the *Guardia Civil* in their patrol boats and helicopters.

It was in Caños that she'd met the American. Though it was low season, temperatures had stayed in the mid-20s and made everyone irritable. Their little village had been overrun that summer. Only the lifers remained, thin drunks and meth addicts, many of them skint. Nora had been there to surf. Slowly, from watching the water each day, her eyes had turned flat, as if she observed without judgement. It was one of the reasons troubled men were drawn to her.

She worked in a little surfer's bar. She was staying on past summer as a favour to the owner, who'd wanted a holiday. It hadn't been a difficult decision. She knew the locals and had earned their trust. Her bar was one of many along the waterfront offering tapas and fino from barrels against the wall. Each displayed posters of the owner's favourite toreadors and flamenco stars.

Caños was full of madmen. There was Ernesto the human squirrel, a tiny thing made of sinews and teeth, who climbed the fences and clifftop rocks along the beach, then slipped into swish hotel bars for the free drinks. There was Fuelgencio, who compulsively filled plastic bottles from the sea to splash across the main road. The locals gave him money. Back and forth he went, cleaning the road with seawater, day and night. His trousers were soiled, his bare feet covered with unspeakable sores. Eventually he'd pass out face down in the sand, like an exhausted bull before the sword was plunged between his shoulders. In Caños there were plenty of actual retired matadors. These men had painted whole arenas with blood. The longer she stayed, the more Nora was lured by them, educated by them, drawn in by their *banderillas*, multi-coloured harpoons and *muletas*.

At the end of each shift she drank at her favourite watering hole, *La Esposa de Barbate*. Unlike her tourist bar, it was where locals drank cheaply inside a windowless block of white concrete. The American had been drinking there. He was one of the oddballs Encarna accepted without asking questions. Like the ancient Greeks, the owners of Spanish bars rarely turned away vagrants for fear they were gods in disguise.

The American looked like he'd been occupying his stool for years. Plunked on the end of the bar with his shoulders forward, he surveyed his world with deep-set, watery eyes. Above his head hung a joint of Iberico on a hook. Encarna held a weekly meat lottery. While the man drank his fino, the locals were buying tickets.

'A full bottle he's had already,' Encarna said, following Nora's gaze.

'And you are telling me that why?'

'You are lonely in this town.'

'No, I most certainly am not.'

'This is my friend Nora,' Encarna said to the American, and pointing down the bar at her. 'She is also speaking English here.'

'A friend,' Nora said to Encarna in Spanish, 'who knows what you're up to.'

The American got up from his stool and plodded over to join her. He was both more drunk and more handsome than she'd thought. There had been a beard until recently. She could tell by the sunburn under his ears.

'Nora's a surfer,' Encarna said. She poured them both fino.

The American tried to smile, but it was really a grimace. Something dropped in her throat. It was a foreboding that they would be entangled, that it might be bad for her.

'Is it true,' he asked, 'what they say about this coast? Good for surfing, but it can't be developed on, because of the relentless wind?'

'Yes. A lucky thing. Nature sometimes saves itself.'

They sat together a while. As they talked, Nora decided she'd been wrong about being wary. He was a washed-up and haunted specimen. It would be an act of generosity to be with him. His desperation seeped out to infect her, and as they shared a drink she felt lonelier.

She asked, 'What are you doing in Caños?'

'I was working down in Tarifa.' He turned in the direction of the sea, as if watching it through the concrete. 'I came to this village to dry out.'

She laughed. 'Here?'

He shrugged. 'My ex came to Caños years ago, for the outdoor activities. She said it gave her peace.'

'And you've taken advantage of these . . . outdoor activities?'

'The first couple of days I did.'

'And then?'

'Then I stayed in. But I couldn't bear being in my apartment.'

There was a commotion at the end of the bar. Where the American had been sitting, a couple started shouting at each other.

The sound of their argument travelled across the room like a series of explosions. The American looked at Nora steadily, then reached for his glass. His hand was trembling badly. The couple exploded – a bottle smashed, stools tipped over, and everyone jumped to their feet.

Encarna came out from behind the bar with a baseball bat. She was small but fearless. Nora had witnessed her passion for throwing people out. At *La Esposa*, the nights always wore on until morning. Anyone still there saw the hidden edges of things become exposed.

'What about you?' he asked Nora. 'Is that all you do – surf?'

'I run a bar. You know the *El Gato de Playa*?' Down under the hooked Iberico, Encarna was threatening to use the bat on the couple if they didn't shut up.

Nora put her hand on the man's wrist. It was strangely cold. 'Want to go?'

She felt like taking care of him a while. It was an easy decision, but once it was made, it seemed there could even be pleasure in it. He left the money, she took the fino. They hurried out like kids escaping parents.

They took the crumbling concrete steps to the beach, past where Fuelgencio was still splashing the road with his bottles of seawater. The commotion in the bar had set off the local dogs. The sound of barking faded as they walked down to the sand past the last of the wild olive trees. These trees grew in the hills, along the beach and over the tops of graves. He stumbled on the rocks. Nora slipped her arm around his waist. They would sleep together in the morning, she decided. It would be at her place, after he'd sobered up.

For a while they sat on the sand and faced the receding waves. Nora had the impression she was sitting beside a ghost. She wanted to know where it came from, his particular desolation. In the distance, against the dark slate-grey water, the night ferry was leaving Tarifa for Tangiers.

The next morning, the ceiling fan circled above Nora's bed as she woke beside him. His name, she'd learned, was Ben. It was the first time she'd woken next to someone called Ben. He was a quiet sleeper for a drunk. When he stirred, he was a frightening sight. He was like a delicious bit of food you'd raise to your mouth, then decide against at the last moment. They made love clumsily. After, he threw on his clothes and found the nearest bar.

She got herself ready, had breakfast and went to work. He was there at the *El Gato* ahead of her, drinking fino – and when she finished her shift he was still at it, unmoveable, sitting straight on the stool with his hand clutching his glass, as if frightened someone would take it away.

Let him sink, she told herself, and when he hits bottom your next move will become clear. That night, on foot, she followed Ben home at a distance. He was walking straight into oncoming traffic. Cars honked and went around him, and on he walked, head thrust forward, arms stiffly at his sides. Fuelgencia splashed the road with water after he passed, as if washing away his remains. Later, Nora found them passed out beside each other, directly in the sun.

For a week straight, she watched him drink and walk the roads. Then he wasn't at her bar, and he wasn't at any of the others. It was Encarna who told her. Ben had collided with a car and been taken to a hospital in Malaga.

Nora went to see him. She had been to the same hospital in Malaga years ago, to visit a friend who had had a miscarriage. Then, the waiting room had been full of new mothers, expectant mothers and mothers wanting help to get pregnant again. Now, in the span of just a few years, the women of Spain were having fewer children. This time the waiting room held a woman with a black eye, a man nursing a leg wound, and a long row of thin, emaciated survivors of the tourist season, coming off meth.

She was taken to Ben's bed. He had been struck from behind and somehow avoided serious injury. He was propped on a pillow with his head bandaged. Beside him lay a row of men, some moaning, others asleep.

'This is not the first time,' the doctor had told her. 'He keeps this up, soon you won't be collecting him from a place of the living.'

Ben looked embarrassed. He considered himself out of place beside the meth cases. She brought him home and set about healing him. At first he slept badly, only for a couple of hours at a time. He would wake up suddenly, throw his arms out and make garbled pronouncements. They had to do with seaweeds.

She went to his apartment to collect his things. It was an enormous place. The fridge was empty, and his bed looked like it hadn't been slept in. His clothes were in a pile near the toilet.

The curtains were closed, and when she opened them, the ocean lay before her.

Nora collected the essentials. On the way out, she paused at his desk. Notes were scattered in a drunken hand: *They are trying soft power now. Is anything as deceptive? In our beer and ice cream. No stopping until we become them. Or they become us.*

For seven months she had been working at *El Gato de la Playa* without a holiday. She asked a friend to cover and took Ben by bus to a pretty village up the coast – Zahara de los Atunes, where the Romans had built their whaling and tuna factories. It was a place known for its *almadabra*, the ancient technique of trapping giant Bluefin in shallow water and clubbing them to death.

They took a cabin up in the hills, away from the heat and the temptation of the bars. After three meals a day and gradually watered-down wine, she brought him out of the worst of the shakes. She fed him anchovies in olive oil, manchego and bread. They took long walks until his skin warmed and some colour emerged in his face. He started to sleep through the night. He smiled at the little things. His thoughts didn't run so far aground.

From their terrace they could see the village's white-painted houses and the sea beyond. They took trips – to the prison where Cervantes was held for espionage, to the church where tuna was cut up for sale under the altar. Each night, above the sound of the waves, they could hear helicopters searching for the *migrantes* crossing from Morocco under the cover of darkness.

And each morning, the news revealed thirty or forty more, washed ashore and buried in Tarifa without names.

'You've made me remember my dreams again,' he said to her, one morning in bed. Outside, the swallows and finches were making a chorus. 'I dreamt the *migrantes* had come to the house – and when I woke, I could have sworn one was here, standing outside our window and looking in.'

The window had a view of a young palm tree. 'That's probably what you saw,' she said, pointing at it. 'In the dark, it could look like a person.' She started to get up when he reached for her. It happened a lot. Each time she left the bed, even for a minute, he held on.

She began to believe it was why she'd stayed in Spain past the surfing season, to develop a different form of love. Good God, she thought, watching him fumble with his socks, what sort of mother raised *that*? Ben was so dramatically neglectful, a man practically unable to bathe. Something had obviously gone badly wrong. She learned two things had happened in quick succession – he'd split with his partner, and he'd lost his job at a big multinational that developed pharmaceuticals and biofuels.

In the mornings, they walked the local beach. It was a flat and windless stretch of sand. It seemed the waves only moved in order to prove to Nora that she wasn't dreaming. One day, they woke very early to a stunning full moon.

By the time they reached the sea, the moon had come very close – bright, cold, treacherously near. They walked until the sun rose and its pale counterpart finally retreated, temporarily conceding the sky. The only sound came from the seagulls complaining. Then they came across others on the beach – fishermen, standing motionless at even intervals between the poles they had planted in the sand.

'They never catch anything now,' Ben said. He was walking faster. He stopped every now and then to identify the seaweeds he found. She hadn't known of the different varieties until then.

'Do you like them?' Nora asked.

He looked up, and the lines tightened around his eyes. 'Why do you ask?'

'Just things you said in your sleep.'

'Ah.' He looked away, across the water, as a smile formed. 'For seaweeds, what I like doesn't exactly matter.'

He kept walking. They came to a huge rock twice their size. It was completely covered with green algae, thin and wet, uniformly placed around the surface of the rock like felt on a billiards table. On the sand nearby, tightly grouped in clusters, lay a colony of something bright purple.

'Dulse,' he said, squatting beside them. He looked up, the muscles in his face slack. 'This species is like us. They travel a long way, just to perish.'

He told her that he wanted to get further away. He didn't want to be at the sea any longer. They took another bus up into the countryside, into the communes and windmill farms where cattle and egrets cohabited under the constant hum of spinning blades. Every morning, old men held political arguments in the tavernas over grappa.

She had been to these hills before. Wild horses came right up to the human habitations. Unfixed dogs, their balls hanging, skipped down the streets like young men while the aging dogs sat on sunny rooftops gazing on their creations. Normally in these hilltop towns, the parents and future parents were everywhere. Young couples frequented the pram shops on the street corners. There the latest models were displayed like automobiles in shiny showrooms. Behind their parents, children pushed prams filled with toys and potted plants.

Now the pram shops were gone. The streets and alleys were quiet where a chorus of children usually cried. In the past, there were babies fed, burped and changed. More babies were made behind drawn curtains. Balconies were for courtship, trees for foreplay, beds for procreation. There were families in restaurants and babies brought along to lunch and dinner. This time, it was as if a plague had struck. It was the trend, people said – across Europe, Asia, the Americas, Africa: better contraception, fewer babies, more abortions.

They stumbled on some kind of re-enactment in Vejer de la Frontera, where the blinding white houses, white lanes and alleys were populated by the *Mujer Vejeriega*, women dressed all in black with only their left eyes exposed. This garment, the *cobijada,* had once been banned. Now they silently drifted the *avenidas* and plazas, speaking back the poems written for them, telling how they kept their faces captive for the sake of freedom.

After two weeks away from Caños, Ben's nervous twitches lessened. He stopped reaching for her when she left the bed. His desperate hunger faded. And there it was, in its place – a dangerous thirst. Nora had seen this look in the eyes before. It looked like boredom. It looked like death. She'd seen it among those men who appeared at her bar after long absences. Their thirst had been conquered, only to come back stronger.

They returned to the seaside on their last night. They had planned to go to dinner at a restaurant on the water, a place they had been avoiding because of its tempting wine list. As they walked the sand to the restaurant, she tried to keep the conversation light. They passed men in tailor-made tracksuits and designer sneakers with tiny dogs in their arms. They passed the luxury hotels, closed for the off-season, and wild olive trees growing along the path. Blocks of purpose-built cement had been placed along the shore to stop the sea from entering.

The beach was as white as bones. She felt an urge to surf. It was the moonlight. It was the wind. Gusts came tearing across the sand-swept tennis court, ripping the net into pieces and whipping it against the posts. They ate inside on a table by the window overlooking the sea. Ben refused the wine and started to fidget. They had little left to say now – instead, they spent the dinner eavesdropping on a table of windfarm engineers down from Madrid. These men and women had been fortunate with their turbines, and they were celebrating. Each time the waiter brought a fresh jug of sangria, they toasted each other. Ben stared, longer than was polite.

On the way back, they walked the same stretch of sand. Only this time, something had changed. Ben noticed first. He stood on the shoreline without moving. The water – it was turning pink. Then, as the tide came in, the sea turned red, as bright as fresh cherries. Soon, others had stopped as well.

'That's phytoplankton,' Ben muttered, 'but it isn't supposed to be here until spring.'

People were taking photos. While they did so, the colour dissipated. Then it was just gone. The whole thing might have been their imagination. As the others moved on, Ben was still standing there.

'What happened,' she asked, 'with your ex?'

'Nothing.' He was staring at the incoming waves. 'She didn't want a child with someone who believes humanity's doomed.'

And then she understood. His thirst, his underlying despair – it was something she had once been plagued by. The next morning, staring out the window of the bus, watching the campervans heading in the opposite direction, she decided that she couldn't be with him either, not if he didn't think there was any point to the future. Not if he was determined to drink himself to death.

It was still windy along the coast. The white-capped waves were coming closer to the road. The sea was steadily removing the land, returning all manner of dead things for deposit. They entered Caños. Fuelgencia was the first to greet the bus, standing in his soiled trousers, splashing the road from his bucket of seawater. The bars were filling up. Ben was peering into the open doors.

She had forgotten what it felt like to give herself over completely, with nothing to show for it. He was twitching again. His mouth had already begun tasting fino, amontillado, oloroso – the many drinks she knew he would prefer silently and alone.

There had to be a better way, a voice said. It was a voice that seemed to come from the depths of the sea.

'Come with me,' she said. 'To my bar. We'll have one last drink together.'

He looked at her. 'Why?'

She opened her purse and removed one of the notes she'd taken from his desk. He saw his handwriting and turned pale in the sunlight: *No stopping until we become them. Or they become us.*

The wind had died, the sea turned flat. They sat on stools facing the water with the chalk cliffs in the distance. It was early afternoon, and the bar at *El Gato* was quiet. Nora bought a bottle of amontillado and placed it on the table between them with two glasses. She knew the end was coming, she knew it was inevitable. This time, she wanted it on her terms.

She poured herself a drink and felt the warmth of it in her chest. Ben's eyes darted to his empty glass.

'Why don't you start,' she said, 'with how you first got into seaweeds.'

'It was in Santa Monica,' he said, 'when I was in college and regularly swam in the ocean. One morning I came out of the water and felt something strange inside my mouth. I spat onto the sand. I picked up what I found and took it to my professor in the bio lab. It turned out to be *Gomontia polyrhiza*, a green sporophyte. It lives inside calcareous worm-tubes and dead barnacle shells. Its normal habitat is the estuaries of Sweden.' He looked at her with disgust, as if reliving the experience. 'It found its way into my *mouth*.'

'Some accident of the currents?'

'That's what we thought. But nobody in the lab *knew*. My prof couldn't give me a definitive answer. That little glob – I can still feel its finger-like cilia creeping down my throat, searching for nutrients.' He shuddered.

'So you decided to study seaweeds? And work in the field?'

'I switched to marine biology. But the people involved in phycology – they're mostly interested in classifications. They don't understand, these seaweeds have started to infiltrate human life to such a degree that we're not in charge any longer. They're like Greek gods, amusing themselves with us. They take root in any host they want.'

He reached for the bottle and stopped himself. 'Keep going,' Nora said. She knew it was coming – a bad binge. 'First, go back a little. Where did you work in Tarifa? Before we met.'

'At a research lab. Analysing data from old fossils. Investigating a place called The Island of Doves.'

'I've heard of that. People windsurf near there.'

'Yeah. Its original purpose was a graveyard. It's where the most advanced cultures on Earth planned to face the sea for eternity in underwater caves. Phoenicians, Romans, Spanish Moors and caliphs – all buried their leaders there.'

This time, his hand made it to the bottle of amontillado. He poured a full glass of the honey-brown liquid and held it to his nose.

'The ancient fossils in those caves, they go back a billion years. Think of it! A place littered with sea sponges, tuna, seaweeds. For us, it was like visiting the pyramids.' He pointed across the water at the white cliffs. 'Did you know, in that pile of chalk, in that tall white cliff, lies over a billion years of fossils?'

There flowed a lot of water between where they sat and the cliffs across the sea. She tried to imagine what it was like. Hundreds of millions of years had elapsed, while the cliffs gradually grew higher – each moment without human habitation.

'We realised,' Ben went on, 'that we can use seaweeds as models. Because of their efficiency. Because of their design.' He put his glass down on the table. 'Kelp haven't changed, Nora. Not for a billion years – they travel the oceans and make everything else change for them.'

She watched the sunlight straight on his face. His watery eyes had dried around the edges. The skin had turned papery, almost crispy.

'I think seaweeds come from one common root. Like the aspen's the root of all land trees.'

His bristly whiskers had come alive – but the mouth inside was starting to twist and sneer. The man she'd kissed the night before, it seemed he was practically dead.

'They seem to be acting in concert. They have these air vesicles called pneumatocysts for floating in strong currents. They're expanding their range, Nora. They've come ashore, and placed themselves in everything from cosmetics to fertiliser.'

'*Placed* themselves?'

'Yes.' He studied the surface of the water. 'But it doesn't matter what *I* think. Or what anybody else does. Seaweeds will always be waiting.' He reached for his glass and took a quick, shy sip.

'Go on,' she said. 'Drink up.'

He had another, a big one this time. The muscles in his face jumped to life. The drink made him look younger. 'You'll see. Whichever one you study takes over.'

'Takes over?' She refilled his glass. 'You mean, in a metaphysical sense?'

He nodded. 'You could call it that. Mostly, it's a psychological thing. At the start. Then . . .'

'Then what?'

'They're preparing for the end. They're *luring* us. Down in the caves in Tarifa, there were warnings.'

Nora's regulars had appeared at the nearby tables. Her shift was starting soon. I won't be serving you again, she'd tell them, because I'm not coming back. The longer she had sat there with Ben, the more it dawned on her how much time she'd wasted on drunks.

He gulped down the rest. 'I knew you wouldn't believe me.' Without pausing, he poured another. 'Humanity's doomed. The faster we die off, the better.'

She listened as he listed one proof after the next: the steady loss of aquatic biodiversity, environmental catastrophe, deep ecology and the pointlessness of more children. A strange thing happened – the more she listened, the more she realised she wanted to be with someone sane, in a loving relationship and raising a baby.

MANFRED

He left the car park as the sound of the farmers' market faded behind him. With his shopping basket he weaved through the oncoming late arrivals, past the musician with her open guitar case scattered with coins.

When he reached the road, Manfred stepped over the retaining wall toward the sea. He peered into his basket, where the tub of dulse waited. He wanted to be far away from anyone when he opened it. The black logo on the paper bag, with its coiled bladderwrack, seemed to shift and dance in the sunlight.

He gained the beach and walked faster. The shifting sand, the waves and constant mizzle – the squishy sounds of water and fish – soon he'd reach the mouth of the estuary, abandoned boats and mud flats. He would have to arrive at his house. Then he would have to go inside the garden.

The abandoned fish factory stood in the distance. It gave him hope. He wanted to be among hard things, unmoving things, man-made steel and concrete. When he reached the turn to his house, he kept going toward the quay. The tide was coming in.

The fish factory had a high retaining wall. Drainpipes poked out of the stone where run-off dribbled into the sand. Manfred found comfort in the walls and railings and metal sluice gates. High above his head were windows – and through these windows he could see fluorescent lights along the ceiling. He pictured the way it would have been, with its cutting floors and blood, its workers milling around steel separating tanks. Vats of fish, sorted, beheaded, stacked. Up there, somewhere in that hulking monstrosity the size of a container ship – it was where her Cornish seaweeds start-up had established itself.

The waves came lapping up to his ankles as he opened up the bag and withdrew the card she'd given him. Sure enough, there was her mobile number on the back. It was right next to her name – Nora. Standing there on the wet sand, with the seagulls screaming overhead, he was struck by how easy it had been, speaking with her. She lived *here*, in Gweek? When could he ring her? How long could he wait?

This time, the way home felt different, the mizzle almost delightful. This time he had things to be proud of. He opened the gate to the back garden. He didn't want to linger. He passed the tub without once looking inside.

In the kitchen he put his shopping basket down, right on the linoleum. Something had changed. He stood there a moment. He listened to the hum of his refrigerator, and the birds, and the sound of his beating heart. Inside his basket lay his salad greens, potatoes and mackerel. The hunger he'd had this morning – it was still there, and it had grown stronger. But instead of eating to stave it off, even something small, he couldn't bear the thought of what would come next. He would prepare the food, then eat and digest it. Then what?

Outside, he'd been excited about life. Now he was only exhausted. It was the idea of getting out his pots and pans. It was the *act* of eating and the cleaning up after – as if there was a logic, or a necessary sequence to it all. The only thing left in the end would be that same fateful awareness of his body, as if man's sole function was to mechanically digest food.

He went upstairs to bed. Along the way, he avoided his worst thoughts, and he listened to those governed by self-preservation. It was important to concentrate on the little things, to focus on each shoe on each step, all the way up to his room.

Later, in the night, he woke fully clothed. He'd left the lights on. It felt like there was something sneaking toward him, a presence he couldn't see. He lay there a while, blinking at the wall. There had to be new arrivals out in the shallows, plotting.

His hunger was a dull ache, with sharp pangs when he moved. Then he remembered all his shopping in the kitchen. Stupid – there would be insects coming, flies and ants crawling toward his mackerel and salad greens. He still couldn't imagine cooking. Maybe he would have some cheese on a cracker, just a little to stave off the cramps. It was the weekends that always bothered him. Saturdays and Sundays, with nothing to do but age. He simply had to get up and eat. Otherwise, over time, he *would* eventually die. Using all his effort – an inordinate amount, considering how simple it was – he left the bed.

Downstairs, his shopping lay on the linoleum where he'd left it. There were no insects. Nothing on the ground seemed to be moving toward the fish. The tub of dulse was still buried in the basket, partially covered by the salad greens. He'd had a handful, but now, at home, the idea of eating *more* seaweeds seemed wrong, somehow. He stood there a moment, staring out the kitchen window. In the garden, the white tub gleamed faintly in the mist. Something was urging him to do it – open the door. Go outside.

It was colder. In the moonlight he went squelching across the garden. When he reached the tub, there were footsteps there in the wet grass. They were the size of his own shoes. He wondered if he'd gotten up in the night and forgotten.

He stared into the water. The kelp's outline was barely visible. He didn't really want to look. He walked over to the pine tree under a sky that shone brightly in the clear cold evening.

'So you thought you'd go to the market, did you?'

Manfred turned. It was just as he'd feared. Inside the tub, the kelp had raised its head above the taps. Its rubbery flesh had developed spots, probably from the brackish water.

'Why don't you come over here? That's it. Come closer, so I can have a look at you.'

He went all the way to the tub. He wasn't all that surprised that it had spoken. It was possible the kelp had been talking to him all along, and he just hadn't been listening closely.

'Why did you go to the market?'

Manfred sat on the edge of the tub. The kelp had a Mediterranean accent – Greek, perhaps Spanish. It didn't sound particularly male or female.

'I needed to do some shopping,' he admitted.

'Oh? What did you get?'

He shrugged. 'Just the basics.'

'You came home looking very pleased with yourself.'

'I did?'

'And you went out the night before.' The kelp flattened one of its blades on the water and splashed Manfred a little.

'You mean, with Simon? I suppose I did. I thought I'd try one last time . . .' He looked over his garden. He could feel the kelp's round head staring.

'Go on.'

'To look on the brighter side of things. To try my hand again. That's all. It turned out to be pointless.'

'Of course it was. You should have stayed here with me.' The kelp wiggled closer to him under the water.

Manfred smiled. He peeled a leaf from the long rubbery neck. It *would* have been much nicer. 'You ever felt like you've known someone longer than you actually have?'

The kelp gave a little gurgle. 'What, in another life?'

'For some time now, I've felt that way. Ever since we met.'

'Yes. We're both of us old souls.'

'Yes – foreign and familiar at the same time.' Manfred glanced over at his neighbour's house. The curtains moved. He turned his back and brought his voice down to a whisper. 'So why do you think we're meeting now?'

'Maybe our spirits have entered new bodies. Or maybe something larger brought us together at last.'

'What would have done that?'

'Nature.'

Manfred looked out at the rising river. The sound of the waves against the shore almost made him sick.

The kelp gave another gurgle. 'What was in that extra bag you brought back from the market?'

Manfred could feel himself going red. He kept his face turned. 'What extra bag?'

'Hiding something, aren't you? Under those salad greens.'

Manfred shook his head. 'I don't know what you're on about.' He wiped his eyes with the heels of his hands.

'Go on. You can tell me.'

'You know what? I'm ill all of a sudden. I think it's your smell, in that stinking seawater.'

'Thanks a lot. What do you expect *me* to do about it?'

'Come up with something,' Manfred said, but he suspected the kelp knew why he'd changed the subject. He couldn't stop his face from burning, and he hurried back inside before the kelp had a chance to reply.

At times, lying in bed at night, it felt like the waves came right up beneath him. In the distance, where the river met the sea, the life forms multiplied. All he'd ever wanted to know was why, what for, what next. The kelp knew. It came from the depths. As he left the bed in the morning he sensed it out there harbouring secrets. He saw its shadows in the mirror when he brushed his teeth. It would be the kelp that determined how long he had to live. As he came downstairs, he heard it calling to him from the garden.

'Why did you bother to shave? You look fine. And nobody cares, not in the long run.' There followed a snort, and a gurgle.

By early afternoon he'd finally got out his pots and pans. He cooked up the mackerel and potatoes, and he ate them along with the salad greens.

For the rest of the day he stayed in the safety of the lounge overlooking his front garden. As a precaution, he hid the dulse in the back of his kitchen cupboard behind the spices. As he did so, he could feel himself starting to sweat. It was partly embarrassment, partly shame. His last comment hadn't been very nice, what he'd said about the kelp's smell in the bathwater.

The tub gleamed under the mizzle. Manfred tried to avoid looking at it. After the washing up, he went upstairs. He stayed inside the bathroom, staring at himself in the mirror. The longer he stayed there, practically hiding, the more it looked suspicious. He went into his bedroom and paced back and forth. He'd become trapped – *in his own house.*

He turned out the lights and lay in bed. It was still early, and he had to pretend to be asleep. Eventually the night came on in earnest, and the darkness spread into the room. Half asleep, half awake, he entered into a watery dream of seaweeds and mooring ropes, molluscs, swimmers' legs, warm-water seaweeds that hitchhiked in ship ballasts to expand their range. Cold-water seaweeds floating ever northward to survive. Tall kelp forests marching out of the sea and onto land. There they looked like the wives of ancient Greek warriors, lining the sand and waiting for their husbands to return – either carrying their shields, or as corpses on top of them.

The browns, greens and reds were all there, right underneath his rapid eye movements. They sprawled out in his mind like past lovers, naked in their collective judgement. All night they crawled up his legs and burrowed.

Somehow he made it through the darkness to Monday morning. He was greeted by the bladderwrack logo on the bag of dulse as he reached deep into the kitchen cabinet. He left for work by the front door, and he even said hello to his neighbours as they too were leaving for work. Manfred didn't go down to the beach. He walked along the pavement all the way to campus. His classes went as expected. Some of his students even seemed to be improving.

Before coming home, he texted Nora to see if she wanted to meet up. She replied right away: *Sure! Pint at the Ship?*

He stared at his phone in disbelief. It made him nervous but hopeful. He felt confident enough to come home via the back garden. It was colder out, but he was sweating as he reached his gate. He told himself to walk slowly and steadily across the grass. He told himself not to look. It's possible, he reminded himself again, that he'd imagined the whole thing. His elbows at his sides, walking as straight and even as a soldier, he'd almost passed the tub.

'Hello again.'

He stayed at a distance. The kelp rose out of the water and stared. Its dripping head looked bigger – like it had eaten something.

'I heard you cooking food yesterday. I smelled it.'

'Oh?'

'I have to say, I felt a bit neglected. Stuck here in this nasty tub. My poor head, it's bloated with air.'

Manfred felt himself go pale. He didn't want to think of the kelp's bladder popping.

'I'll bring you some fresh seawater. Okay? After I go inside and change.'

'Must be nice, having all that room inside.' The kelp squished down into the murky water. 'It's not my fault I stink. It was *you* who brought me here.'

'I know.'

'We won't dwell on it.' The kelp sunk further into the tub. It rested its enormous head against the taps. 'I once went five months without really eating.'

'Are you hungry now, then?'

'Maybe. That special surprise you picked up from the market – was it for me?'

Manfred didn't move. He looked around the garden, as if the kelp had addressed someone else.

'Well?'

'I don't have to answer your questions. Each time I go to the market I don't have to come home to an interrogation.' He came closer. The kelp bobbed up a little and shook its blades dry.

'Salt,' Manfred blurted. 'It's a special kind of salt.'

'Ooh,' the kelp said, wriggling in the water. 'Bring it out. Shake some into my suckers.'

'It's expensive. Used as a garnish. I can't just dump it into a bathtub.' He tried to sound hurt. It was the best way – to invent a lesser failing to cover up the bigger one. 'You wouldn't be able to taste it anyway. You're used to the sea!'

The kelp let out a long, slow gurgle. It submerged itself entirely, slipped its head below the water and stayed under. It seemed to be intentionally drowning itself.

Manfred inched closer, toward the taps. 'Hey,' he said. 'Come on up.' He sat on the edge of the tub. The water had gone dark. He started to put his hand in.

Suddenly, the enormous head surfaced. It was covered with open sores.

'Oh!' Manfred said, flinching back. 'Does it hurt?'

'The least you could do is dab a little into my mouth.'

'I'm not sure if that's wise. I start touching those pneumatocysts of yours, I'll be coating you all over.'

'Ooh. Really?'

'Tell you what. When I get paid, at the end of the month, I'll buy you a whole bag of some nice kosher salt. The chunky kind.'

They sat together in silence a moment. The sores in the kelp's head vented putrid gas. 'This reminds me of the old days,' it said, 'when we'd keep each other company without needing to speak.'

The kelp went under again. Manfred went straight down to the water with the empty buckets. He carried them back full of fresh seawater and poured them in.

Soon the kelp emerged, flattened all of its broad blades and splashed around. 'I am back in the depths now. I can practically smell the caves.'

'Which caves are those?'

The kelp looked at him. 'Where we all come from. If you're good to me, one day I'll tell you about it.'

The Ship was almost empty – there were only a couple of men at the bar. Manfred stayed quiet as he sat across from Nora, and they made their way through their drinks.

'I've got a confession,' she said. 'Before we met at the market, I'd already spotted you.'

Manfred leaned in, his voice low. 'Where?'

'On the beach.' She stretched her arms out wide and laughed. 'Collecting a ginormous piece of kelp!'

He gave her a half smile. 'You saw that?'

'And I'll never forget it.'

'For a while there, I was trying to make my garden interesting. Then I realised it was just a junkyard.' He reached for his beer. 'One more cider?'

'Go on, then.'

Manfred headed for the bar. As Nora's glass was getting filled, he stared at the rising bubbles. Each of these bubbles, as they neared the top, told him the same thing – to deliver her drink, make an excuse and go home. He was doomed. She'd *seen* him with his kelp.

He paid for the round and returned to their table. He sat across from her and kept his eyes on a poster of shipwrecks on the wall.

'So – what did you do with it?'

'With what?'

'That massive seaweed.'

'Oh. I don't know.'

'Did you take it to bed? Fling it on the sofa?'

He laughed nervously. 'Sowhat do you do with yourself? I mean, when you're not at the market?'

'Seriously. You dragged it all the way home . . .'

He had told himself to come up with some story, but he hadn't. 'You ask a lot of questions.'

'I've been told.' Her lips slightly parted, she took out a packet of tobacco and rolling papers. 'At least I got *my* confession out of the way. Smoke?'

'No, thanks.'

While she was outside, more men came in. They had seen Nora sitting there, and now they were all glancing at him from the bar as he waited there alone.

'Right,' she said, when she came back. She pulled her chair closer. 'This is going to sound weird.'

'Okay.'

'But I just want to hear one thing. If we're going to get to know each other.'

'Go on.'

'What did you do with that great honking piece of kelp?'

His hand trembled. He spilled beer down his mouth and wiped it clean with his shirtsleeve.

'I'm sorry,' she said, 'but I have to know what you were *doing*, dragging it away. It's what I do, after all. I have to admit, it's partly why I was attracted to you.' Her eyes flashed. 'I think seaweeds are amazing.'

'You do?'

'That one you had, it was a Bullwhip, wasn't it? That's not a common species here. Are you some kind of collector?'

Up at the bar, the men were still staring. 'That's right.'

'Well – why didn't you say?' Nora slapped the table with the palm of her hand. 'I mean, what are the chances? What's your favourite type?'

'I *do* like dulse. It's just so unusual, with that bright purple colouring.'

'But at the market, you acted so ignorant.'

'That wasn't exactly an act. You could say I'm just starting out.'

'Listen, I can help if you like. With identification, I mean. Hey, did you know that the best collectors have been women? The first seaweed album in the nineteenth century was put together by women. They pressed them into a book and shared discoveries.'

'The head of the Phycological Society's female,' Manfred added.

'Mary-Margaret Dennison? She's one of my closest friends.'

Manfred stared. This piece of information seemed to take on physical shape in the back of his throat. 'You *know* her? I've used her field guide for years.'

'I wonder what it is about women. Maybe we identify a wider range of colours.' She grabbed her glass and stood up. 'My round.'

He downed what was left of his beer, and she took their empties to the bar. The men there greeted her by name. As they closed in on either side, she endured a series of inane jokes and innuendos. Somehow Nora adeptly removed herself without insulting them.

They sat in The Ship for another hour, and he became almost ill with nerves. He deflected more of her questions, and outside the pub, when he was about to say goodnight, she kissed him on the mouth. It was his first kiss in over a year. He had so many past mistakes – but her ease with him gave him hope.

Before he knew it, they were walking back to her place. He kept wrestling with various scenarios and wondered how he'd explain it to the kelp if he stayed over. Each minute felt precious, like the last ones of his life.

Nora lived in a big shared house on the other end of Gweek. Her housemates, she told him, all worked for various environmental projects. They were old friends – they shared food, art projects and the care of two house cats.

Her room was at the top of the stairs. Some of her housemates were in the kitchen, but she put her finger to her lips and sneaked him through, as if determined not have any unnecessary conversations. It was a comfortable room. She had books on various seaweed recipes and a poster of edible algae on the wall. He was looking at this when she turned off the lights and started taking off his clothes.

He started to hyperventilate. As they were slipping into bed, he could hear her housemates outside the door. They had entered a protracted discussion, seemingly aimed straight at his ear, about whose turn it was to clean the toilet.

'Mate, it was my turn last week.'

'You were up in London. And you didn't do it, remember?'

'That's because I was up in *London*. Your turn now.'

'Nora cleaned the loo all last week, when you were away. It wasn't her turn.'

'Exactly, it *wasn't* her turn. Why did she go and clean it, then?'

Under the covers, Nora placed her hand flat on his chest. 'Maybe I can put on some music,' she whispered.

'But then they'll know what we're doing.'

After the cleaning rota was resolved, a deadening silence took hold. It coincided with the application of the condom. Manfred kept picturing himself as her friends would see him, the naked interloper in the upstairs bedroom. He endured in the face of defeat. She encouraged him, but he'd become fatefully embarrassed.

Finally she gave up and lay motionless, her eyes taking in the ceiling tiles as he continued to work away like a heart surgeon, unable to accept the death of his patient. It wasn't until she'd physically removed him with her hand that he flopped on his back.

'Probably best to stop,' he said, as if it had been his decision all along.

It was Nora's idea to meet up again the following night. He was relieved, and he was also terrified. This time nobody was home. And this time, they were successful.

In terms of effort, she was the one who made it happen. They didn't talk about it much, but if she had asked, he would have said it wasn't the act of sex that troubled him – it was what sex represented. Despite the condom, there was always the possibility of *reproduction*. It was the idea of *one more* of him, as if someone, or some thing, was out there in charge of cloning. His sperm was probably tainted anyway. Past failures loomed like ghosts above each bed.

Despite this, Nora ushered him through the difficulties. She was both patient and alluring. She seemed to understand his plight, as if she had her own long-term vision.

He began to see her regularly. She liked to greet him at the top of the stairs, naked except for a Fair Isle jumper badly riddled with holes. Her blonde hair was so long, she could make a hat out of it. He spent long stretches of time just staring into her pellucid eyes, a colour of blue that looked asleep while taking him in. Sometimes she would draw doodles on her thighs with a pen, or write long notes, all the way down her legs, for him to read.

He didn't need the kelp to tell him the obvious. He was in danger of falling for her. Late each night he returned home in the early hours, entering quietly by the front door. Each morning, on his way to work, he told the kelp he'd been working late, that he didn't want to wake it. The kelp didn't question him. Like a patient wife who knew her husband was cheating, it seemed to be biding its time, waiting the situation out until he came to his senses. Its quiet dignity made Manfred even more melancholy. When he sat by the tub, their small talk was strained. The kelp seemed saddened by its knowledge, its bladder-head tightened like a dried prune.

Compared to the Bullwhip, Manfred was a primitive, a barbarian. Both of them ultimately came from the ocean, a vast and ancient realm with laws that predated its current inhabitants. If either of them was closer to these laws, it was the kelp. Manfred's species was both new and on the way out. His legs often felt useless when he sat down. He was as much a victim of nature's shifting hierarchy as the dodo bird had been to the colonisers of Australia.

Nora invited him to see where she worked. She introduced him to her colleagues, young hippies driving company vans with their windows down and their music blasting over the bladderwrack logo. The managing director had arranged a little territory for himself along the Cornish coast. The government had given him a temporary licence for one year, and that year had become ten. By farming something free, his profit margins were high. The seaweed harvesters just cut their crops off the rocks before the rats, flies and seagulls got to them.

Manfred's favourite thing to do was watch Nora at the shredder. After the harvested seaweeds had dried out, her job was to reduce and mix them into customised bags for what she called 'posh salads'. She stood at the machine in shorts and goggles. The size of a motorcycle engine, the shredder was mounted on a stand with a chute out the back. It was a bright red machine from the 1970s called the Apex Comminuting Mill. Nora stood behind it, shredding and filling her plastic bags, one after the other, making her pleasing roar of continual destruction. Clouds of dust filled the old fish factory with a thick vegetal smell. Even after she'd finished, and taken off her hairnet, bits of seaweed still clung to her long blonde hair.

She loved taking apart the Apex Comminuting Mill. After each shift she swept up the debris around the machine. 'This thing once powdered paracetamol,' she told him, demonstrating how she cleaned and fit the parts back together. Every day the blades had to be sharpened, the guts emptied, the mouth wiped dry. Her company sent her posh salads to customers all over the world.

For lunch they often drove out into the country for pasties. They went to a tiny farm shop in her friend Daisy's dirty old Volkswagen. Daisy was one of the company's harvesters, and her car was always full of what looked like gardening equipment – long-handled loppers, waterproof gloves, sharp saws attached to adjustable sticks. Outside the farm shop, they ate their pasties overlooking the fields. Daisy had a degree in biology. She explained to them how the living world was broken down.

'First,' she said, holding her pasty in its paper sack, 'there are the primary producers such as seaweeds and other plants. They make energy from the sun. Then come the secondary consumers, like fish and plankton. After that are the tertiary consumers, the humans and higher animals. When these levels interact properly, they're balanced.'

'Only they *aren't* interacting properly,' Nora said. 'Not any longer. That's why humans might have to give way.' She sat on the wall and kicked her feet in her runners. 'In Spain, I joined a sailing crew once, and we went way out to sea for days. Somehow, these buntings decided to maroon themselves with us. They'd circle all the way back to land, then return to our boat each night as we sailed further away. They got more and more exhausted. Eventually we left food out on deck for them, but they didn't eat. They just gave up and died. The captain didn't understand. Why were birds killing themselves to be with us?'

'Suicide?' Manfred said. It just tumbled out. He noticed Nora studying him with a look he hadn't seen before.

'Whatever,' said Daisy. She popped the last of her pasty in her mouth. 'I suppose we see a lot of dead things rejected by the sea. That's why, when you walk through seaweeds on the shore, they smell like corpses.'

Manfred spoke again before he could stop himself. 'I think some seaweeds have cognition.'

A customer leaving the farm shop overheard. 'Did you say *cognition*?' The man was tall, in wellington boots with a Labrador retriever at his side. The dog kept turning its head from Manfred to the hot pasty in the man's hand.

'I don't know for certain,' Manfred said.

The man glanced at the logo on Daisy's car. 'Either way, surely they need protecting, not commercial harvesting.'

'How delightfully simple an idea,' Nora said. She reached for Manfred's hand and traced her finger across his palm. Then she caught the man with her flat blue eyes. 'How do you know they aren't connected? Harvesting stimulates regrowth.'

The man just blinked at her with his mouth open. He called his dog and kept moving.

They returned in Daisy's car to the fish factory. Their start-up operated out of a few Portakabins on site. One of them was used for the break room, where they had a cup of tea. The room was strewn with customer orders, sample packets of seaweeds, old coffee mugs and historic photographs on the wall. The largest was a black-and-white taken in Shetland, where women were raking seaweeds into wicker baskets.

Nora walked over to the photo, gliding and unhurried as usual, never looking back. 'After a gale,' she told Manfred, 'lots of seaweed comes ashore. In Shetland, they used it for manure when it was rotting. If it was dry, it became animal fodder.'

They went to the packaging Portakabin, where Daisy worked. She was studying for her master's, and textbooks on photo-synthesis were stacked on top of a desk. On the shelves lay hundreds of white plastic bags, tied at the ends and labelled: sea greens, gutweed, purple dulse, kelp kombu, sea spaghetti, bladderwrack, carrageen, Irish moss, special nori from Sennen. The whole cabin smelled like a briny stew. Daisy switched on the radio and started to weigh the kombu.

'Try this,' she said, popping a piece into Manfred's mouth. It tasted like dried fish.

'Come on,' Nora said, leading him back outside. He noticed, as she walked ahead of him, fresh markings on her legs. 'What are those?' he asked.

Nora stopped. She fingered the tiny gouges along her thighs. 'I sometimes take care of this bloke's geese. I herd them back to their little house at the end of the day, and the nasty buggers peck at me. I know, it's ugly.'

He went and put his arms around her. There isn't a part of you, he wanted to say, that I don't consider beautiful. They stood on the jetty outside the fish factory, and he could see all the way to his cottage on the shore. As they stood together he could feel the warmth of her skin, her inner life. He wondered if she could feel the warmth in him. And then it struck him – of course she could, he wasn't dead yet.

The tide was coming in. The wind rippled the surface of the rising water. Manfred held Nora tighter, as if they were setting out by boat up the tributaries of the Helford toward the sea. In the distant garden, behind his cottage on the shore, something nefarious lurked in his bathtub. He wondered if it would ever be possible to tell Nora about the kelp. If he *could* tell her, one day in the future – then, he decided, he would be truly in love. And to be truly in love, one had to believe there was something to live for.

The next morning, he tried to walk quickly past the tub. Within seconds, the kelp had sprung out of the water.

'Going to work?'

'Yes.'

'Why not sit with me a moment?'

He perched on the edge of the tub. The Bullwhip's long brown stipe, completely uncurled, looked thicker than he remembered. 'I am running a bit late.'

The kelp's head stayed by the taps. Then it slithered a long blade out of the water and encircled Manfred's wrist. 'I'm on to you.'

'What do you mean?'

'You know.'

'I don't.'

'You're seeing someone, aren't you?'

The kelp tightened its blade and held him fast. The bladder-head floated closer. 'Do you know, carbon monoxide is one of the gases that makes me buoyant? What do you think that would feel like, sprayed into your eyes?'

'Please . . .'

'Do you remember what we agreed?'

'I have to go to work.'

'*Not when my sperm is still viable.* Your words. Remember?'

He did – it was a private agreement, made long before he'd met Nora. The blade pinched tighter. His wrist was turning blue. 'Please let go.'

The kelp squeezed even tighter. 'It's time to stop delaying things. Time to make concrete plans. Time to *end* it.'

The bladder-head floated by the taps. The blade unwound and slipped back under the water. Manfred stood up and held his trembling wrist, covered with welts.

'End it,' the kelp gurgled again.

Manfred circled the tub behind the taps. He hadn't changed the water in a few days, and it was covered with black flies. He plunged his hands in, despite the smell. He pulled the kelp out by the shoulders and shook its slimy head.

They struggled as the neighbour's cat came out to watch. The kelp unfurled its blades, wound them around his wrists and pulled him toward the tub. Manfred wrestled free. He flung the kelp to the grass, where it lay limp and sickly.

'What if I end *you*?' he said.

He seized a spade leaning against the house. Chest heaving, he glanced over at the cat. It was staring at him with its eyes wide.

'Coward,' the kelp cried.

'Don't tempt me.'

'Go ahead and do it! You'll lose your only voice of reason.'

One blow would have done it – he would have decapitated the thing. But the kelp was right. He *was* a coward. He dropped the spade on the grass. Holding his breath at the stink, he collected the kelp in his arms and flung back it into the tub.

The kelp needed to be in water. It didn't waste time stretching itself out. 'This is *my* home too,' it said, bobbing its brown head. '*You* brought me here.'

Manfred stood there panting with his hands on his knees, water dripping down his trousers. 'I know,' he said. 'There's no excuse.'

'I refuse to be intimidated like that again.'

'You're right. I'm sorry—'

'After all I've done for you.'

'It was stupid of me. I was afraid, that's all.'

'Nothing new.'

'I'm sorry.'

'Maybe you are, maybe you're not. But I'd rather not discuss it right this minute, if you don't mind.'

Manfred waited, head lowered. The cat had left the garden. Along the road, front doors were opening – parents taking their kids to school, others leaving for work. 'I promise I'll bring you fresh seawater tonight, okay?'

'Just go.'

'I said I was sorry.'

'And I said, I'd rather not talk about it right now.'

The kelp curled its long stipe under its blades and made a kind of nest. 'Go on, you don't want to be late for your first class.' It started to sink to the bottom of the tub and added, 'We'll discuss this when you get home.'

The sun was going down sooner. By four o'clock, as he made his way home along the beach, it was nearly pitch black.

He collected two buckets of fresh seawater. Part of him wanted to be with Nora. The older, wiser part wanted to be alone with the kelp. He scrabbled around along the waterline and found a few seashells for a gift. Then he came home through the back garden gate and hurried to the tub.

'Hello.' He peered into the murky water, and there was no movement. 'Can we be friends again?'

It was too dark to see very well. A new fear struck him, an outcome he'd been aware of, but had never allowed himself to fully plan for.

'Hello? You down there?' He leaned closer to the water. There was no gurgle, no voice, nothing. He put down the buckets and searched the garden for evidence of an escape.

'Hey! Where are you?'

Manfred sat on the tub. He rolled up his sleeve, slipped his hand into the water and fished around.

The kelp had returned to the sea. He was seized by a strange but familiar panic, worse than ever before – a visceral fear that when his new relationship with Nora ended, he'd have nobody to talk to.

He searched the garden. He couldn't find a trace of the Bullwhip. In his pockets he found the seashells he'd brought as a gift, and he placed them beside the taps. One minute he was an old, grief-stricken man, the next he was young and nervous about the future – like experiencing someone's death after secretly hoping for it. He wouldn't have to tell Nora after all. From now on, he would succeed or fail *on his own terms*.

He headed back to the house. In his bedroom window, a shape appeared. The kelp was up there, staring down at him. Manfred's throat tightened. It wasn't possible – the kelp couldn't live outside the water too long.

There was a horrible wet laugh behind him. He turned and found the kelp standing at a distance in the moonlight. It was casting its long shadow up to the window in silhouette.

'Tricked you!'

He wiped his eyes with joy. Waves of relief washed over him – a reassurance that the kelp was still *here*, his better conscience, his bosom friend. He wouldn't have to decide his fate alone.

'Of all the seaweeds, I had to find you?'

The kelp slipped back into the tub. It giggled like an infant.

Manfred's eyes were still watering. He turned his face away. 'You had me *worried*. What were you thinking, staying out so long?' He fetched the buckets of seawater and poured them in.

'Aah.' The kelp fanned out its blades as the water cascaded around its head. 'Aah.'

'Did you notice those shells I brought you?'

'They're pretty.'

Manfred sat on the edge of the tub. The neighbours had opened their curtains, so he lowered his voice. 'You *will* be happy here, won't you?'

'I suppose.'

'I have a bit of gossip. Remember that girl at the pub that Simon met, Ruth? Well, they're still together.'

'I knew you couldn't count on him as a friend. You were like that yourself, not long ago. Out meeting women.' The kelp whacked the water with its flattened blades and splashed Manfred's face. 'Where did *that* get you?'

Manfred wiped his eyes. He pretended, for a moment, that Nora didn't exist. 'Those days are long gone, I suppose.'

'I only bring it up,' the kelp said, 'because you seem to have forgotten. Just remember, there *is* such a thing as a good death.'

Together, they stared out at the river stretching to the sea. A little later the kelp slipped back into the water, and Manfred crept back inside.

That night he woke to a voice calling out to him. It flew over the clinking masts in the harbour like the chimes of a distant church bell.

'Think twice! Think twice!'

Yes, he did need to be warned. He *had* imagined a child with Nora. The kelp was being good enough to remind him of a couple of statistics. One was sixty million, the other was three. The former was the estimate of miscarriages and terminations each year. The latter was the number he'd contributed.

Three different partners, three miscarriages. Each ate at him. Not only because of what might have been, but because these women went on to have children with other men.

Below Manfred's window the kelp sat taller in the tub, and in its round bladder-head turning toward him, he saw the faces of his exes. Their eyes carried the suspicion of blame. He had told the second about the first, and the third about the other two. All three, without undue delay, had found their next partners more family-minded, with effective sperm at last. In the town where they all lived, Manfred had heard of their progress. They had given birth to healthy children while he became known as that unfortunate soul with the broken seeds. He couldn't exactly pull aside shopkeepers and passers-by and wave the tests that showed his sperm had normal count and 'optimal' motility. It seemed something deeper lurked, some combination of sadistic alchemical forces preventing him from fatherhood. Or maybe he'd been set aside by the gods, saved especially for seaweeds.

Secretly he started eating more of the dulse Nora had given him. He had it before breakfast – just a pinch, like a sailor taking snuff. Dulse gave him vitality, just as she'd promised. He had seaweed in the morning, went home and faced a different seaweed at night.

Now that he was seeing Nora, life became almost rewarding. People spotted them together. Locals and work colleagues treated him with respect. Back and forth he went, out the front door toward the promise of life and back home through the garden of death. Ultimately one of them would eventually come out on top – Nora, or the kelp.

Then, mid-December at the end of term, Nora asked if he'd like to go to London for the weekend.

They were in her room, lying in bed. He had come to prefer it there, especially the view of her back garden. It wasn't beset by crashing waves but by gentle pine trees, fields of lettuce and warm earth.

'I'm going up there for a conference on algae,' Nora said. 'Nutritionists, evolutionary biologist panels, phycologists, marine biologists.'

'An academic conference?' At first he was excited by the idea, and the implication that their relationship was developing. Then he thought of the kelp. How would explain such a long absence? He wouldn't be able to refresh the tub. 'I don't think I could manage it,' he said. 'I'd be out of my depth.'

'Don't go to the talks, then. Just join me in the hotel. We can visit the Herbarium under the Museum of Living History. Where Mary-Margaret Dennison works.'

'Really?'

'You could meet her, if you'd like.' Nora rolled over in bed. 'Let's see,' she said, reaching for the programme on her desk. 'There's a panel on conservation trends. One on kelp forest biodiversity . . .'

'That does sound interesting.'

'. . . and my boss Pete, he's got the industry talk on his collaboration with Cornwall Council. Protecting intertidal coastal zones.'

Manfred looked over her bare shoulder. The conference programme was in her hands, partly draped by her long blonde hair. Whenever she talked about seaweeds he became more excited than usual. He put his arms around her waist and turned her toward him. In seconds, their legs were entwined. Then they were more fully ensnared, entangled, stuck. They separated briefly, then slowly came together again and made love.

Immediately after, Nora fell asleep. Manfred lay on his back, almost breathless in her shadowy little room. Her nightstand was strewn with the seashells he'd brought her from the beach. As gently as he could, he reached under the duvet. He moved his hand like a spider slowly down her chest, all the way to her stomach. For a moment he let it rest where their baby would be. They hadn't used protection this time. He'd also been very close to telling her about the kelp.

He left the bed. He wandered around her room, glancing at her things. She wasn't a tidy person. Recipes were stuck on index cards and Post-its. Books of star constellations lay open on the floor. Tubs of seaweed samples sat around half-eaten. Bits of green sea lettuce spilled onto her desk, down her chair and onto the floor. It was as if he stood in a densely wooded forest, trees swaying overhead, only to notice the shrubs and bushes and moss underfoot.

Some handwritten notes were tucked at the back of her desk. They were sticking out of a guidebook on Spain. The handwriting, he noticed, wasn't hers.

He peered at her asleep in bed. She lay on her side with her mouth slightly open, her eyelids dancing across the surface of a dream. He reached for the book. It was dog-eared, marked up with a few restaurants circled and beaches ticked. He pulled out one of the notes: *No stopping until we become them. Or they become us.*

Outside the door there was a loud commotion. It was her roommates, chasing each other up the stairs with manic laughter. Nora stirred – quickly, he put the note back into the book.

'You're awake.' Manfred realised he was naked and covered himself with his hands.

She laughed. 'You were just fucking me like a bloody rhino. Now you're modest?' She reached over and pulled him back to bed.

They lay there together as he blinked at the ceiling. 'Can I ask you something?' he said. She yawned and turned toward him. 'When did you first get interested in seaweeds?'

'Why do you ask?'

'Just curious.'

She sat up and crossed her legs. Her hesitation was very brief. Then she delivered to him a tidily packaged story – a little tale to do with Spain, surfing and collecting things on the beach.

Later that night, when he reached the tub, he shone a torch near the taps until the head came slowly to the surface.

'Hello.' Water dripped down the kelp's stipe. Its blades curled inward. 'I won't ask where *you've* been.'

'Nowhere in particular,' Manfred said.

The kelp gave him a sarcastic hiss. 'You've allowed yourself to get carried away.'

'I've been learning a few things. Things to do with you.'

'Oh? Like what?'

'Like maybe you're not dead after all.'

'If you'd *wanted* to preserve me, you wouldn't have left me in the garden. You would have brought me inside and put me in the freezer.'

Manfred sat and put his arm around the kelp's shoulders. 'Maybe. What if you have certain dormant characteristics?'

'What are you getting at, please?'

He crossed his legs. He looked away and tried to make his voice calm, even casual. 'I've been invited to a conference. All kinds of experts will be there. There's even a panel on *you*. Did you know, you might be an invasive species?' He took the programme out of his pocket and held it under the torch. 'Here it is: *The American Kelp are Coming: Why Should We Care, and What Can We Do?*'

The Bullwhip hissed again. One of its longer blades came creeping over the porcelain. This time, something gaseous seeped out of its pneumatocysts. The programme in Manfred's hand sizzled and smoked.

'Tell me what else is on offer.' The blade curled around the programme, as if trying to read by touch. 'Where and when is this so-called *conference* taking place?'

'London.' Manfred pulled the programme away. 'This weekend.'

'Ooh!' The kelp wriggled, and bobbed its head. 'I've always wanted to see London.'

'I could speak to experts about you. Maybe they'll have advice.'

'They'll want to examine me. Put their *hands* on me. See how it was I came here in the first place. I'll come with you.'

Manfred thought of the kelp in their hotel room. It would sleep in their bath. It would eavesdrop as they talked in bed. 'I don't think that's a good idea,' he said.

'Why not?'

'Well, how in the world would I get you there?'

'A big plastic tub?'

'What – on the train? I'd need three or four people to help.'

'They have extra staff on trains.'

'They wouldn't even let me on.'

The kelp floated closer to him. It stuck its round head out of the water. 'I thought you said you cared about my life.'

'Of course I do.'

The kelp went quiet. It seemed to be thinking. 'Who told you about this conference?'

'A friend.' Right after he said it, he could feel himself turning pale.

The kelp snorted. 'And this *friend's* going as well?'

Manfred pointed his torch into the water. He could see the long stipe, curling like a snake under the head. 'Hey. Come back. We were having a conversation.'

The kelp stayed under water. Across the garden, the wind picked up and made white horses in the roiling river.

'Please. I want to talk to you.'

The kelp sat up beneath the taps. 'You've taken me for a fool.' It had cleaned itself off. Its face was proudly scrubbed, almost puritanical. 'Of course, I only have myself to blame.'

'I just wanted to try to live once more.' He stood up. 'Is that so horrible?'

'To *live*?' The kelp's voice was low, almost inaudible. 'My ancestors are from another continent. I've dodged cliffs crumbling into the sea and slept inside shipwrecks. I've crossed the Gibraltar Strait!'

77

'I know.'

'You can't dream of what I've seen and done. I come from the place your people left – the place you'll return to, one day.'

Manfred wandered over to the gate and looked out over the waves.

'I came ashore for *you*,' the kelp said. 'Not her.'

'And I'm grateful for that.'

'Have you told her of your track record? You asked me, remember, on the first night we met. You asked me to promise—'

'Don't bring it up. Not now.'

'Promise me, you said, if I ever dupe myself again—'

'Don't.' He put his head in his hands.

'Your words, not mine: *Not when my sperm is still viable. Do anything you can to stop me.*'

He lowered his eyes and tried to calm himself. Behind him, he heard a pop. It sounded like a bottle being uncorked.

'What have you done?' He rushed to the tub. The water was draining away, the kelp had shrivelled into itself. He ran for the hose, turned it on and dragged it over.

'Where's the plug?' Manfred cried.

The water kept draining away. The kelp was shrinking into a sickly damp pile, like something you'd find on the beach. He stepped into the tub. He reached down and held the kelp in his arms.

'Tell me what you want. Please.'

He had no idea how much he'd needed it, not until the tears came. 'I'll do anything, just don't leave me like this. I can't trust her. I only love you . . .'

The shrivelled little head that was cradled in his hands turned toward him. It was already much smaller, no bigger than his fist. 'Do you mean it? You really love me?'

Manfred nodded. 'Yes!'

'Then take me inside.'

He peered over at his cottage. 'What, now?'

'I want to feel like a resident. A *partner*. Not some vagrant you keep in the garden.'

The slimy blades crept around his back and hips. Almost gagging at the smell, Manfred stepped out of the tub toward the house. The long stipe trailed behind in the grass.

He kicked open the back door. Up in his neighbour's house, he saw the lights switch on. His neighbours were watching, and he didn't care. He brought the kelp across the threshold and into the kitchen.

'Tell me the truth,' the kelp said, looking around. 'Has *she* ever been here?'

Manfred shook his head. 'Never.'

'I want us to lie down together. In your bedroom. Each and every room in the house. First let's get out of this horrid kitchen.'

He carried the kelp through. He went into the lounge and hoisted it up on his shoulder, so that their heads were right beside each other as they walked.

'That's right. Keep going, past that *vile* chair. Right up the stairs. Ooh! There's the tub. It can wait. That's your bedroom? You just throw your socks on the carpet, do you? Who's that on your dresser, your little family?'

The kelp stuck out its neck toward Manfred's framed photos. It smirked at his parents. 'I've had enough. Time to lie down together. In bed.'

Manfred drew back the blankets. As they lay together he could feel the kelp curling tight around his body. The stipe shot up his back, the blades encircled his legs. He was trapped.

'Now,' the kelp said, turning its rancid head on the pillow. Up close, Manfred could see the prunish wrinkles. 'You've been thinking about your place in nature, haven't you?'

'Yes.'

'It's a waste of time. Nature doesn't need your thoughts. It's only human pride, what you're doing. Your so-called *thinking* makes no difference at all. Repeat that, please.'

'My so-called thinking makes no difference at all.'

'That's right. And to have a child – that's a crime. Nod your head, please. Repeat what I've said.'

Manfred looked at the kelp and nodded. 'To have a child is a crime.'

'The world is full and overflowing. Far too many humans, all of them superfluous. I shouldn't have to tell you that. The desire for reproduction is a *sickness*, Manfred, it only results in more people and a limitless capacity for atrocities. There's only one instance where being a father is acceptable, and that's when the child is not your own. When it's an orphan. Understand?'

'Yes.'

'That's what every living thing is,' the kelp said. 'An orphan. Tell me again how awful your life has been. I want details.'

Manfred lay there exhausted. Turning toward the kelp's rubbery mouth, he offered it his most embarrassing confessions. The kelp had heard some of them already.

'Remember,' the kelp said, 'how you concluded that all people have useless lives? You're smart. Yet you still lie here beside me, your eyelashes damp with self-pity. Aren't you capable of making correct decisions?'

'Yes.'

'Tell me, then. Tell me exactly how.'

The kelp wanted to hear each of his imagined methods. It hissed quietly as he described them. It emanated carbon monoxide from its pneumatocysts.

'Good,' it said, after Manfred had finished. 'I'm glad this is your decision. Now go off to London. Meet more idiots who give us names and put us into categories. When you return, you can tell me what you've learned, then make good on your promise.'

Manfred nodded, spent. The night had been long and was far from over. The kelp insisted on initiating every room in the house, each time with more confessions and pledges. Finally, it demanded to be left alone in the bathtub with plenty of fresh seawater.

NORA

She sat on the sofa waiting for Manfred to come down to the lobby of their South Kensington hotel. As a well-dressed elderly man rolled his suitcase across the gleaming floor, Nora realised happily that she had fallen deeply in love. Finally she'd found someone normal. People from all over the world were coming and going – it felt like she was having an affair. Only this time, she was with a man she wanted to share a future with.

Manfred never talked over her. He didn't need to be in charge and didn't have a drinking problem. That he was into her obscure world of seaweeds was a plus. She was even looking forward to introducing him to Mary-Margaret – a relationship she'd played down. In truth Mary-Margaret was like a mother and a mentor rolled into one.

It had been over three years since she'd left Caños, and all the nonsense that went with it. She'd left her dead-end job at the surfer bar, along with her daily diet of tapas and fino, and her co-dependent friendships which centred mostly around drink and recovering from drink. Most importantly, she'd finally left Ben. What hadn't left her – what had only grown – was her interest in seaweeds.

In many ways, she had Ben to thank. It had been his mania, paranoia and alcohol-infused delusions that had forced her to realise how she'd been wasting her time with men like him, men too self-absorbed and self-destructive for anyone's good. In the end it was the seaweeds themselves that saved her. The more she'd learned about them, the more they'd provided a way out. Who could have imagined Cornwall, a place she'd only thought of for its surfing, could have offered a job in seaweeds?

This would be her third visit to the annual phycology conference. The first time had been something of an accident – a friend of a friend had needed a plus-one for the conference dinner – and from then on, she'd become rooted to the whole business, probably for life. She'd made friends, taken lovers, found jobs. It was all very incestuous.

It was why she'd been attracted to Manfred. He had a healthy interest in seaweeds. They were his hobby. He wanted to learn without being monomaniacal. And he wasn't part of those tight-knit research circles who only socialised with each other and created a stultifying atmosphere. It had taken her a while, but she realised she needed *balance* in relation to seaweeds. Manfred helped with that. She could bring him along to the seaweed party, so to speak, then leave together.

Manfred came out of the lift and nervously hung back. It had taken some doing to convince him to come. He confessed to being intimidated by her professional colleagues – and what had eventually convinced him was the promise of a tour of the Herbarium.

They went hand-in-hand, out of the hotel and across the street. The Museum of Living History was a short walk. Under the security cameras they proceeded through the ornate brick and stone entrance, through the metal detectors and into the great hall. Visitors came and went, carrying tote bags and taking pictures with their phones. Manfred moved timidly, green around the gills. He stopped at a giant squid over the doorway and peered up at its great beak and long tentacles. She laughed as he flinched from it, as if the squid might still be feeding.

They took the lift down. When they reached the basement Mary-Margaret was waiting for them in khakis and a white silk shirt halfway unbuttoned. She had thick curly hair and green eyes.

'Hello, love.' Mary-Margaret embraced her.

Nora held on a little longer than she'd planned. She felt accepted, and at the same time fortunate to be friends with Mary-Margaret, one of the most important living experts in phycology.

Manfred was visibly blushing as he held out his hand. 'I've read your book many times. I have to admit, I'm a fan.'

'Go on. That thing's so outdated – I've been working on the next edition, but it never seems to get any bloody closer to completion. Now come inside my subterranean domain . . .'

Mary-Margaret unlocked the door and went ahead. The Herbarium grew out of one long, central corridor. Wooden cabinets stretched from floor to ceiling, with rolling ladders on tracks. There was a strong smell of mercury and iodine.

As they walked behind Mary-Margaret, Manfred kept staring. Nora became aware of a slight jealousy – because of her friend's experience, and powers of seduction. Mary-Margaret had no regular partner, no children. She'd devoted her life to algae, and not without a cost. Along the way, many had been loved and abandoned.

'We don't get too many visitors down here,' Mary-Margaret said over her shoulder. 'They all want to see the stuffed tigers and bears. Nobody talks about it, but the mammals up there are under constant attack from carpet beetles. And worms. The vertebrates are being eaten from inside out. Soon they'll have nothing left in their guts!'

Nora peered into the wings, where the lab assistants sat hunched over microscopes and specimens. When Manfred paused at a taxonomy exhibit, Mary-Margaret slid her hand under his arm. 'Nora tells me you're interested in kelp. I want to show you one of our oldest specimens.'

She unlocked a cabinet with a key attached to her waist and pulled out the top drawer. 'This,' she said, opening the manila folder, 'is *Nereocystis luetkeana* . . .'

Under the fluorescent lights, the three of them came closer. Laid flat, squashed and pressed on the page, the dried brown kelp peered back at them. It was withered, ancient, mute.

'The first of its kind collected in continental Europe, back in 1815.' She tapped her slender fingers near the stem. 'Look how careful they were, preserving this elegant shape. They were religious about nature then.'

Manfred looked at her. 'Religious?'

'Scientists thought every aspect of the natural world formed part of a larger design. Each plant and animal – every living thing shared a common destiny.'

'They don't think that any longer?'

'Oh, no.' She laughed. 'Now, apparently, God can't exist!'

Nora leaned closer. The specimen was over two hundred years old, and it seemed to return her gaze. 'Manfred found a Bullwhip recently,' she said. 'A big one.'

'Where?'

'Cornwall,' he said. 'Gweek.'

Mary-Margaret didn't move. 'That's unusual.'

Nora studied the faint handwriting under the specimen. 'And where was this one found?'

'Spain, I believe.' Mary-Margaret slipped on her spectacles to read the collection list. 'Let's see. Yes. A place called Caños de Meca.'

'Caños?' Nora felt herself tilting. She was suddenly sent sideways and back, as if time had wrapped itself around her.

'Must be the iodine,' Mary-Margaret said, peering at her. 'It can have a strong effect.'

A couple of lab workers hurried over. Everything had gone blurry – she could feel Manfred's arm around her shoulder, holding her up. Nora's eyes rolled back. In her mind's eye she saw Ben's glass of golden fino and the rolling surf off Tarifa.

~

She came to in a large armchair. A window opened onto a courtyard, and a breeze was blowing in. The two of them were having tea – Mary-Margaret sitting forward behind her desk, and Manfred across from her, propped up straight like a schoolboy in a tutorial.

'Destinations are important for your genus.'

'Why?'

'That Bullwhip's a traveller. Even for kelp with a wide domain, it's unusually active.'

Nora gripped the arms of her chair. She told herself that lots of seaweeds were found in Caños, that it was a confluence, after all. She leaned back among the files and specimens in their plastic sleeves. A large shelf against the wall held books on marine ecology, taxonomy and genetics. There were multiple copies of *The Future of British Seaweeds*.

'Ah,' Mary-Margaret said, noticing her awake. 'Feeling better?'

Manfred came over and felt her forehead. He handed her a cup of tea. 'We thought you just needed to rest a moment,' he said, hurrying back to his chair.

'Normally,' Mary-Margaret continued, 'we'll see Bullwhip along the Pacific coast of North America – Oregon, Washington, British Columbia. It also pops up in northern Africa, along the Gibraltar Strait.'

'Caños de Meca,' Nora said, thinking out loud. 'Like Cornwall, a coastline with multiple waterways. A waystation.'

'Exactly. Recently, a Bullwhip was spotted up in the Arctic, though this hasn't been verified. If it starts arriving in Cornwall in greater numbers, that would be news.'

Manfred got up and started to pace. 'The Arctic? Surely kelp can't survive there?'

'The oceans are warming faster and faster. They'll have better territory domination where it's cold and remote.'

'That far from its habitat?'

'It drifts. It hitchhikes on distance swimmers, like whales.'

'Intentionally?' Manfred and Nora asked, at the same time.

'Well – yes. It both anticipates and responds. It predicts changes to the environment and adjusts. Very quickly.'

'Evolving, then?' Nora said.

'They adjust their trajectory. Not necessarily their shape.'

Manfred was staring at Nora, as if for help. 'I'm afraid I don't understand.'

'Tell you what,' Mary-Margaret said, 'instead of describing this, I'll show you.'

They followed her out of the office. Mary-Margaret swiped her key card, and they entered the inner chambers of the Herbarium. It turned much colder. They passed a series of labs until they reached a sign that read, *Cryptographic Research*. Through the door's window, Nora could see lab workers taking plastic tubs from tall refrigerators along the wall.

Mary-Margaret brought them inside. The room was very bright. 'Every living species we've ever known of,' she said, 'ends in extinction. On average, after about five million years.' She waved her hand down the length of the lab. 'Seaweeds are the exception. They've been around more or less unchanged for over a billion and a half years.'

Manfred's eyes darted to the plastic tubs on the work stations. 'They pre-date practically everything we know.'

'That's right. And their fossil deposits look remarkably similar to seaweeds of today.'

Mary-Margaret led them along the lab. The workstations in the middle were divided into sections: reds, greens and browns. 'Red seaweeds are the oldest, most abundant and diverse. Browns are the largest. Greens, probably the least understood.'

'The freshwater seaweeds,' Manfred said. He glanced quickly at Nora. 'I studied botany.'

'That explains your sex appeal,' Mary-Margaret said, walking over to a plastic tub. 'You're right, greens aren't normally found in marine environments. But recently we've been seeing more of them in the oceans.' She dropped her hand straight into the water. Inside, the small seaweed seemed to float up to her touch. 'Such a pretty little sea lettuce.'

'That is pretty,' Manfred said, coming closer. 'Hello, there.'

'Its blades change colours closer to the surface of the water. See it go from dark to bright green, under the light?'

Nora watched the two of them. She'd seen Mary-Margaret give these kinds of tours before. Now she felt oddly displaced.

'Look closely at these lighter coloured cells.' Mary-Margaret scooped up the sea lettuce and stretched it out between her fingers. 'They're the females. The darker ones, males. Right now, these cells are using the plant, the vegetal part, as a vehicle before jumping off to spore. They can do it on a stick or a rock, makes no difference. That's what I mean by expert adjustment. They keep colonising, no matter what.'

Manfred was following the silky substance between her fingers. Mary-Margaret locked eyes with him, openly flirting. She'd had so many partners, Nora thought, she didn't need another. It was how people gained power – insatiable hunger. Mary-Margaret *ate* men, the rumours went, and each volunteered. She was the phycological equivalent of the male fertility doctor who impregnated unsuspecting clients.

'Why are you studying this specimen?' Manfred asked her.

'To see how it protects itself from stress.' Mary-Margaret dropped her hand back in the tub and released it. The sea lettuce floated for a while, then drifted to the bottom away from the light. 'It avoids heat, bright light and toxins. It isolates its infected cells so that the bad part stays dead, and the healthy part keeps on growing.'

'That brings us back to the idea of design, doesn't it?' Nora said. 'It has its own internal rules.'

'The perfect life form.' Mary-Margaret looked Manfred up and down. 'A seaweed can evolve, or stay the same. It can reproduce sexually or asexually. That Bullwhip of yours – do you mind if I ask what you did with it?'

Manfred stepped back, bumping against the tubs of specimens that sloshed about in the water. He glanced at Nora then back to Mary-Margaret, his mouth in a tight circle. 'It's at home.'

'Still?' Nora asked. 'You didn't tell me that.'

'I thought I did.'

Mary-Margaret laughed. 'You mean you've never seen his kelp, love? I would have thought he'd have shown you ages ago.'

'He hasn't invited me over.'

'It's natural to be possessive of discoveries.' Mary-Margaret patted Manfred's shoulder. 'Bullwhips can get quite large. Ten, maybe eleven meters? Where do you keep it?'

'In my bathtub.'

Nora snickered. 'What, you bathe with it?'

'No, the tub in my back garden. It seems to get along there.'

She studied him. 'But I thought that kelp was dead.'

'Don't worry, I've heard of stranger things,' Mary-Margaret said. 'Where collectors keep their algae would surprise most anyone. Studying them becomes something of an obsession, I'm afraid.'

The talks, poster sessions and corporate coffee breaks were held in a climate-controlled, windowless conference room. A petrochemicals firm called Motilion had underwritten the whole thing. The firm's banner, with its bright orange sun-like ball, hung beside the lectern. Their reps manned an information booth with glossy brochures, office supply grab bags and biodegradable pens.

They had arrived late. Nora wanted to sit down, but Manfred kept pacing in front of the research posters. It had been a struggle convincing him to leave their hotel room – he'd sat fixedly, almost immobile, on the edge of the bed. 'I'll embarrass you,' he kept saying, as she tried to reassure him.

It was the first time she'd heard him speak like this. His eyes had gone darker, hollow. 'Just go,' he told her. 'Leave me here.'

She shook her head. 'I'm not going anywhere, you know.' She noticed something else, then – her attunement to his changing moods. It reminded her of Ben, and the way she'd become so attached. With Manfred, it was more like enmeshment, where it wasn't possible any longer to decide only for herself. She didn't *want* to go to the conference alone. She would go with him, or not at all.

Nora did her best to make him feel whole again. She heard out his anxieties, she praised him and made him feel worthy. At last he got himself dressed. He combed his hair and readied himself for the very world he was afraid of.

The first speaker was almost finished. 'Let's sit down,' Nora said. She'd spotted Mary-Margaret in the front row, surrounded by young stars. They came to these conferences in droves, most of them early career researchers chasing grant proposals, job references and co-authored publications.

Manfred took two empty seats at the back. Nora knew the first speaker at the podium – an older man from Greece who had the remarkable name of Aristotle. His thick grey hair was parted in the centre, and his open linen shirt exposed his chest. He was an ex-boyfriend of Mary-Margaret's and was rumoured to have had many children with different partners.

Aristotle was describing the resilience strategies of seaweeds in the south Pacific. In sweeping, almost poetic language, he described their 'exodus' in a series of interactive and multi-coloured maps that ran in a loop on the screen projector, and set to a musical score. Special effects in presenting algae research had become increasingly the norm.

Manfred was turning pale. 'Incredible,' he said, as Aristotle left the podium to applause. Nora checked her programme. The next talk was *Sustainable Aquaculture Practice*. The speaker, as it happened, was an ex of her own.

Luke came to the podium in the same corduroys he'd worn when they'd met. Though now a university professor, Luke was young. He was *too* young, emotionally. Egotistical and self-involved, he'd never understood the meaning of sacrifice, even in such simple activities as sharing a platter of cheese.

Luke fixed his eyes on the audience. He ran his hand through his cropped hair and tugged at his beard. He put up a graphic on the depths of the oceans and opened with an anecdote about kelp forest regrowth that Nora had heard before. She thumbed through the programme and found an afternoon panel on *Wildemania*, a red seaweed with very thin blades recently found in northern Russia.

'Right – over ten thousand kinds of seaweeds on the planet, according to the most recent estimate.'

Nora looked up. Luke had come out from behind the podium. He had his hands in the pockets of his cardigan, and was striding up the middle of the aisle and glancing at her. She had broken up with him long ago, but she'd heard he was still referring to her as his 'on-again, off-again.'

'Aquaculture tells us which seaweeds prefer which oceanic depths. So. You might ask, do sexually reproductive seaweeds seek out partners there? Is it like swiping a dating app?'

The audience laughed. Luke was openly staring at her now – and Manfred had noticed. He had sunk into his chair, his head retracted like a turtle's.

With a laser pointer, Luke hovered his red dot on the south coast of England. 'Here's where I live outside London,' he said, 'and here's the English Channel. Which seaweeds are flourishing here? And why?' He shifted west to Cornwall. 'Ocean placement is important. In Falmouth, the third-deepest natural harbour in the world, seaweeds reject those literally out of their depth. So, can we say that seaweeds show a preference for certain partners?'

A woman up front raised her hand. 'Can you talk about the challenges of sustainable harvesting? Now that the business has grown – to what, billions of pounds annually?'

'We're victims of our own success. We have to balance demand against conservation. Kelp forests can be enormous, almost the size of their territorial cousins in the Amazon. We do have to conserve, yes. But we've also an obligation to strap on those goggles and work that shredder – as my friend from Cornwall over there knows.' He gave a deep, melodramatic bow.

During the applause, some turned for Nora's reaction. She clapped politely and shook her head – Luke was still a boy pulling stunts. It was time for the coffee break. 'Ready?' She stood up, but Manfred didn't move.

'What was *that* about?'

Nora sat back down. 'Nothing.'

'Were you two . . .'

'A while ago, yes.'

'And you didn't tell me?'

His face twisted into a grimace. He sat there bloodless, bereft. Meanwhile the more ambitious delegates were pushing toward

Mary-Margaret – company reps and grad students, stepping on each other's toes. Over their heads, she caught Nora's eye and pointed at the Cornish Seaweeds banner. There, premium canaps were being offered on an invitation-only basis.

'Come on,' Nora said, taking Manfred's elbow. The best course was to jolt him out of his funk. She brought him quickly past the delegates and through her firm's cordon. Catering staff circled with platters of puff pastries, sautéed mushrooms and dried seaweeds sprinkled over poached eggs. The printed recipe books she'd put together stood on their own table.

Mary-Margaret stood at the edge of a break-out session being delivered by Nora's boss Pete. A small group had gathered, mostly potential investors. Pete was giving his growth spiel, waving his arms, sleeves rolled up to his pale elbows, hair plastered wetly to his forehead. Manfred drifted away.

'He's struggling at the moment,' Nora whispered to Mary-Margaret. 'He thinks he's embarrassing me.'

'Everyone has their rough patches.'

'I suppose.' Nora watched Manfred wander off, toward the corner of the reception, where he found a stretch of empty wall to lean against.

'Does he still teach?'

'Yes.'

'He might serve a better function elsewhere.'

Nora drew in her breath. 'That's a bit harsh, isn't it?'

'I'm just saying. There are reasons for behaviours.' The green of Mary-Margaret's eyes darkened. 'The best ones want whatever *you* want without feeling insecure.'

'Thanks for the advice.'

'Don't get defensive, love. I'm just making an observation. Now, that Bullwhip of his.'

'Yes?'

'If it hasn't completely dried out, it might actually be salvageable. He's got to store it away from the light or it will disintegrate.'

'I know.'

'He's welcome to bring it to the Herbarium any time he likes.'

'I'll be sure to tell him.' For the first time, Nora didn't want more guidance from her mentor. 'I should go and collect him.'

'You might want to wait. Look.'

At the entrance to the reception, Luke had made it past the cordon along with Aristotle. The two were coming straight for them.

Manfred's anxiety across the room was palpable. Nora felt the pull of her attachment, her entwining. It was *why* she liked him, she told herself. He wasn't of this crowd – it would make anyone uncomfortable. She headed over to save him, but halfway there she felt two hands turning her around. One was Luke's, the other Aristotle's.

'Where do you think you're going?'

'Come on, show us the latest recipes!'

They practically dragged her toward the table with her seaweed recipe book, and began quizzing her on its contents. Laughing nervously, Nora was too surprised to react. She caught a glimpse of Manfred rigidly pressed against the wall, like a man in front of a firing squad.

~

Their train shot along the Devon coast, toward the crumbling red cliffs of Teignmouth and its flat expanse of sea. Nora felt frightened by what she was returning to, as though passing into a landscape she no longer recognised. Manfred, on the window seat beside her, seemed miles away.

She had to confront what happened the previous weekend. How, for the first time in her life, she'd consciously, even blithely, opted out of contraception. They hadn't even spoken about it since. She'd felt certain this wasn't based on an impulse but a belief – a sense, a kind of premonition, that her love for Manfred was stronger, and healthier than it had been for anyone else.

Now she wasn't sure. Manfred sat pressed against the glass with his eyes fixed on the passing countryside. He asked no questions, refused food. Nothing in his expression resembled life. They passed Teignmouth, followed by the raised tracks over Dawlish. In the distance, past the red cliffs, fishing boats were coming back to shore – and further out, at the edges of the horizon, the long dark line of container ships. They looked like hearses waiting at a funeral. She could see Manfred's reflection in the window. He was searching the water as if for survivors.

'Hey.' She reached for his arm, and he flinched. 'So what do you think? I mean, what's next?'

'What do you mean – *next*?' He turned, his mouth strangely contorted.

At that moment Nora saw Ben in the *Esposa*, sitting under the Iberico ham with his hands between bottle and glass. Three years it had been, since she'd left him to stumble back to England alone. When had she known, exactly, when *that* was over?

'I was just making conversation.' She decided not to say anything for a while. As they crossed the Tamar bridge, the windows became streaked with scum and mizzle. It was as if the weather knew the border, as if all of Cornwall lay contained in the same thin film. Rain slanted sideways, gusts of wind shook the train on its tracks. They reached Bodmin moor, where the sky dropped and darkened. Press on, she decided. Don't lose your nerve and stop, like last time, without saying what you think.

'I want to tell you something,' she said. 'I like you. Very much. It's different from romantic love, I think. I mean, I think we might *have* something here. But before we go any further, I need to know a few things.'

'What things are those,' he said softly. He still had his face turned away.

'I'm not interested in just carrying on. Not casually, as if I don't care about our future.'

The back of his head was motionless. 'Go on.'

'Remember the other day, when we didn't use protection? Well – maybe I want a family one day. There. I said it.'

He turned. His eyes were moist. 'I didn't think you were actually considering it. Not with me, anyway.'

'What? Who did you *think* I was considering it with?'

'Plenty at that conference to choose from.'

'Don't be silly, Manfred.'

'I wasn't counting. But if I *had* been—'

'Then you would have counted nobody! Not one. I wasn't *ever* serious about any of my exes. I know, in some ways, it's far too soon for us to be talking about this. But I told myself a while back that I would be straight with the next person in my life.'

'I respect that.'

'It wouldn't be fair if I didn't let you know in advance.'

The train was leaving the moor as they plunged into clay country. The white conical tips of the derelict clay pits gleamed under the stars. He was crying as he reached over and held her hands. He squeezed her tightly, as if something suddenly possessed him.

'Stop.' She was trembling. He was gripping her hands so tightly, she almost cried out. Finally he released her.

Manfred looked back out the window, his shoulders hunched to his ears. He needed reassurance, she decided. 'It was *nice* sharing that hotel. I have an idea. What if we went over to yours tonight? You know, for a bit of privacy? I could cook us dinner in your kitchen.'

He didn't reply, just turned away. A new silence came over him, dark and pointed.

'Maybe not tonight,' she said. 'Sometime soon, then?'

His silence deepened in the endless countryside. Finally, lights appeared in the distance. Out of the darkness, twin cathedral spires rose up out of the city, glowing sickly yellow in the night. The train jolted them into the bright white lights of the terminal.

'Truro at last,' he said. He sounded like a doctor delivering a fatal diagnosis.

It was all she could do not to shout – why can't you be *nicer*? Why, after months, *couldn't* she go to his house? Then it struck her. She'd been so blind. He was probably having a relationship with someone else.

They reached the station and gathered their things. It didn't seem possible, suddenly, that she was right. He wasn't with someone else, he was just old and miserable. Certain men spent their days postponing the grimace that formed on their faces at night. At the end of their lives, that grimace took over entirely. Manfred was one of those. He wasn't even speaking to her now, not even politely. She had another foreboding that here, at the end of their first holiday, she'd never see him again.

A taxi pulled up as they left the station. The window came down, and she'd gone mute. The driver leaned out the window. His head was as big as a cow's, and his cow eyes travelled over them.

'Where to?'

It was Manfred who finally answered. He spoke dully, staring up at the fog. 'Gweek.'

She was dropped off first at the top of the main road. They were in view of Manfred's house, and it was a short walk up the hill to her own. She said goodbye through the window. They kissed briefly, made vague plans to chat the next day. Then the driver continued down the road, down through town toward Manfred's cottage.

Nora stood there with her rucksack and watched the taxi turn the corner and disappear. Instead of going home, she walked down to the beach. In the distance, through the mizzle, she could see the outline of the old fish factory. She had thought Cornwall would be the place to begin a new stage of her life. Now she wanted only to be back in London.

She rolled a cigarette and smoked overlooking the river. By the time she'd finished it, thicker clouds had arrived. Back and forth she walked along the sand near his house, waiting for his lights to go on. Maybe he'd gone out for food. Maybe he was meeting someone. If so, her night had just become much longer.

She smoked another cigarette. Then, his house lights came on at last. She wanted to reach his door soon after he did – to catch him in his element, to find out what it was hiding.

Keeping low, she crept up the sand. The gate to his back garden was standing wide open. The wind off the water was blowing in, straight over the grass toward the bathtub. It was a bigger garden than she'd thought, with a lane of trampled muddy grass leading to the kitchen door. The tub lay under a tree. She came over, taking care not to slip on the wet. When she reached the edge of the tub, she peered inside.

It was empty. There was no bathwater, just a few leaves scattered around the drain. So he had lied about this as well. She was fishing around in the leaves when there *was* something. A bit of kelp that tumbled into her hand. It was a twisted withered thing, desiccated from time. Its tiny bladder was no bigger than a radish. Surely this wasn't the Bullwhip he'd found – it had to be an offshoot.

Over at the house, there was a scream.

'Oh, God. No! What have you done?'

She froze. It was Manfred's voice. He *did* live with someone. She dropped the bit of kelp on the grass and came toward his house along the wall. The kitchen door was open, the lights on.

'God – I knew it! Why? Why did you do this?'

His voice had gone shrill, like a woman frightened to death. Then another voice followed – and this one was deeper.

'I told you not to bother. Someone else should be with her, someone more suitable. Now go on and end it.'

Nora came closer, keeping low in the shadows. She could hear something smash. Then a creature moved near the kitchen door – a cat, crouched as she was, with a direct view of what was happening beyond the kitchen. It looked petrified, and unable to turn away. From inside the house came another smash, followed by a scream.

Nora looked into the cat's eyes. She tried to imagine what it saw. There was another scream. This one carried sharp, continuous pain. The cat jumped straight over the wall.

She couldn't leave. It sounded like Manfred was abusing someone. Possibly, *he* was being abused. The upstairs lights went on and flooded the garden. She ducked, crept closer, peered into the kitchen and gasped.

Inside, seaweeds were everywhere. Kelp hung from the walls and lay in heaps on the floor. They came spilling out of the open cabinets. The washing machine, fridge, dishwasher – all stood open with more seaweeds rotting inside. On a window, someone had made a ghoulish face out of wet kelp and dulse for the eyes. Her business card, the one she'd given him at the market, had been stuck into the gaping mouth.

Upstairs, there was a long howl. Nora came through the kitchen, stepping over mounds of wet kelp. In the lounge above the fire, a bag with the Cornish Seaweeds logo hung on the wall, impaled by a kitchen knife.

She hurried up the stairs. She had to stop whatever was happening in that bedroom. At the end of the hall, a light was on. She came toward it. She braced herself and looked inside.

Manfred stood completely naked on a wooden chair. He was alone. Above his head, tied to a rafter, hung a long strand of kelp, the end tied into a noose.

'No,' she said. 'Don't!'

Manfred looked into her eyes. He didn't seem surprised. He didn't seem anything. The muscles in his face had gone slack, as if he'd become inhabited. Mechanically, without hesitation, he placed his head into the noose and stepped off.

A few days later, after the worst was over, Nora visited the seal sanctuary. She'd gone once before, just after moving to Gweek. She hadn't been sure about relocating to Cornwall, and being in the presence of so many injured but recovering seals had given her reassurance.

This time it was Family Day. Half price for all adults accompanied by kids. Nora came alone, paid full admission and followed the sounds of excited children. The first convalescent pool was indoors. The keepers had just finished feeding, and the seals were mostly lying about on the cement. A sign read, *Did you know? A group of seals on land is called a Colony. In water, it's called a Raft!*

There were about a dozen grey seals and a couple of common seals. The older ones were lounging on their sides like obese sunbathers. Some had visible scars from motor boats and fishing trawlers. Under their gaze, the pups dived and splashed in the water. These younger seals had been abandoned or lost. Now they were learning to interact with adults again before being released back into the sea.

Nora waited while the children asked the keeper questions. They wanted to know how much food the seals ate, how long they typically slept. The keeper put down her bucket and replied that seals ate about seven kilos, or five per cent of their body weight each day. They were on a balanced diet meant to replicate their typical intake in the wild.

While the kids asked more questions Nora read the placard in front of her. It said that the oldest seal in the sanctuary was called Baby. There was a photo of him with his bearded face turned to the camera. The placard claimed he was the oldest common seal in captivity and estimated to be forty-four.

It didn't take long for Nora to find Baby under the fluorescent lights, somewhat away from the others. He lay directly on his flippers and had long white whiskers. His eyes seemed aware of what lay squarely in front of him and engrossed with events far in the past, as if reliving the trauma he'd suffered.

As the family in front of her moved on, Nora came up to the rail. Then she did something she'd never done before. She asked a seal for advice.

'Hey, Baby?' she called. 'What do I do next?'

Baby looked straight at her. In the thickets of his beard were fish scales from the keeper's bucket. There were also green tendrils of sea lettuce.

Baby rolled sideways and stood up on his flippers. He bobbed his head at Nora and barked in a raspy wheeze. With a front flipper he rubbed his face until the bits of sea lettuce dropped to the cement. Then he doggedly finished each bite, as if aware of the dietary importance of seaweeds for healthy aging.

MANFRED

The first few days of his stay in Bodmin, he experienced divine grace. There was light coming through the windows. The rain was fresh and clean. Was he dreaming? How could it be that he was still alive?

The window of his room looked out over a row of houses. They were all made of stone and slate. He could smell the air and its arid mineral landscape. There were no seaweeds near here, not in the surrounding bogs and marshlands. No algae lurked in the grassy fields and derelict clay mines. He had been lifted off his grounds like a seedling, transported by the wind, deposited eighty miles inland for his own benefit.

Where he lived wasn't called an asylum any longer. It was called Greenways. The building was an open-door facility, with curfews but no locks. There was a communal garden, regular visitors and work placements. Everyone signed up to a cleaning rota and regular therapy. It was an older building with two floors of patients' rooms, a lounge and shared bathrooms. The clinic was made even gloomier by its tepid attempts at cheer – framed pictures of sailboats on the walls, plastic flowers in chipped vases and light classical music wafting the corridors.

Occasionally he went into town with the other residents. They were all men of various ages. They sat in groups on wooden benches. From this vantage point they watched the heroin and meth users, the emaciated wanderers of Bodmin's high street beg their fix before bedding down in the doorways of the derelict Methodist church. The town was populated by the ghostly and the half-dead. When their little group had made it back inside the walls of Greenways, they knew they were lucky.

Each morning a staff member asked what he wanted for breakfast. It didn't matter. It was always the same, no matter what he replied: orange juice, toast and tea, served on a plastic tray. Once, he asked for grapefruit juice and got orange juice. On another day he asked specifically for porridge and got toast. If he asked for coffee, he did sometimes get coffee, but other times he got tea.

He gained weight from all the medication. His hands grew puffy and his mouth dry as sand. From the noose there were still red contusions on his neck. They felt hot, like raw burns from a fire.

Later, he realised what had happened in Gweek. He had been taken, for a time, into the manipulative mind of the Bullwhip. He had seen inside that rubbery bladder-head and tasted its poisonous brine. The kelp had almost taken him into its clutches for good, penetrated him with its blades and used him for a vessel. Luckily, he hadn't been ready. A truly manipulative Bullwhip wouldn't have been stymied by anyone, not even Nora.

Of course there would come a time when he would enter the consciousness of the Great Seaweed Brain – the unifying entity Mary-Margaret outlined in her book – but this would have to happen later, with a more appropriate species. He had to develop his mind further. He had to make sure his body was primed. Until then, he had to be on guard. There were too many malicious seaweeds like that Bullwhip. They didn't care a jot for proper planning.

At times Manfred felt that all seaweeds had treated him badly, like a disillusioned youth selected for a terrorist mission. He'd been poorly trained, destined to fail. In the clinic there were plenty like him. They formed a protected group of failures. They were like once-lethal tigers, declawed but still dangerous, secluded for study.

Time moved slowly. He ate his breakfast and stopped answering when asked what he wanted for breakfast. Some days, he hoped a superior seaweed would hurry up and tell him what he was destined for. Other days he just wanted to be left alone, deep in the moorland, forever. His worst fear was waking up one day and not knowing the difference.

What he often thought of, lying in bed and trying to make sense of it all, was Nora. She'd saved his life – and in so doing, she had also made possible the extension of his species. She had probably been instructed. He wasn't sure how, exactly. He just had a hunch. What he objected to, when he was in therapy, was the contention that he had done it to himself. Or at least, *all by* himself. He understood the need for this sort of reasoning. People wanted clarity, the rudiments of plot. It made them feel better to skip any additional thought. His therapist's opinion made him laugh. He didn't laugh out loud, of course – he kept it inside, where the seaweeds were laughing along with him. What, he'd dragged that Bullwhip into his own house on his own volition? Anyone who spent time with algae knew one thing – they were always in control.

He wasn't completely bored, he had things to do. He wandered the grounds, sat in therapy sessions. Even under the influence of the meds, he tried to keep his mind sharp. There were newspapers and magazines, radio and television broadcasts, books in the clinic's library. It didn't take long for him to discover new secrets. They were left in his path, like breadcrumbs to find his way home.

One of the nature magazines stuffed in the back of a bookcase had an article on newly discovered seaweeds. He almost threw the magazine against the wall. What were they trying to do, drive him out? There were already seaweeds in their shampoo, in the jam he put on his toast, in the ice cream served on Sundays. Now they were in his reading material? After a while, he calmed down. He read the article all the way through and remembered there were others in the same predicament.

The article profiled a new red called Rosy Dew Drops. It was an obscure asexual species with hidden microscopic power. The enlarged photos were startling. They leapt off the page like fire. Up until recently, the article said, Rosy Dew Drops had been mistaken for other reds because it was capable of sudden shifts in its appearance. Most of the time it looked delicate, like a red rose, with beautiful petal-like blades. Other times, it crumpled

itself into a tight red cocoon and seemed to anticipate changes
to its environment. Rosy Dew Drops normally thrived in the
tropics, but it was moving north to British waters and possibly
beyond. Somehow it drifted in the bubbles created by its tiny
fronds. If it could change its morphology *based on threats to its
habitat,* what, the author asked, was this mysterious algae up to?

As Manfred sat in the library, with the sound of a radio
drifting out of a nearby room, he became aware of a warm tin-
gling all over his skin. Rosy Dew Drops had revealed itself to
him for a reason. It had anticipated the need for its own discov-
ery. It was even possible that the algae had prefigured *his own
awareness.* He put the magazine back and tried to forget all
about it. That is to say, he forgot about Rosy Dew Drops while
keeping the algae secretly in the back of his mind, like a squirrel
with an acorn.

He bided his time. He ate and shat and smiled on cue. As the
cold mists of February enveloped Bodmin moor, he dreamt of
ice fields and glaciers. If Rosy was heading north, it would be
off to the Arctic next. He would chase it there, he decided, right
up to the deepest ocean, a place devoid of colour and human
footprint.

'Do you want to talk about seaweeds today?' his therapist
Gwen asked. It was the first time *she'd* brought it up since he'd
arrived. They were in her office for their regular session.

'I'll talk about seaweeds any time you like,' Manfred said.

Gwen was director of Greenways. She was roughly Manfred's
age and walked with the stooped posture of a librarian. She

wore a cheap plastic digital watch and clunky black shoes that looked a size too big for her feet. It was his good fortune, the others said, to be counselled by her. Gwen was a woman of the earth. Everything about her demonstrated firm groundedness – her plodding gait, her steady temperament and dry, shrub-like hair. It was doubtful she ever visited the sea, or even swam in indoor pools. Yet she never voiced a particular dislike for sea-weeds – in fact, she seemed to be doing an increasing amount of research on them.

'I'd like to collect seaweeds in the Arctic,' Manfred said, by way of an answer to her question. She was looking at him almost sadly. He added, 'One of my long-term goals.'

He could tell she was a little alarmed. She didn't bother to ask what kinds of seaweeds could be found there. So he told her more about it.

'The most unusual discoveries,' he explained, 'are the epontic browns on the bottom of ice sheets. The sea ice holds lots of ecosystems, including algae forests. Cod and herring float underneath, often to catch some sleep far away from the fulmars and kittiwakes.'

Of course, he was also thinking of his secret microscopic algae. He didn't mention what he'd learned since reading the article – that traces of Rosy Dew Drops had been found inside broken narwhal tusks. They were encrusted there like cavity fillings.

'We *can* talk about the Arctic,' Gwen said. 'But first I'd like us to arrive at a healthier understanding of your past. In order to better address your future.'

He suppressed a smile. The idea of combing through his past for the sake of his future – it was too funny. 'How would that happen, exactly?'

'By breaking what we call destructive thought chains.'

'Come again?'

'Retraining the mind. Engaging and establishing healthier patterns. Let's set aside the Arctic for a moment. Go back to your kelp in Cornwall.'

'*Ecklonia maxima*, of the order *laminariales*. Also known as Devil's apron. That's the Bullwhip, the one I found in Gweek. What do you want to know?' He smiled as if to say that he wouldn't offer the slightest resistance. He would allow her to probe all she wanted because this kelp was long dead to him.

'What do you think about it now?'

'Not much.'

'Do you wonder where it is?'

He shrugged. 'Part of the food chain, I expect.' He imagined the Bullwhip separated into molecules, repurposed in the Atlantic.

'For the sake of your therapy,' Gwen said, 'we should discuss certain aspects of your relationship.'

'My relationship?'

'With the kelp.'

'Fine.' His palms were moist. He placed them on the chair under his legs.

'We call it 'systematic desensitisation'. For instance, if you had a phobia of spiders, you would slowly be brought into tolerable exposure. We might start with pictures of a spider. Then you'd enter the same room as a spider. Then, you would see a spider up close but in a cage. Finally you'd be fine with a spider crawling up your arm.'

'I understand.'

'We'll do the same with seaweeds, all right? Eventually you'll be able to discuss them without any adverse reaction. You'll demonstrate mastery over them . . . now you're laughing. Why?'

'Sorry.' He couldn't help it. He did feel a growing affinity for Gwen. 'That kelp didn't ever intend to be my friend. I just didn't realise until it was too late. The seaweed I'd talked to, every day for months, was replaced by a monster . . .' He looked out the window. He could have sworn he heard the ocean in the distance, past the moor.

'Yes?'

'But my so-called insecurities, they can't be mastered. Not if they're *valid*.'

Gwen was nodding, but she really had no idea. She'd never been torn between a woman and a sadistic Bullwhip. Even as she sat in her office with her diplomas and certificates, she was oblivious to the water rising below her feet, right beneath the floorboards.

After it snowed, Gwen took them on a field trip. They bundled up in hats and gloves and crunched across the white grass toward the moor. Their destination was Dozmary Pool.

The roads in and out of Bodmin sloped downward and formed two sides of a valley, as if taking separate paths to the insides of the earth. As the group walked out of Greenways and onto the verge, the motorists passed on their way to Wadebridge or Truro. It made for a dangerous intersection. Drivers honked or yelled at them as they tried to cross. Gwen wore a reflector jacket and stayed in front like a mother hen.

Dozmary Pool wasn't far from the road. There was a footpath to it through low-lying trees, where the pool lay under the shadows of the misty moorland. The residents stood around the water and stared into its depths. The pool was rumoured to be bottomless. There were stories about it being connected to other pools in Bodmin through underground rivers. Gwen hadn't imagined, it seemed, that some of them might be frightened by this. Maybe she *had* imagined it and brought her patients regularly for that purpose. She admitted conducting her own research on the side. Some of the men were weeping quietly into their coat sleeves.

At first, Manfred stood at a distance. Traces of sulphuric gas emanated from the water and made you ill if you came too close. With the wind in his face, the remnants of snow swirling and the cold in his bones, there was only one thing to really think about – that Britain was more or less a boat, floating on a vast sea. In the corner of that boat was a place called Cornwall, with a pond so deep it reached all the way to the sea. Surely intelligent marine life would one day find this passage and invade.

Were algae already preparing? As all life forms moved to colder waters, what was left would feast on each other. Seaweeds had nourished humans for a reason. Gradually the light would dwindle. After the sun was extinguished, and the whole world went white, they would be the last remaining living things, still faintly green – before they too would calcify, freeze and crack. They would turn to dust, spin out into the cosmos, drift and settle like ash in distant galaxies. The seaweeds would be the last off the boat. They were preparing for it now, the final jump.

Manfred stepped closer to the pond. He stared into its black depths. There were layers of grey within the black ripples, like vestiges of sunlight. Behind him Gwen seemed to be silently encouraging him to look down, back into his past and into a different future.

The others were watching him too, he could sense it. An hour earlier they had all been in the common room playing backgammon, reading and watching television. Now they were at this place they'd warned him about, and they'd want to know what he thought about it. He was the most recent resident. He was the alien. He would tell them that Dozmary Pool was black because of its pure reflection of outer space. Any creatures living under those sulphuric waters would detest humans. No species was more vicious, none more worthy of detestation than humans, he would tell them – and the proof lay in those columns of anti-human vapour, like cathedral spires, rising from the pond's surface. It would be kelp that emerged, kelp that would creep toward the people asleep in their beds.

'Time to go.' Gwen stepped up onto a little hillock, and the men huddled close. 'Hello, Manfred! You ready? This trip has been really nice, hasn't it?'

From the edge of the pond, Manfred waved at them. They couldn't see it on his face, but he'd reached the next stage of understanding.

Time was not his enemy. It was his fatal companion. It continued to pass by, minute by minute, leaving him behind as it simultaneously brought him closer to the end. He tried to become friends with it, but it rose like a giant monolith in his path. It took effort to get out of bed, to get dressed. The monolith was always there. Come on, it said, drop into a hole in the earth where you'll never move again.

There in Bodmin, he could smell rich soil under the trees and dense sod. The smell repulsed him. He was used to having his nostrils scorched by saltwater and tidal mud. To get away from the sharp ponk of fertility, he stayed indoors. He kept to the lounge and made his way through the books in the library. He found another crucial text of relevance. It was on display, as if left by a former patient.

The clinic had a decent collection of books. There were geology textbooks with pull-out maps that described the earth's surface. There were romance novels and psychology primers. The one he found was a naughty little volume. It was a longitudinal study on the sociological factors of suicide. Each suicide had its own psychoanalytic definition. The book broke them down into categories: altruistic, egoistic, impulsive, maniacal, melancholy and obsessive. Then there were the raw facts. If you suffered from hallucinations and delusions, you were at high risk. At the same time, suicide was correlated with a complete lack of sensation. The manic and especially excitable were in considerable danger of suicide. Then again, if you were particularly careful about killing yourself, and you steadily considered the right steps, over and over in a kind of script, you were very likely to kill yourself. It was also true that many people killed themselves impulsively, for no apparent reason, as if taken by a powerful idea that wasn't their own.

Protestants had a higher suicide rate than Catholics. This was supposedly because Protestants had a more repressive treatment of sin. Also, Catholics who suddenly confessed their worst sins often killed themselves immediately. Of all the religions considered, Judaism had the lowest rate of suicide. This was true, the author noted, even though the Jewish faith had a higher rate of insanity.

There were 'cosmic' risk factors that included winter, economic conditions and birth order – firstborns were at the greatest risk. One body of data demonstrated that poverty significantly correlated with suicide. Other data showed that increases in wealth led to an inexplicable spike in suicide rates across time. Regional differences were demonstrated. The countryside made people particularly susceptible to suicide. So did living in the city for extended lengths of time. There was a very high risk of suicide among the young – but as one grew older, toward 'natural' death, the risks also increased. Apparently it helped to be in some vague area in the middle, during the relatively tranquil stretch between youth and retirement, though these parameters kept shifting suspiciously as if trying to avoid detection.

117

Recent studies pointed to a high rate of male suicides, though historically females were still firmly in the lead. This gender competition had been going on a while. The book claimed there was only one point of rare agreement among all the available data, collapsed over time in a meta-analysis. The highest risk factor for suicide across demographic categories and cultures – a factor that was statistically indisputable – was being a childless male. In Paris alone, over the course of twenty years, men without children were fished out of the Seine about once a week.

Manfred finished the book and held it in his lap. The pages seemed to burn into the crotch of his trousers. He suspected with good reason that seaweeds were really to blame for suicide.

Next he chose a romance novel. The complication in the book came quite early, when the young woman became pregnant. Her lover was hunted down by her family for an assault on her honour. In the end, the two ran away to an island where nobody could find them. After he'd finished, Manfred held this book in his lap. The pages were comparatively cold against his crotch. He spent the rest of the afternoon staring at a framed picture of a sailboat on the wall. He noticed there was also a miniature wooden sailboat on the bookcase shelf. The cold romance novel, and the picture of the sailboat, and the wooden sailboat on the shelf all made him more depressed, and more likely to kill himself than the textbook on suicide. Here again, he suspected seaweeds were to blame.

Two men were playing backgammon nearby – Jacko the rape-seed farmer in his fake leather jacket, and young Miles, the former mathematician still in his bathrobe. From the bookcase, Manfred began to tell them his thoughts on Dozmary Pool. They weren't exactly paying attention, so he shifted his delivery to the sofa where John and Gary were watching TV. At least, they seemed to be watching – the volume was turned off.

John was a middle-aged former estate agent prone to nervous, mostly silent giggles. Gary had lived at Greenways the longest. He walked the corridors of the clinic with a self-possession that bordered on contentment. Manfred was afraid of getting to know him for fear that this comfort might be infectious.

'No, I won't tell you my thoughts on Dozmary Pool after all,' Manfred said to them. He projected his voice from the book-shelf as if delivering a lecture to his students. 'Instead, I'll tell you about Nora.'

At the mention of a woman's name, all the men turned in his direction. They were a mixed batch – crusting reds, hardy browns and a few floating greens. They had been forgotten. There was something sadly obsolete about them.

'Nora, she saved my life,' Manfred said.

Jacko and Miles went back to their backgammon game. Gary turned back to the television and sighed. 'Tell us something we don't know,' he said, and John giggled loudly.

'All right. Then I'll tell you how we met. Some people meet at work, or in bars. Or on-line, I suppose. I met Nora at the farmer's market.'

The only sound came from the dice on the backgammon board. 'She was selling something. Something in particular,' Manfred added.

They didn't exactly ignore him. They just didn't ask. 'Do you know what it was she was selling?' he asked.

'Seaweeds,' they said in unison.

After that encounter in the lounge, Manfred realised there were others like him, *aware* of seaweeds. He became more comfortable discussing their incursion with Gwen. Gradually, as he opened up about his past, he was allowed to receive visitors and accept outside gifts. The first item was a tub of dried dulse from Nora. She enclosed a photo of herself in shorts and goggles, shredding at the Apex Comminuting Mill.

The second gift was a packet from Mary-Margaret. She enclosed a note with recent research papers on algae and suggested he look into upcoming volunteer roles. Every so often, she wrote, her colleagues needed additional crew for research expeditions. If he wanted, she could help him obtain a place.

During his next session with Gwen, Manfred didn't mention what Mary-Margaret had sent him. He brought up something else that was on his mind.

'Can we talk about suicide today?'

'All right.' Gwen didn't seem surprised. They had reached a new level of trust. Apart from his most private thoughts, Manfred was completely forthcoming.

'I've been reading about a psychologist named Rossman who claims farmers have an instinctive need to feed others – something called the agrarian imperative. But when they're faced with the impossibility of feeding the planet, they feel inadequate and kill themselves. Apparently, more than any other profession. Can this be true?'

Gwen stopped writing in her notebook. 'Everyone assumes it's dentists. But it's true that farmers do have the highest occupational risk of suicide.' She leaned back in her chair and looked out the window at the setting sun. 'Makes you wonder about the early days of man – when most of us would have been farmers.' She shrugged. 'Full moon tonight.'

'Oh?' Manfred thought of the high tides back in Gweek. 'The waves will be picking up, then.'

'Yes.' Gwen parted her straw-like hair. 'Did you know, not long after the Earth formed, the moon was much closer than it is now? So close, in fact, that it created ten-thousand foot tides every two hours.'

'My God.'

That evening, as he sat at his window, he thought about ten-thousand foot waves churning the primordial soup. Ten-foot waves he could imagine. A hundred feet – well, it was a very large amount, but he could almost picture the magnitude of it. Ten times a hundred was an inconceivably large wave, and ten times *that* was what seaweeds came from.

The full moon slipped into view. He could practically feel its pull. He made a telescope of his hand and traced the dark shape of its craters, its portals to the other side.

When Simon came for a visit, it took Manfred a moment to place him. Gweek College had become buried in the past like a corpse with soil on top.

They sat opposite each other at a table in the lounge. At the next table, Jacko and young Miles were preparing to play back-gammon. They were waiting, it seemed, for someone to tell them to begin. Their pieces were arranged, and the dice just sat on the felt.

Manfred felt self-conscious, seeing Simon. He raised the collar of his shirt so that it covered his neck. 'I've gained weight. It's these drugs, they make me lethargic.'

'You look just fine,' Simon said, reaching a hand toward him. 'You'll be back teaching soon.'

Manfred noticed something in Simon's eyes – a twinkle. 'Tell me what's going on with you.'

'I'm going to be a father, mate.' He placed his hands across his stomach, as if protecting a baby. 'It all kicked off that night we went to that pub. I have to thank you, I wouldn't have met Ruth otherwise.'

'Wonderful news,' Manfred said. Beside him, Jacko and Miles stayed motionless, the dice still waiting on the board.

'Who's that?' Simon asked, glancing at Gwen who lingered nearby.

'She's in charge.' The way she stood there reminded Manfred of a little girl he'd once seen on a beach. As she'd stood there, a wave had knocked the bucket and spade out of her hands and swept them out to sea.

'Ruth's almost four months along,' Simon said. 'A boy.'

Seaweeds, Manfred thought, were inside infants. Greens and browns and reds, pigments shaped by the sea and sun. The juveniles steadily thickened into adolescents, formed filaments and twisted into rope-like clumps.

'I don't know that we're *totally* prepared. She's moving into my house in Bristol . . .'

Manfred nodded. From a distance, the greens were waving at him from the shallow rock pools. These greens had long, interwoven strands. They extended with cylindrical tubes and basal cells in mollusc shells, pebbles and driftwood. They produced thousands of themselves in an instant, detached from their hosts, formed spongy masses and roamed the coastlines and beaches in cushion-like colonies. Only waves had the strength to move them. Only the strongest of currents made them float like clouds. They lived like nomads. They were equally at home covering a stationary boulder as they were inside an unsuspecting periwinkle.

'. . . but we'll get a bigger place eventually,' Simon was saying, glancing at Gwen. She had come closer to them along the wall. Jacko and Miles still hadn't started their game. 'You know, so he'll have a place to play. A proper garden. Not some shit little square of grass.'

Manfred nodded. The browns were on him now. What he would have given to be floating with them in the Scilly Isles, those olive Dabberlocks with thick midribs and claw-like holdfasts. To swim among the eerie Bootlace Weeds growing vertically in tubes, or the rubbery wet browns with little popping balls named Creeping, Tough and Hairy. Then again, the Straggle Weeds could have him and he wouldn't complain.

He could even entangle himself in the stiff stipes of Forest Kelp. The giant redwoods of the sea would entwine him only to spit him out after a storm. He could also mingle with the wracks – Egg, Two-headed, devilish Horned Wrack with its fronds in the shape of pitchforks. Or he could spread himself thin among the encrusting browns, encasing rock after rock with its Marmite-coloured paste. The feathery browns of the mudflats, the bushy browns of the bright, sun-dappled shallows. To roll naked in a bed of wormweed, among the slippery and squishy jellies—

'She'll take some time away from work. Ruth's good that way. She knows how to use the system you know, instead of having the system use her. Me, I'll have a few weeks of paternity leave as well. We're already starting to look at schools.'

—but the most abundant were the reds, over seven thousand species to fall in love with. They were capable of the great double whammy, the ambidextrous switcheroo, releasing spores to form their own blades. The reds were as androgynous as waves. If they felt so inclined, they could do it the old-fashioned way. Weekdays, self-replication. Weekends, shooting their sperm and making hair-like structures to bore vigorously into the hardest shells on the planet.

'It's early days, I know, but we're thinking of a second one. Down the road. Ruth says she wouldn't mind a girl.'

'They say a second child's a good insurance policy,' Manfred said.

He would join the slippery, fragile varieties, the feather weeds branching in purple fronds. How firm, how juicy they were, with their ripe cylindrical bases and whorled branches, gripping tight to their hosts and never letting go. Stubby, sturdy Little Fat Sausage Weed. Steadfast Rosy Fan Weeds with its thick flat blades high on the cliffs. From there, they peered down at their cousins the crusty reds, content on the rocks, soaking wet, nearly drowned, waiting for the outgoing tide to dry in the sun. Crusty, parched and crispy, gasping helpless for water, only to become bathed in waves again. Or to swim among Sandy Creephorn, to stick out your tongue for a gob of Sticky Tubeweed floating by in bright red sheets like pools of blood.

Manfred sat up. The shape of things had changed. The sun was bathing the empty chairs around him in warm light. He had only to blink and it was over, like centuries passed. Jacko and Miles had abandoned their game without moving a single piece. Gwen was no longer at the wall – and Simon had gone.

The corners of Manfred's eyes began spilling over. Down within the buried reservoirs, the tears rippled out. Once there had been a secret place in his heart, a sanctuary devoid of seaweeds. Now that place was filling up, like a submerged cave in rising water.

'Why do you think you're here, Manfred?' Gwen crossed her legs, glanced at her watch and opened her notebook. 'I mean, at Greenways.'

Manfred shrugged. He wanted to say that humans and sea-weeds had guided each other for as long as they'd shared the planet. This was the main fact. People started out with seaweed carousels in their cribs then learned to classify the types. Everything else was secondary – window dressing for the main stage.

'I suppose I was in a dark place.' They were just words he'd learned. They added nothing to general understanding.

'Tell me more about that. I want to know more about your unique situation,' she added. 'Your *own* dark space, and nobody else's.'

'I suppose there are certain origins.' He looked at his hands, which weren't shaking any longer. 'But only one main one.' Gwen knew. The proof was right there in her office, behind all the certificates and diplomas. She was the psychologist. Why else *would* they be continuing to discuss seaweeds if they weren't so important? He squeezed his eyes tight.

'When you do that, Manfred, what is it you see?'

'A few reds.' They were in front of him now, floating across his line of vision.

'Okay. Would you like to talk about red seaweeds today?'

'Of course I would!' His answer came out louder than he'd liked. He opened his eyes, and she was waiting for him to continue. 'But I don't *need* to talk about them. There are greens as well. And browns.'

'I understand. First maybe you can tell me how it all began?'

'You mean, me and seaweeds? They were in my toys. And in my books. Plus, I liked to collect them.'

'I see.' She nodded benignly, like a grandmother. 'Tell me the first time they sent you into that dark space.'

'Oh, that's easy enough.' It seemed Gwen really wanted to know. So he told her.

In the town where Manfred lived, the urgent care clinic wasn't far from the beach. His girlfriend, the first of the three, had gone into premature labour. After it was over, and they'd lost the baby, she stayed in bed, sitting up and drinking a cup of orange juice through a straw.

It was just as well what had happened, she said, pressing his hand after the operation. She had always been the braver one. It was a shame, she'd said, but they could try again, or they could have a life without children. His waves of nausea wouldn't go away. He kept thinking of where the foetus had gone. He wondered what gender it had been, and if it might have had the dark green eyes of its mother.

He went outside and walked down toward the beach. He could smell the sea. As he passed the tourists he tried to take his mind from the high-pitched pneumatic sound of the clinic. The whole time in the waiting room, there had been a chorus of vacuums.

When he returned from his walk, he peered down the lane that ran alongside the clinic. Something about it called to him. It was as if he had been directed there. Then he saw them – two seagulls by the wall, furtive thieves taking turns pecking at the bottom of the drainpipe. It was almost romantic, the way they were sharing what was coming out. They were probably parents filling their stomachs to feed their chicks. And what they were eating called out to him.

'Help! I could have offered something to the world. My brain would have grown, I could have played the piano, solved cross-word puzzles, fallen in love. Instead I'm being slurped into the stomach of a seagull!'

He watched until the bird parents finished eating. Then they flew away, one after the other, up to the opposite roof where their nest was. The drainpipe kept dripping. Then there was a great flushing sound, and more gunk from the clinic streamed into the drain. Maybe the first one hadn't been their foetus after all. Maybe it was in this second flush.

Manfred left the lane and walked to the beach. He followed the sewer line down to a big storm drain. A black taste of bile rose in the back of his throat. It should have been sufficient warning. He should have paid attention.

There was a wall above the storm drain. In the distance, waves were crashing into the wet grey sand. He peered below. Water was foaming under the metal grate, bubbling over and pooling out. There were seaweeds down there, heaped around this organic material and teeming with black flies. The sea-weeds had trapped the clinic's waste. Eventually all three of his miscarriages would go to them, three sets of miniature hands and feet, three pitter-pattering hearts.

After the tests showed his count and motility to be normal, the doctor suggested that his sperm could still be at fault, perhaps tainted by antibiotics, microplastics and pesticides. Mother Nature was always being guided by something. It was a population-control framework that could make procreation difficult.

Manfred had made a poor joke after the third one. He said that he'd been fated to fall for women whose biochemistry was incompatible with his own. It wasn't really a joke. Each miscarriage led to the end of a relationship, which in turn made him more detached. Less human. More like seaweeds.

In the morning, he went for a walk down the corridors. He passed the rooms and peered through the windows at the sleeping shapes inside, dark mounds under blankets. He imagined someone in the future, walking the same corridor and looking in on him, a sleeping mound. He pictured himself growing old at Greenways, and for the first time this didn't bother him much. The meds had placed a warm blanket around his brain. He felt calmer, in control, with an acceptance of what had happened before Greenways.

He'd long known that seaweeds were impossible to predict. The events in Gweek no longer felt abnormal. Around the clinic there was a saying – they'll mourn you if the noose holds; if it breaks, they'll call you a nut.

Passing the potted plants and framed pictures of sailboats, he wondered about his future role with seaweeds. He thought of eighteenth-century beachcomber Amelia Griffiths, a woman who turned to seaweeds in grief and made rare discoveries in the sands of Torquay. He thought of amateur botanist Anna Atkins, so beguiled by algae that she created the first cyanotype images of them. Some seaweeds pushed you to death, others turned your life around. Still others taught you that you were never meant to procreate by heaping around storm drains.

Maybe humans were destined to become like their seaweed progenitors if they wanted to evolve.

He stopped at a room with the door open. In the bed was a dark sleeping shape. It must have heard him standing there – the shape rose under its blanket. 'One day,' it said, 'someone will be me, and I'll be you.'

Manfred kept walking. The greatest mysteries *always* involved seaweeds: the purpose of the narwhal tusk, the images on the world's oldest prehistoric caves, the toxicity of the seas and its effect on sperm, the cosmic risk factors for farming and even self-destruction itself.

At their next session, Gwen asked if he wanted to expand on anything they had discussed the last time.

'Yes,' Manfred said, 'I should have mentioned that there were always valid reasons for the ending of each relationship. I don't blame any of my exes.'

'Is that all?'

He nodded. 'I think so.'

'Let's set aside the miscarriages for a moment. Why do you think those relationships ended? Was it a different reason each time, or were there common factors?'

'I don't know. I was told I was self-destructive.'

'*Told*? As in, you didn't believe it?'

He shrugged. 'Over time, something inside me hardened. There was something *not there* when I looked in the mirror. No person, no atom of substance. The doctor was right when she suggested it was me to blame.'

'How so?'

'I've never felt in control. I've always felt *watched*. Used, maybe. Like something else is in charge. The virus, the pathology. Whatever you want to call it.'

'What would *you* call it?'

'Seaweeds.'

Gwen nodded. 'Seaweeds.'

'Yes. They're the ones who designed all this, right?' He waved his hand around her office. 'I'm not that ambitious, okay? Not without clear answers why anyone should bother. Each of my girlfriends must have known that. They saw the futility of it all.'

Gwen got her notebook out and placed it across her lap. 'I should tell you that Nora has written. Asking if it's possible to visit.'

Suddenly the room grew cold and bright. It was as if the blanket around his brain had been removed. 'Did she say anything else? When would this be?'

'She's been in Spain, Manfred. She's passing through, on the way back to Gweek. Do you think you'll want to see her?'

'I really don't know.'

'Do you feel ready?'

'To see the person I love more than anyone on the planet?'

Gwen turned to a new page in her notebook. 'Maybe we should talk about that night now. After you and Nora came back from London.'

'Okay.'

'What were the things going on in your mind? Before, during, after?'

He took a deep breath and let it out slowly. 'I had kept it a secret from her. How seaweeds had been making themselves known.'

Gwen had no change in her expression – as if she almost *believed* him. 'Go on.'

'Outside campus, for instance. Or in class. The students had changed. Then seeing them in other places where they shouldn't have been.'

'And London?'

'I became aware of other things. I had a strong desire to come back to Cornwall. Back to Gweek. To the tub.' He closed his eyes and shuddered. 'It wasn't just the seaweeds this time, it was their human representatives.'

'Who are they?'

'The ones who do their bidding.'

'And you were planning all along what to do?'

'The kelp asked . . .' He opened his eyes. Gwen was watching him, but he turned to the door. Out loud, it sounded too strange.

She leaned forward. 'It's hard to think about, isn't it? What happened that night.'

He nodded. It was harder to imagine what he must have looked like to Nora.

'Don't worry about how it all sounds. Just tell me what happened, if you can.'

'I didn't struggle. I was tired of resisting.' He thought of how he had come home and seen what the kelp had done to his house. 'I had to tell it about all those successful people in

London, with their children. Their careers. The next step was easy. I just got on the chair . . .' He closed his eyes again.

'Manfred. I want to ask you something. And I want you to be honest, okay? Did you make that noose?'

'I don't remember.' He put his hand to his neck. 'All I know is, I stepped off the chair and the room went dark. Then . . . I was lying on the floor. Nora must have fetched a kitchen knife. She cut the kelp's head and flung it to the floor. She told me everything was going to be all right.'

Manfred opened his eyes and looked at his trousers. He had wiped his palms and left damp blotches.

'Describe how this episode affects you now. Describe what you hear, what you see.'

He could still hear Nora answering the kelp as it lay on the floor. The decapitated bladder-head was mocking him, saying it was just a matter of time. 'I still see the waves. I smell the watery depths. I don't regret it. At that moment, I was hurtling toward something. It was truer than any of *this*. I saw the source, do you know? It's not always terrifying, the great seaweed brain. It can be benevolent.'

Gwen scribbled in her notebook. 'Thank you,' she said, 'that's all for now.'

Manfred sunk into his chair. He was tired of trying to explain. He could have described his dream of taking Rosy Dew Drops into his body and turning into space dust, and Gwen wouldn't have grasped the beauty. She might have been helping with his memories, but she didn't have the right tools to interpret them.

'Thank *you*,' he said, standing. 'That's all for now!'

Gwen looked up at him. Maybe she did have the right tools – she was smirking as if grasping everything he'd said. It seemed, in fact, that she'd heard it all before.

At the end of the corridor, the light was brighter. It was as if he was walking toward a new beginning. Then he had to turn the corner, at the same potted plants and framed sailboat pictures, back to where he started. This return to the beginning of his journey gave him a sinking feeling.

After his last session with Gwen, Manfred was hollowed out. He had never really discussed those elements of his past with anyone. Describing his emptiness, his spiritual vacancy – it made him feel worse than ever. Was this how therapy was supposed to work?

It was midday. Most residents of Greenways had their doors open, and he could hear a chorus of televisions and radios. He had completed his third lap when he became aware of an echo. The normal sounds of the wing had reached a new place, an open chamber somewhere. As he neared the end of the corridor, the echo was louder. It was coming from Gwen's office.

Her door was wide open. She didn't appear to be in. Her cardigan hung from the back of her chair and her laptop was open. He looked around and saw that her coffee mug wasn't on its coaster. Maybe she'd popped to the kitchen for a refill. He looked up and down the corridor. If sound waves could go in and out, why couldn't he?

It didn't take long to locate his file in the cabinet against the wall. He'd seen where she kept them, and the names were neatly alphabetised.

Manfred Drake
49, White British
College lecturer. Gweek, Cornwall

Provisional Diagnosis: Axis Three Delusional Psychosis. Acute chronic paranoia of atypical variety.

Affect/Cognition: Generalised melancholia, but with a perceived single source, pursuing the patient like a bête noire. Patient harbours paranoid and systemic delusions concerning a plot by seaweeds to use selected bodies as vessels before eradicating all other human life. Suicidal inclinations do not appear to be linked to clinical depression, but to a conviction that he, and perhaps all humans, are unfit to populate the planet.

Axis Two: Highly functioning (primary personality) capable of sustaining employment and intermittent short-term friendships, possibly assisted by interpersonal deceptions and internal self-deception. Narcissistic rationalisation schema relating to former relationships. Secondary (delusional) personality carries discrete and coherent speech patterns (reported by ex-girlfriend) which are projected onto select seaweeds. Through therapy, primary personality becoming gradually aware of secondary personality.

. Case Notes: Suicidal ideation and fixation. One known attempt (by hanging) prior to intake. Patient presented as initially withdrawn and unresponsive to verbal cues. Response to tricyclic antidepressants combined with cognitive behavioural therapy provisionally positive.

Observations (other): Patient has experienced three failed pregnancies in past relationships which may be nexus of the 'malicious seaweeds' delusion.

Holding his file, Manfred laughed. The tidy psychological profile, the classic *bête noire* – how romantic! It solved all the thorniest problems to do with algae, even explaining their lack of guile. If they were already inside us, seaweeds were the calmest, most confident assassins. They didn't need to over-exert themselves and leisurely stalked their prey while waiting for the right moment to strike.

He opened Gwen's notebook and skimmed to the most recent entries. He wasn't prepared for what he found. Seeing what she'd written after their last session, he grew very cold – as if a third person had emerged, one that wanted to survive, if only to understand exactly what it was he was seeing.

Note: Patient exhibits characteristics of other noted algae-philia disorders recorded at Greenways. Ideation parallels with seaweed intentionality, serving as a saviour vessel for rare specimens and apprehension of a 'great seaweed brain'; check with Mary-Margaret and pursue as case study/ continued research links.

There were footsteps in the corridor. He put his file back in the cabinet just before Gwen walked in with her coffee mug. He wandered over to the chair opposite her desk and sat down.

'Manfred, what are you doing, please?'

He smiled. 'Don't you remember? We had an appointment.'

Her face changed. Around the eyes and mouth were hard lines. 'We saw each other yesterday, Manfred.'

'I forgot.'

She glanced around her office to the cabinet. 'How long have you been here?'

'I just walked in.'

Watching him closely, she stood behind her desk. 'Please don't come here without permission.'

'Of course,' he said, hurrying out of his chair. At the door, he turned. 'I'm sorry, may I ask – do you think I might be able to contact Mary-Margaret soon?'

Gwen just looked at him blankly. 'Who?'

'Dr Mary-Margaret Dennison.'

It was then that he knew, watching her dissemble. The reality was much worse than he'd expected. 'Oh, yes. That woman who sent you her research on algae? What for?'

'It's just that I've been wondering if there have been others she might know about. Others in my situation.'

'Let me have a think, Manfred. I don't see why not. But we'll chat about it next time, all right?'

The lights at the end of the corridor had grown darker. The further he made it from Gwen's office, the safer he felt. He realised there were only a few people who could help him now, and one of them was Nora.

NORA

Not long after taking Manfred to the clinic, Nora had booked a flight to Spain. It all came back to her, outside Malaga airport – the endless glasses of *vino tinto* and amontillado, the plates of Iberico and olives stretching into the afternoon. The heat, even for February, was scorching. She remembered how she'd felt when she'd first visited Andalusia to join the surfing scene.

This time she went straight to Tarifa. After unpacking she lay in her hotel bed with a bottle of Rioja. In the morning she would be meeting Enrique the dive master at the small boat wharf. From her folder she took out the sketches once more, the maps of underwater caves beyond the Island of the Doves. On her phone, she checked the weather. It was a good forecast. The moon was distant, the tides calm. But there was no predicting the whipping levant winds, the strong cross-currents and busy shipping lanes, all of which conspired against exploration. Still, someone had found those caves fifteen years before. The proof lay before her, the fruits of her library research from the last diver to investigate.

Nora had taken time off from work. Her boss Pete, after hearing how she'd taken Manfred to hospital, told her to take as much time as she needed. Coming back to Spain was something of a reverse pilgrimage. The state of Manfred's cottage had been too disturbing, too macabre – especially finding him up on that chair, naked and hanging from the rafters by a rope of kelp. Something *other* was going on.

The sketches across her bed showed kelp forests stretching out of the cave mouth toward the surface of the sea. The last diver hadn't been able to penetrate. But there were faint images he'd spotted inside the largest chamber, before the waves had prevented him going further – a moon and sun and stars, giant flowers across the cave walls that looked like seaweeds. She'd asked Ben, long ago, what *were* those warnings you mentioned? The ones written on the caves of Tarifa?

'Do you know about the kelp highway hypothesis,' he'd said, pouring himself a glass of fino, 'that early humans migrated toward seaweeds on the coastlines on the promise of vegetation?'

'Makes sense.'

'An ingenious decision – *probably made by seaweeds*. Humans populated the interiors and returned to the coasts to create cities. Only now, the oceans have hundreds of dead zones. Sewage and fertiliser run-offs that create massive algal blooms. Soon we'll be entirely surrounded by our own toxic stew. And some seaweeds will use us for recycling.'

'Come on.'

'It's true. It's already happening.'

'Okay. And those warnings?'

'We're becoming them. Or they're becoming us. They'll enter our gut bacteria, then go into the sea caves and wait.'

'For what?'

Sitting in her hotel room, the maps showed the place. The Mediterranean used to be a lake, one story went, with land encircling it. Where the Strait of Gibraltar was now, there was a bridge built by the ancient Mesopotamians. This story had been passed down through generations – how men had been instructed by messages reflected in the water, sent down by the night stars – to build first a bridge, then a transport vessel to the sky to join a passing asteroid.

The timing was wrong. What was known about these civilisations and the formation of seas didn't exactly track. However, the Arab dealers in antiquities traded lamps, bowls and urns that depicted the same story of the bridge, the vessel, the asteroid. There were also remnants of a construction site where an ancient bridge had been started. The canals and viaducts were still partly visible, the fortifications right above the location of the seaweed caves. Years of rising waves had stopped the construction forever. The waterways had opened, followed by the great submergence that covered the wharves and Mesopotamian settlements. The sketches showed the original viaducts, now over a mile out to sea. These viaduct walls showed more recent pictures of seaweeds and *monster marina* figures, outsized aquatic animals with open mouths swallowing ships.

The waterways had only widened since. The straits had grown deeper, the distance between the two continents greater, the original bridge submerged and forgotten. It was the cave system underneath, where the oldest seaweed fossils in the world had been found, that she hoped to explore.

The next morning her dive master was waiting on the wharf. Enrique was short and broad-shouldered with dark wet hair plastered to his forehead. Nora had known him from her first years working at *El Gato*, where he had come to drink beer after taking British tourists on excursions to the wrecks off the Trafalgar coast. He had never been too talkative. And now wordlessly he set out their oxygen tanks and checked the seals. Behind him, on the water, his speedboat was tied to its mooring.

They went over their plan once more and set out. Their destination was barely a mile off the coast. It was just a spot on a nautical chart. There were no markers, no places for navigation. Enrique had heard of the ancient bridge fortifications and believed they were possible to locate. The water was flat and bright as they motored south out of the harbour toward the Strait of Gibraltar. The levant had subsided and left the waves manageable.

Gradually, Tarifa grew smaller behind them. They passed the last of the fishing boats and pleasure cruisers hugging the Trafalgar coast. Soon they were quite alone in their direction of travel. There didn't seem anyone else on the ocean. With her binoculars, Nora stood up out of the boat, and in front of her lay only a stretch of grey-blue water. The mountains of Morocco stood far in the distance – lumps of contrasting colours as if daubed on the horizon by a painter. She felt she was entering a mystery for which she was only partly prepared.

Enrique kept the speedboat skipping across the waves. Finally he slowed the engine. He checked the depth finder against his GPS, turned into the wind and neared the area they'd identified on the map. 'Here is where we are,' he said, and he cut the engine.

There was suddenly no sound as they floated in the waves. The sun had risen, the heat blasting across the open sea. They approached a red triangular buoy.

Enrique turned to her. 'That, I have not seen before.' He pointed in the distance. There were more shapes bobbing toward them in the water.

'What is it?'

Soon the buoy was followed by another, and another. On all of them was written, *Prohibido*.

'We cannot dive,' Enrique said. 'Not within this area.' He stood up out of the cockpit and shook his head. 'We should not even be found here.'

She looked around. There were no boats, no surfers, no ships – the conditions for their dive were perfect. 'Why not?'

Enrique just shrugged. When he spoke, his eyes flicked away. 'I am sorry, but *Prohibido* is the places of national interest.'

They floated a moment on the flat sea. There was not even the mast of a sailboat for miles. They drifted into the middle of what looked like a circular perimeter of buoys. Viaducts and bridge fortifications and fossils of seaweeds – all of it just below, their access sealed. Enrique was the best diver in Andalusia, and he wasn't prepared to break the surface?

'This is ridiculous.' She turned to him. 'There's *nobody* here. Not anyone at all.'

'We cannot dive,' he said.

Nora dropped onto her seat. From her rucksack she found her cigarettes, and her hands trembled as she shook one out. Blank astonishment turned to anger.

She smoked furiously and glared at the sun. She had travelled from Cornwall to London, flown to Malaga and now Tarifa – for this. It seemed to her that Spain was a country of routine and arbitrary injustice. Enrique hadn't sat back down. He was standing right by the wheel, just watching her as she let the embers fall on his deck.

'Maybe you cannot.' Her anger had become defiance. She stood up and started zipping up her suit. 'Thirty minutes, that's all I want.' She went over to the back of the boat and strapped on her tank.

'I can be arrested,' he said. 'Stop, *por favor.*'

His eyes looked guilty. He'd known all along they wouldn't be able to dive. He had taken her money and wasted her time.

'I'm going down there,' Nora said. She fastened her weight belt tight around her waist. She put on her fins and ignored him as he protested.

'No,' he said again. 'You must stop.'

Her mask had fogged up. She spat and wiped clean the surface. If Enrique tried to stop her, she decided, she would fight.

Surely the ones in the know, the ones with access to the ocean's secrets – surely they weren't *chosen*.

'Thirty minutes,' she said, and sat on the top rung of the ladder with her back to the sea. 'One dive, then we go back.' He advanced toward her across the deck.

She had a knife strapped to her leg, and she reached for it. He stopped and stood above her, glaring. As she swung her legs over the side and put her fins in the water, the red *Prohibido* buoy bobbing right beside her.

Enrique turned. There was the whine of an engine. A large speedboat came quickly toward them. It looked like the *Guardia Civil*. There were mounted surveillance equipment and antennae. The boat blared a loud horn, and its oncoming wake came surging toward them, bobbing them on the water like a cork.

The *guardia* pulled alongside them. He stood at the wheel in his boat, a tall man with a narrow waist and narrow hips. He cut his engine and said something to Enrique, who produced his identity papers. The *guardia* didn't bother looking at them.

'*Hola.*' He glanced at Nora on the ladder, still in her dive suit. '*Que es?*' he asked Enrique.

'It's not his fault,' Nora said, 'I hired him as a guide.'

'Here? *Prohibido.*'

'We didn't know that.'

He wasn't listening. 'This boat, it stays here. You will go back to Tarifa now with me.' The man lifted the receiver on his belt and got on the radio.

145

Nora looked out over the horizon and traced the wind rippling against the waves. Then she placed the respirator in her mouth, checked her watch and slipped backward into the sea.

It happened as soon as she plunged into the darkness. She realised how reckless she'd been. Enrique was supposed to navigate, to judge the currents and mark their safety stops for the way back up. She had committed herself to a plummet, a death dive into the unknown.

The temperature kept dropping. Her heart thrummed in her ears as she searched for signs in the dark. The truth was in her mind at last. She was mad. These were the unpredictable waters the *migrantes* crossed, and she was joining the ones who hadn't made it. Gradually the water became less murky. In the far, far depths was a ring of bluish light. Shapes were coming toward her – shadows that advanced out of the depths. She used the buoy ropes to guide herself down.

The ancient bridge was supposed to have been built on a hill, now a shelf at the bottom of the sea. She checked her dive watch. Enrique had estimated thirty-six meters, and at her estimation she was nearly there. Soon it rose up out of the water, the outline of a long arched wall, crumbled and broken, a floating ghostly thing covered with thick layers of barnacles and algae.

Boulders and broken rock lay heaped about. She could see the structure clearly because it was lit from below. Beneath the ruins, at the base of what was once the hill, the bright blue ring glowed in a hollow. She flattened herself out and drifted, keeping the ropes in sight. Plumes of gas bubbles steadily rose as if from an underwater stream. She kicked and dived down below the bridge walls, down toward the blue.

A little later, the ropes disappeared into a forest of kelp. The stipes were thick and glistening with sea worms, growing straight up from the source of the light. With her hands, Nora parted the kelp. The blades hid floating fish as if they were suspended in air. Then the current changed – a swell caught her, and she let herself be taken down in the draught, out of the kelp and into a clearing. She could see everything now. And what she saw almost made her hyperventilate.

On the ocean floor were half a dozen geodesic biomes. They were lit brightly from within and connected by a network of pipes. Each biome was the size of a greenhouse, made of thick Plexiglas and steel. As she swam closer she saw that each had been built over the mouth of a cave, as if to absorb its contents for processing. She held onto one of the biome's steel frames and pulled herself along. Through the Plexiglas all she could see was bright white light, billowing in milky clouds.

She let go and bobbed a moment. It was much warmer where she was. From the ocean floor, the steaming gases were bubbling up from thermal vents. Schools of tiny narrow fish were feasting on the rising vapours. She kicked along the ocean floor and came to a few smaller caves. These were uncovered. One of them was just wide enough to swim into. From its mouth she could see stalactites further inside. She made her way through the narrow opening. Ghoulish lumpy fish with bulging eyes swam straight at her and darted away. The temperature rose – she could feel her arms and legs expanding in her suit. Above her head were luminous chambers and hanging tapestries of brown kelp like dripping monsters that shone briefly before retreating into the darkness.

She was breathing too rapidly, her oxygen draining. She didn't know where to look, or what to make of what she saw. The cave seemed a gateway. She was between continents, between species and known worlds. The light kept changing – as if its source was alive and adapting to her. Beautiful delicate fan weeds floated by with undulating filament branches. They were young and green, just born, as if created out of nothing. Balls of luminous light passed through her outstretched hands, internally propelled by bright rolling orbs. They were rising out of a thermal spring bursting into the ocean.

For all the creatures she could see, there had to be hundreds of microscopic phytoplankton she couldn't. It was increasingly hot. She bumped against a wall. She turned and saw the paintings of dripping hands and faces, scattered limbs. Below them had been painted giant bladders and suckers grasping at the escaping light and pulsing like stars. Strange colours collided with each other on the cave walls. She had never seen such colours before.

Nora checked her watch. Four minutes of oxygen left, she estimated, including the safety stop. She wiggled back out of the cave and hovered one last time over the biomes with their eerie milky light. The kelp forest rose above her. She kicked her way up, parting it with her hands. The further she went, the more kelp surrounded her. The currents that had helped her down were not helping her back up.

Each direction she turned, there was more kelp. The thick stipes entwined her legs and grasped at her arms. She wriggled inside them like a fish in a net.

'I've got her now.'

'One blade, slipped between the legs?'

'I'll have a nice home in that tummy.'

Hearing these words, her mind began to separate – these were the waters where her ancestors began. Don't give in, Nora told herself, get yourself free.

She unfastened her weight belt and let go. She rose higher, up through the middle of the twisting green trunks and sea worms, before being jerked back. Her ankle had slipped into a noose. A stipe held her like a giant closed hand. She kicked and struggled and ran through her oxygen. This was where she would die, this grave for foolish people who disobeyed.

Nora reached for her knife. Bending at the waist, she unstrapped it from her leg and hacked the kelp around her ankle. Something had been released from Manfred as he'd stepped off the chair that night, some obscene horror, visible and stinking on the floor. Now the same thing was giving way. The water streamed blood – she'd nicked her ankle, but she was free.

She followed the ropes up this time. All her oxygen was depleted. There was nothing in the tank, only the mask. Then that too was gone, leaving only what was left in her lungs. The safety stop was too short, halfway up where the temperature plunged and her lungs began to burst. Just half a minute to decompress, with her ears ringing and her eyes aching in their sockets. Six of them she counted, six white hulls on the surface of the sea, flashing their rudder lights to guide her.

Nora woke to a man sitting outside her cell, watching her through the bars. At first she didn't recognise him. His eyes were jewel-like and clear. He was leaner, self-possessed.

'Ben?' she asked, sitting up. Her ankle had been bandaged. It wasn't a deep wound – the medic had patched her up after she'd surfaced.

Ben motioned to the guard. They had a short conversation in Spanish. 'Don't worry,' he said to her. 'You're being released.' For a moment they regarded each other through the bars. 'You saved me once. I'm glad you're okay, but what in the world were you doing, diving down there?'

'I wanted to look at the cave walls.'

'That's the most protected site in Spain.'

Looking into those hardened eyes, Nora could see how far he'd come up in the world. 'And how do you know that?'

'Because I manage it.'

The guard unlocked the door to her cell. Nora limped out. She and Ben followed the guard through another locked door and down a corridor crowded with dazed women, children, half-starved men. She was processed first. In a small hot office, she was presented with a large cardboard box that held her rucksack and money, her identification, cigarettes and maps. Through the window she could see Ben speaking to the officer who had itemised everything the day before. Here he was again, returning everything without a word.

'And Enrique?'

'His charges are dropped as well,' Ben said. 'I've covered the fines.'

They went out of the station. She could hear the helicopters overhead, returning from their sweeps. Petitioners for the *migrantes* were crowding the entrance to the jail and waving documents. There was a news team outside, filming.

Out in the car park Ben opened the door to his new luxury sedan. She settled into leather seats scattered with paperwork. She picked them up – they concerned biofuel.

'We are doing work on environmental preservation,' he said, as if to counter the opinions she was forming.

'Preserving what?'

'Those caves.'

'Humour me,' she said. 'What else would I have found down there? Where the biomes are.'

'Fossils. Specimens embedded in rocks. But nobody's allowed any archaeological research right now.'

'*Prohibido*?'

Ben looked at her. His eyebrows were trimmed, his skin brown and papery crisp. He started the car, and as the air conditioning whispered out, she had a quick chill. Was there anything left of the man who got drunk every night under that Iberico ham?

'I can tell you a little about it,' he said, as he pulled out of the car park. 'But you must be hungry?'

'Well . . .' She hadn't eaten since breakfast the day before.

'There's a place I like nearby. First, we'll get you into a bath.'

'Oh really?'

Ben gave her a quick smile. There was something patronising in it. 'A public bath, I mean.'

He drove along the water. Lots of tourists were about. The levant had returned with a force – buffeting the windows, playing havoc with hats and hair. Beyond the pier, the windsurfers were skimming across the water and launching off the waves. Ben pulled up in front of a blue-tiled building with a Moorish roof.

'I have an account here,' he said, guiding her inside. The place had high-vaulted ceilings, brass sculptures and marble fountains. 'Go ahead. Everything you want. I'll be working in the café until you're ready.'

A woman at the desk handed Nora a robe. It had only been one night in that jail, but her body was tight and compressed. She limped down the corridor, sunk into one hot bath after another, and allowed her muscles to relax in the mineral water. In one of the larger pools, she sat dazed on the stone steps and stared at the system of pipes delivering hot water in steady drips above her head. She was offered and accepted a full body massage.

Soon, her hunger became a pleasant empty ache. She shampooed her hair and softened her skin with the variety of lotions. When she emerged in the lobby, she was glowing – she could feel it emanating from her pores. Ben stood up from his table in the café. For a moment his eyes flashed.

They walked from the baths to a tapas bar overlooking the water. They sat at a table on the outdoor terrace, from where they had a view of the towering palm trees lining the seafront.

He ordered their food and wine. She asked about his work, and he told her the places he'd recently visited – Greece, Egypt, Venice.

'In the last two years I've realised the opportunity I have. What we're doing now with spirulina, it's opening up world markets. Not just the commercial side of biofuels, but philanthropic work in developing countries, too. I suppose I've really started to think about the difference I can make, leveraging the ocean's bounty into wellness.'

Here it was, Nora thought as she reached for her wine, the corporate-speak evangelism, the executive's born-again narrative. He'd become one of those corporate Americans abroad. Still, a part of her was impressed.

'This product. What market impact are you talking about?'

'Beyond imagination. We're doing research and impact assessments for this biofuel on every continent now. Without boasting, we're forecasting billions in returns. In less than a decade.'

'*Billions?*'

'I know. And I'm being conservative. And I'm not even talking about remote places, where there could be enormous algae deposits.'

'What exactly *is* this product?'

He gave her a quick smile. 'You're not the competition, I hope?'

It was the same patronising smile he'd given her in the car. 'I'm still putting together my lowly sea-lettuce salads. But I am curious about this product. A compound of spirulina?'

The waiter arrived with their food. The plates came one after the other – *pulpo*, anchovies, Manchego, Padrón peppers, roasted potatoes, bread and olives. She ate, he talked.

'It's a biodiesel made from blue-green microalgae. Other outfits are developing similar products, but theirs are mostly based on alternative feedstock. Ours is incredibly efficient, and very high in oil. We still don't quite understand it, so we've been separating primitive spirulina cells to see how they thrive. And how they ward off attacks. In the lab we built glass containers with walls so thick, nothing can pass through. But these algae can still detect any foreign agent and release sugars to kill off threats to growth – like coral, or other seaweeds. What's left behind is energy,' he said, tapping the tablecloth. 'Pure, potent energy. Harnessing more of this energy is the technology that's coming next. Nothing touches it for potential. Not wind, not wave, not nuclear.'

'And the caves?'

'Let's just say the fossils contain some very old specimens that are guiding our research.'

'So the Spanish government's allowed your firm to effectively seal it off? Until your patents are filed?'

The waiter brought a bottle of white. 'Tell me about *you*,' Ben said, pouring it out.

Nora allowed the dodge to her question. She described her life with a touch of self-pity, working for a small start-up in Cornwall, shredding dulse for posh salads. Not once did she mention Manfred. By her second glass she noticed Ben neglecting his wine altogether. When the bottle of red came he poured her some and left his glass alone.

'Where do you live these days?' she asked.

'There.' He pointed, over the water, to the villa perched on a nearby cliff.

'Oh,' she said, without knowing what else to say. 'Quite a change from your old flat.'

He gave her a gentle laugh. It struck her that no matter what she did, no matter how hard she worked or believed in what she was doing, she would still have only the tiniest impact on the world. She wondered how she'd react if he suddenly said, *Join me, Nora, and if you work hard, I'll give you a life like this.*

He checked his phone. 'I'm afraid I must run.'

'What?' The table was still covered with plates of food.

'I'm so sorry. My wife just reminded me. Our son has to be collected early today.'

'I see.' In the uncomfortable silence, she reached for her glass a few times.

'You have kids, Nora?'

'Not exactly on track at this rate, am I?'

He was already getting his things together. 'Can I drop you somewhere?'

'No. You've been kind,' she added, more meekly than she would have liked.

He stood up. 'I've taken care of the bill. Stay as long as you like. Relax, enjoy yourself. It's been good to catch up.' He dropped his card beside her plate and wrote a number on the back. 'You need anything at all when you're here . . .'

She nodded. Her eyes moistened as she looked out over the water.

155

'I can't tell you what to do, Nora. But if you get in trouble again, the police will call it trespassing, and I'm not sure I'd be able to help.'

Nora stood up and hugged him goodbye. Then she sat down and tried to understand exactly what had happened. She felt as if she'd been made plastic, poured into a mould and reconfigured over lunch. She wanted Ben to come back, just for a little longer. She had planned on staying in the country all week, but she knew what would happen if she did. She would ring his mobile, tell him where she was staying and wait pathetically for him to call. She'd be like a feudal peasant in tattered clothing, peering through the hedgerows at the mansion.

Leaving the table, Nora headed for the toilet. In the mirror she already looked less radiant than an hour ago. There was a curtain hanging over the window. She opened it a little, and peered down at the lane between the buildings, where some bottles and tin cans lay heaped below. It reminded her of Britain.

She had never been a materialist. She rarely pined for things, not for their own sake. But that villa across the bay, the one that was his – she'd known of that place since she'd first arrived in Andalusía years ago. It was a tree-enclosed paradise, built for a Spanish royal. One of her windsurfing friends had been invited to a party there, and she'd come back the next morning bubbling over with descriptions of the terraces, the ocean views from the lawn, the shaded olive gardens.

'A place like that,' her friend had said, 'well, it just makes you feel human again.'

Nora looked at herself more closely in the mirror. Her eyes drooped at the corners, her mouth hung slack. She reached for her cigarettes and tried to remember how she'd felt in the mineral baths – like someone who mattered.

As she walked the promenade to the pier, she was surrounded by lost tourists. She wished she could be taken bodily out of the slot in time she inhabited. Forward or backward, anywhere would do. It was too hot, too dry. Her hair crackled, her eyes burned.

The pier had a plaque that said it was built a century ago, then rebuilt. How many times was this needed, because of the waves, the storms, the wind? This one was evidently meant to last. This one used reinforced concrete. The Island of the Doves, with their network of caves, lay far out to sea. She thought of the gloomy ruins under the water, the eroding fragments of pre-Roman villas, archways and galleries. Even the earliest bridges and seaweed caves were steadily being lost to time.

The levant had kept most of the tourists from the pier. She put her head down and kept walking. Wind whipped across the railings and created tunnels of eye-watering strength. The levant had its own spirit, people said. It brought the *migrantes*, and it left behind ghosts.

Down on the water, the windsurfers were out in force. They went skimming across the sea in coloured sails, performing jumps and somersaults. They recorded each other on phones as they hung in the air. That had been her once. Hands above her eyes, Nora watched these young men and women of the future.

Ben hadn't progressed at all, she realised. He'd gone backwards if anything. His near-death experience had given him a rebirth, and he'd become a grasping, one-dimensional technocrat. Maybe the reason he once drank so much was the fear he'd had, the anticipation of the inevitable.

She had to keep moving through the wind tunnels. A square concrete pylon on the pier offered a refuge from the wind – and as she hunkered down behind it, she had a feeling she was being watched. There at her feet, hiding in the metal crossworks, two pigeons were shielding themselves and staring at her with hard little eyes. All through lunch Ben never once asked what she thought about the caves, or what she was reading in her spare time, or what she hoped for her future. Staring at the huddled pigeons, she remembered a conversation they'd had back in the hills of Caños de Meca. It was during his attempt to dry out. Ben had told her about a team-building exercise he'd had at the first company he'd worked for. The exercise was called 'God Box.'

'Each of us,' he said, 'was given a white paper box, like there was a gift inside. Only it was empty. On it we were supposed to write down – or draw – our idea of the divine.'

'And what did you put?'

'I looked at the others. One guy was making a flower. Someone drew a rainbow, someone else the Buddha. I couldn't think of anything. Then we were given an index card. We were supposed to write what we wanted to be released from, then fold this up and put it inside. I wrote *fino* and placed it inside. Then I realised it also worked for the outside of the box, so I drew a bottle on each side.'

She had liked that story of his. She had been attracted to its dark possibilities, its mystery of a man struggling against his demons. Now, as the sheltering pigeons shivered at her feet, she realised there hadn't been any mystery to the story at all. Ben had just substituted his love of booze for money. And behind this money lay seaweeds.

The wind changed direction. It was coming from behind now. She said goodbye to the pigeons and started back to the promenade. Maybe she was just bitter that Ben hadn't been interested in her. That he had found his calling. She'd always believed there was something *there*, that if the scales fell from everyone's eyes they'd see it, lurking beneath the surface – the world as it really was. Ben had seen his world. Strangely, when it turned out he was married with a child, she hadn't really cared. If anything, she pitied his wife and child. He'd talked more about spirulina than about them.

As she limped along the road to her hotel, she wondered if she could ever be consumed by anything. Even the concept of biodiversity – what she'd wanted to believe in as an inherent truth – only seemed *relatively* so. To care about conservation seemed futile when companies could purchase entire reefs.

She'd reached another wind tunnel. Behind the tallest buildings of Tarifa, the levant was so strong that your mouth could fill with sand. People coming from the opposite direction had streaming eyes. They were walking statues, turning into salt like Lot's wife. Soon, of course, everything would be desert – diversity wasn't threatened, it was routinely decimated. What was there to do? She needed to be re-inspired.

159

At her hotel was an arriving shuttle van. It parked and started dispensing people like exhaust – surfers and windsurfers with wild bohemian stares, sunscreen-dabbed noses, board shorts and flip-flops. They could have been from Cornwall. Nora realised as she watched them that she was about to leave another job. Shredding dulse was only a bridge – to where, she still needed to find out. Mary-Margaret would guide her, Nora thought as she watched the last surfer tumble out. She would go back to London in the morning and ask about upcoming research expeditions. With luck, she'd find a rare specimen struggling against the Bens and spirulinas of the world.

The last surfer locked eyes with her. He was cute enough. She smiled as he struggled to get his board out. He was tall and blond, a male version of herself ten years ago, and she decided at that moment that she would sleep with him.

'Need a hand with your board?' Nora asked, moving quickly toward him to hide her bandaged ankle.

'Ah, thank you,' he said. 'It is a tricky one.' He had some sort of European accent.

She held onto the front of his board while he dived back into the van. New, powerful forces were guiding her. It was like riding on a motorcycle and gripping the dark leather jacket of the driver and sinking lower as they picked up speed.

Strange, how her urge for a child only strengthened when she returned to London. The cold, the mist, the filthy air as she rode the escalator up from the Tube – it was as if she'd returned to her spawning grounds.

She had done something immoral with the surfer. It hardly counted as an intimate experience. At one point during the night, when their mouths advanced toward each other, she'd lost all feeling, interest, motivation – yet she had continued out of a fear that a night alone would have been worse.

The escalator placed her at South Kensington. She glanced up the road toward the museum where Mary-Margaret awaited. First she needed to find a chemist's. The immorality wasn't in sleeping with him, it was falsely telling him she was on the pill. It made no sense to have children in this world, yet this was what she wanted. She wanted one *badly*. For some time now she had fixed this concrete goal, like a number of sit-ups each morning, or a certain number of pounds in the bank. A child. One.

There was a Boots outside the station. Nora found the test and waited in the queue for the register. She was obliged to review her own beginnings – her mum had told her the details – how she'd been conceived one night after an Indian takeaway. Of course I knew it wouldn't last with your dad, her mum had told her, and sighed heavily. One too many ciders, probably. As she advanced toward the register, Nora added a bar of chocolate from a shelf to make her purchase less conspicuous. The woman in front of her had both a coffee and a green tea. Each person in the queue stood alone and sunk into themselves, their faces lined with exhaustion.

The test in her bag, she headed for the museum. Being in London felt bittersweet. The deep isolation of crowds affected her more than usually – the group silence, the ingrained indifference. Occasionally, if you listened closely, you could hear the same sad sigh of her mother's, as if the only affirmative act the British were capable of. One too many ciders, probably. Nora had returned to the blinding void. It was a mystery why she wanted a child *here*, on *this* island, surrounded by *these* people, but she did, for better or for worse.

At the museum she submitted her rucksack for yet another security check – her third of the day, after the airports. She proceeded under the CCTV cameras pointing at her from all directions. Her bag had to be opened for inspection. She turned her head as the guard put his hands on the pregnancy test. She wasn't the only one up to no good, she wanted to explain. Everyone was guilty – each head, each pair of legs spreading out across the museum. They all negotiated the horrible world with the same dubious mission. They did what was necessary to fill the void. The guard handed her bag back. She was motioned through.

Something went off in the metal detector. After she was waved and wanded, she was permitted through to the other side. There was the gift shop, the suspended squid, the blue whale hanging over the gawking children, the corridors of stuffed animals branching in all directions. Nora walked quickly, half blindly, down a corridor at random. Soon she found herself standing in front of an albatross. The bird had been placed beside others of dubious distinction. She never understood why extinct animals were grouped together like performing clowns – the dodo, the musk ox, the woolly mammoth.

She stepped closer to the display case and stared into the eyes of the ox. She could see her reflection. Just get on with it, the musk ox was telling her, don't be like *us*. Do whatever it takes to avoid extinction. Well, why shouldn't she? If not now, when? All her adult life there had been plenty of deceptions *she'd* been on the tail end of. A person needed to take control to bring about the right outcomes. She kept walking to the black bear that was standing on its hind legs with front paws raised. She remembered what Mary-Margaret had said about the vertebrate exhibits. They were being eaten from inside by weevils and beetles. This bear probably had a colony of them in each limb. The beetles would fill each passage in the cranium. One day, a visitor would be standing where she was, only to see the whole bear disintegrate into a swarming mass of insects and fur.

In the corner, half in the dark, a stuffed sage hen stared up at her from its cabinet of straw. Spiders would be inside that one with hundreds of eggs awaiting the right mate. Nora felt someone nearby – an older man, standing close. Even with his wife at his side, he was sneaking his naughty glances. It wouldn't take much effort to cop off with him. It would only take a matter of minutes – and perhaps it was the *right* thing to do, statistically speaking, rather like taking up an insurance policy. In the end, what was one more added to the mix?

Her thoughts circled back. It had been ten weeks since she'd last slept with Manfred. She'd had some spotting a few days ago, nothing too heavy, not really a period per se. Her cycle never followed a regular pattern, so she might have been pregnant already, even before the surfer. If she had to choose a father for her child, she thought she'd go with Manfred. That surfer had such strangely truncated legs. It was something she hadn't noticed, of course, in the car park. It would be the kind of thing that got passed down. Manfred was partly mad, but he was taller, more intelligent.

She kept walking until she found a loo. She got in the stall, opened the box, unwrapped the stick. At the instructions she hesitated. No, she decided, she didn't want this revealed in a museum. The result would be tarnished among the captured animals. Anyway, she had to meet Mary-Margaret with a clear mind.

Nora returned to the exhibits. Strange, underneath all these species, before there were any such things as whales and blue tits and field mice, before even any hint of ancient redwoods, came seaweeds. Nobody knew much about them. The world's largest collection lay in the basement of a museum as if intentionally hiding. Even here on land, they had established their private cave.

She took the lift down. As it dropped to the bottom floor, Nora enumerated her bad behaviours – flying around the world for holidays, avoiding home for Christmas. This one, possibly turning random men into unknowing fathers, *was* much worse. But didn't other species do it? The colourful deceit of the peacock's feathers. The bait and switch of the praying mantis before swallowing its partner.

Mary-Margaret wasn't in her office. Nora lingered at the desk. The office was a museum unto itself. There were sleeves of dried seaweed specimens, sealed tubes of filaments in culture, racks of glass vials. Every corner of the enormous desk was covered with books and grant proposals and periodical articles. The computer was still on. The screen showed what looked like a grainy black-and-white image of outer space. She leaned in for a closer look. It was a screen grab of a NASA feed. The readout originated in Antarctica, and the image was of a submerged rover crawling under the ice pack. Mary-Margaret had mentioned this particular consultation. NASA was using a research station in Antarctica to rehearse an upcoming probe to Europa, Jupiter's icy moon. The rover had collected rare algae under the ice, and Mary-Margaret has been asked to identify it. She'd also been asked to be on hand in case the probe collected algae from Europa.

Nora wandered over to the nearest rack of vials. She picked one at random and held it up to the light. Pale green matter collected at the bottom. The label read, *Ochlochaete hystrix: Almost circular plant with mutually free cells at margin. Sublittoral, epiphytic, turf-forming on pebbles. Studland, Dorset.*

She stared at the filaments. Tiny green segments were immersed in saline – and as she looked at them, they seemed to come alive, as if attracted to the heat of her fingers. The filaments rose in the solution toward the seal. They bounced and danced and frolicked. They looked excited to be chosen at last, to be visible. And in that moment Nora was back down in the caves off Tarifa, in the gateway between worlds where the seaweeds had spoken.

She put the vial back. She could still see the filaments in her mind. She could *feel* them in the pores of her skin, her bloodstream, her neurons. They were watching her, it seemed, through the vial.

She hurried back over to the desk and thumbed through the periodical: a retroactive study of the 'Sargassum incident' in which the entire island of Bermuda was encircled by toxic algae and closed for business; an analysis of sharp rises in Japanese nori consumption; more Norwegian chlorophytes found in Orkney; Brittany's beaches, already coated with green algal blooms, releasing a new hydrogen sulphide. Children and the elderly getting ill, pets dropping dead. Algae thriving on run-offs from fertiliser spread onto nearby wheat fields – wheat cultivated and grown solely as grain for dairy cattle and pigs.

Nora's eyes clouded over. The nausea, it was probably self-created. A kind of wish fulfilment. It was the second time in the Herbarium. The first time, there had also been this sense of being watched. She had been with Manfred. Standing there, her mind racing, she wished she had never become interested in seaweeds. It was Ben's fault for introducing them to her. Then again, before that, it was his parents' fault. It was *her* parents' fault for creating her to begin with – and for passing on a susceptibility to all the men like Ben.

She felt faint. Yet she found herself drifting over to the vials of green filaments on the shelf. Algae was ultimately responsible for her self-destructive impulses. Only algae could stop the endless chain. You must be our mother, the little green filaments seemed to say, dancing with excitement. There was another rack of vials marked *Microscopic Reds*. She picked one at random and felt the glass tube instantly warm to her hand. The saline solution changed colour, the filaments danced as if

happy at being seen. *Rosy Dew Drops*, the label said. *Very rare.*
She held the vial to the light.

Down the corridor, there were footsteps. Nora squinted at
the little dancing colours that spoke through the vial. Go to
Manfred, they said. He needs you as much as we do. Nora peered
around the corner and spotted Mary-Margaret coming. She
returned the vial to the rack and steadied herself.

Mary-Margaret had dyed her hair. It was a golden colour, cut
so the fringe came swooping at an angle across her face. It made
her look slightly ridiculous. She put her things down, and they
hugged. It was a lovers' touch. Nora savoured the smell, the
chemical alignment. It wasn't as much sexual as intimate – their
minds and bodies always seemed to adapt, even to improve
each other. Then the nausea returned in waves.

'Sorry . . .' Nora steadied herself against the wall. 'Tell me,'
she said, 'tell me something that's inherently good. Tell me that
biodiversity counts for something. That life matters . . .'

Mary-Margaret held her by the shoulders rigidly, like a
mother inspecting a wayward hungover daughter. 'Sit there,'
she said, pointing to the armchair. 'I'll fetch you a cup of tea.'

Nora did as she was told. She sat in the corner and waited
to feel less woozy. It didn't seem very long ago, just before the
algae conference, when she'd been in this very spot. Time had
slipped around and claimed her.

'Tell me about Spain,' Mary-Margaret said, as she returned
with their tea.

'I just wanted to see those caves.' Nora glanced at the shelves.
There were more vials – some classified, others with only places

and dates of collection, waiting for identification. It struck her that Mary-Margaret was like Moses, tasked with saving and leading. She had to decide who to name, who to protect.

'Why didn't you come to me and ask for help? Instead, you hire a private dive master and get yourself arrested?'

'Hang on.' Nora sat forward. 'How did *you* know?'

'Ben told me.' Mary-Margaret stood there frowning.

'Ben?'

'Yes. He's a friend.'

'As of when?'

'Long before you two met, love.'

Mary-Margaret wandered back over to her desk. She kept pushing her hand through her hair to change the trajectory of the new fringe. Digesting this information, Nora officially decided that this haircut was not a good look.

'As you probably discovered,' Mary-Margaret said, 'there's really not a lot to see down there. The last survey of those caves came back with nothing new. All the sexy stuff – the murals, mosaics and ancient hieroglyphs, they've mostly been washed away.'

'Okay. Ben must think there's something behind those biomes – his firm wouldn't have paid for them otherwise. And forecasting tons of profit.'

'It's all speculative, Nora.' Mary-Margaret leaned against her desk. Behind her, the Antarctic rover hung frozen on the grainy black-and-white screen. 'One thing's for certain, this particular spirulina can survive whatever's thrown at it – heat, light, drought. It can survive for years in dormancy. Ben's gambling that this makes for a good biofuel. He could be right.'

'You don't think there's anything special about the site itself?'

'About twenty years ago, a fossil was discovered in one of those caves. They used it to sequence the genome of a particular spirulina that can live outside ponds and streams. It shared some genes with land plants. So there was speculation that this species was the missing link. The mythical algae that connects prehistoric seaweeds with the first life on land.'

'And was it?'

Mary-Margaret went over to her bookcase and took down a manuscript. 'This whole line of research is misguided, in my opinion. One species gets a lot of hype, until the next one. Over and over. I don't think such a thing as a missing link exists. When it comes to the development of life, we're dealing with a shrub, not a tree with a single root.'

Nora sipped her tea; it was time, she knew, to ask. 'I need a favour. Can you help me find a different job?'

'Is this connected to what you were asking just now? About biodiversity?'

'I've always assumed it's a good thing, right?'

'Of course it is.' She put the manuscript back in the case. Then she waved her hand across all her books. 'It's *everything*. Everyone agrees on that. In any calamity, you're going to want a wide range of life forms. To withstand a particular virus, say.'

'That's it?'

'Also, to enrich habitats. To broaden the relationships among species. The wider the spectrum, the better chance of evolving life.'

'Right,' Nora said, rather glumly. 'I remember that from school.'

'That's not what you wanted for an answer?'

'I just need to *believe* in something. To do something important. Down in those caves . . . I don't know, it felt like I'd entered some sort of bridge to another land. That seaweeds *were* the bridge.'

Mary-Margaret's expression changed. 'How's that?' Maybe it was Nora's imagination – her face flashed red, then green, and finally brown – until slowly it was drained of all colour, and only a pale shell left behind.

'I just thought . . . there was something more to what I was looking at down there.'

'More.' Mary-Margaret laughed. 'More!' The colour returned to her face, and her eyes gleamed. 'More than life itself?'

Nora shrugged. 'Surely there are processes *behind* life that we don't yet understand.' Nora had to look away now – she could sense Mary-Margaret changing in shape, as if from moss to jelly, to branching ferns. This so frightened her that she had to stare at her shoes. 'Do you know what Ben wrote, in a note I found?' she blurted. 'Before he sobered up and became corporate? *No stopping until we become them. Or they become us.*'

Mary-Margaret went over to her wall of books. She kept her back turned and adjusted a small mirror above a potted plant between the shelves. Then she ran her hand through her fringe. 'You haven't noticed anything different about my hair, have you?' She turned quickly around. 'You hate it, and you're just being discreet.'

'No, it's great! Makes you look younger.'

'Really?' Mary-Margaret smiled happily. 'Come on, let's go get a drink. You've had a rough time of it in Spain. We'll go to a pub and you can tell me all about it.'

'I don't know.' Nora stood up and reached for her bag. She wondered if she could manage taking a pregnancy test in some pub loo.

'You can't go straight back to Cornwall now. Tell me – are you going to see Manfred on your way through?'

Nora sighed. 'I want to. I just don't know if it's too soon.'

'You should.' Margaret slipped behind her desk and reached for a file. 'I have an upcoming expedition he might be right for.'

'But he's still in the clinic.'

'Not for long.'

Nora waited for an explanation. Mary-Margaret sat down and started typing something into her computer.

'I've been in touch with his therapist, you see. Manfred's come through the worst patch. I don't know if he's that delusional, to be honest.'

'What are you *talking* about?' Nora stood up. She had raised her voice, almost to a scream. She searched the office, but all she could see were seaweeds. 'How are *you* speaking to Manfred's therapist?'

'Calm down, Nora, don't be alarmed. Anything to do with algae, I'm usually the first to know. And something interesting's just come my way.' She pointed at the NASA rover on the screen. 'It has to do with Europa. This machine in Antarctica, preparing for the probe landing, got me to thinking. There's a new expedition up to the Arctic in a few weeks. I could use a good range of samples. I need someone with a unique eye to do the collecting.'

'You want Manfred for *that*?'

'I do. These particular scientists, they're funded by another biofuel concern. We wouldn't have our research without private funding. But I wouldn't mind someone on board on behalf of seaweeds more broadly. To collect and identify along the coasts, to be something of a fact-finder.' Mary-Margaret stopped typing and looked up. Her face had returned to its normal colour, her voice even. 'You think Manfred would be interested?'

'That's putting it mildly.'

'The rarest species are often found by rare people. And his therapist, she thinks an experience like this – out on a boat, searching for a new species – could be good for him.'

Nora could only stand there, gripping her bag. 'Where's this expedition going, exactly?'

'Svalbard. The northernmost islands of the archipelago. The ship's doing advance work to see if any spirulina or kelp's there, in the sort of numbers to support future expeditions. The others along for the ride are aquafarmers.' She stood and handed Nora a small wooden press – two slats of wood bound by string, filled with sheets of white gossamer. 'Tell him to preserve what he finds. This will help with identification.' She handed her a copy of *The Future of British Seaweeds*. 'I've added a few of the latest entries, marked it up.'

'I'm sure he'll want to go,' Nora said, numbly. 'Svalbard. Aren't there more polar bears than people?'

'There are guides. He'll be fine. And if he finds something rare, it could mean conservation zones. Maybe he'll get an entry in the second edition!' Mary-Margaret collected a manuscript from her desk. 'Come on, I'll read you my new prologue. Over that drink.'

The pub across from the museum turned out to be perfect for a reading. They sat at an empty table in the corner with their pints. Down by the bar, it was only elderly men.

Nora felt warm and her skin tingled. It had been satisfying to pee on that stick and to watch the two blue lines form. She drank her cider with tranquillity, overlooking the aging ale drinkers spouting provincial politics. They could all bugger off. The father of *her* child was either a seaweed empath or a European surf god. It was as if she and Mary-Margaret had achieved the result together.

'The prologue, I admit, reads a bit like science fiction.' Mary-Margaret put on her reading glasses and opened her manuscript.

'Deep within Earth's waters, over a billion years ago, the first families separated from their common ancestor. They would become known as the reds and the greens. The cataclysms came and went. Each of them dispatched the majority of life. The reds and the greens survived. They reproduced asexually and sexually. They floated freely and in groups. Out of them a new species was conceived.

'Then came the end-Permian extinction event – an asteroid collision creating toxic clouds that blocked sunlight and froze the waters. Within the ocean's darkest caves, the reds and greens huddled. Surrounded by pumping fulmars and shadowed by the luminescent stalagmites and stalactites of their ancient microbial ancestors, they waited years for the coming thaw. After the clouds finally dissipated, the majority of life was gone.

'Out of the ashes a new species surfaced – intelligent, hardy and brown. The browns increased competition among the reds and the greens. They identified new hosts. They spread their beds across the ocean floor.

'Lands rose, continents formed, oceans divided. The reds, greens and browns established territorial domains. For millions of years they flourished in symbiosis with other creatures of the planet. Then the humans walked out of the jungles and forests. They burned and farmed and destroyed, on land and in the waters. They threatened all life with cataclysms of their own creation.

'Down in the oldest caves, at the confluence of the Mediterranean and the Atlantic, the ancients huddled once more. Now it was not enough to be indispensable. A new species was needed. This time, it would need an end plan . . .'

MANFRED

He lay motionless in bed, and across the chambers of his mind the dream took shape, delivering the phycology conference keynote with his own prologue to the next edition.

'. . . and so the Great Seaweed Brain led their encroachment onto land. It recruited human agents, most of them unaware, to further its cause. These agents were dispatched to the inner workings of farming, law, poetry, aesthetics, banking, sociology, science, food, medicine – every aspect of industry and human culture.'

At the podium, Manfred looked up from his manuscript. All the notable scientists were gathered. They were rapt, speechless. 'Should I continue?'

'Yes.' A woman near the front nodded vigorously. 'You must!'

'By the twentieth century, humans had dangerously increased the toxicity of the oceans. The diversity of algae was threatened, leading to a competition among seaweeds for dominance. Wireweed choked out riverine habitats. Sargassum controlled an entire sea and threatened to expand. The major species hastened to their final outposts and ramped up infiltration in biofuels, technology, drug manufacturing.

'These forces are now increasing in strength. Perhaps they are even behind infertility. They continue to feed off the fertilisers we dump into our streams and oceans. They've entered our food stocks, our beef and pasta and ice cream. The Sargassum has grown so thick in the Caribbean, the locals are building booms to keep it away. Blue-green algae feed off the sewage of Mumbai and attract flamingos to feast. Up and down the north Atlantic, pink *Palmaria palmate* is being gobbled so quickly, soon they'll be using mechanical dredgers and seabed rakes to remove the holdfasts, churn up the sand.

'It doesn't have to be this way. When humans become monoculture puppets of just one or two species, the rarest and most vulnerable are threatened. The so-called insignificant algae – how can we be sure they do not hold the key to some future disaster, some unforeseen disease? To perseverate in the face of destruction – that is our mission. We are all orphans in the grand scheme of things. We are *all* the future of seaweeds. In the next century, we need to establish diverse frontiers for humans and algae to thrive. Only then can we establish a staging ground for interstellar evolution.'

Scattered claps grew into roars of applause. Manfred beamed from behind the podium. He had communed with the Great Seaweed Brain. He had channelled its message to take algae out of the seas and into the heavens. Then he woke up.

He lay in bed staring at the ceiling. The dream had come unbidden. It seemed to contain everything he needed to face the future. He turned on his side and braved the walls, the crusty curtains, the framed sailboat picture.

Mid-March – he'd been in the clinic two months. Nora was coming, and how could he prepare? As Manfred got dressed, he felt both pale and plump. It was all the starchy foods and anti-depressants. He made his way to the lounge, waited for her to come through the door and nodded off after breakfast. Then, right before lunch, Nora stood in the entryway.

He waved, but she didn't see him. She had her hair up. Finally he stood and pulled his shirt down over his tummy. She came toward him, her flat blue eyes calmly taking everything in. They hugged. He held the back of her neck and almost wept as he smelled the sea. It had been too long since he'd touched her skin. The others were nice enough to leave them alone, and the sofa clear.

They sat together in front of the television. 'How's Gweek?' he asked.

'I don't know how much longer I'll stay on.'

'Really? Work's not going okay, or – ' Manfred turned. Gwen had taken up a position along the wall behind them. She stood stooped, with her messy hair almost covering her eyes.

Nora scooted closer, her legs very near. 'How is it in here?'

'Fine. There's food, sleep, conversation.'

'Are you worried you might get used to it?'

He smiled. Then he realised she was serious. 'At first, I was.'

'How long do most people stay?'

He glanced at the chair in the corner, where Gary the lifer slept. Facing him was Jacko the former rapeseed farmer, snoring into the lapels of his fake leather jacket. 'We're not meant to compare.' Nora's eyes tracked him with their peaceful blueness. 'Some people have come and gone since I arrived. Others have been here a bit longer. I do have things yet to accomplish, Nora.' He reached for her hand. 'I do have dreams.'

She withdrew and put her fingers over her eyes. 'I'm sorry,' she said, finding a tissue. 'I knew this would be hard.'

'I'm the one who should be saying sorry,' he said. 'It must have been horrible, discovering me like that. I wouldn't have blamed you if you'd wanted nothing more to do with me.'

'I would have visited sooner.' She wiped her eyes. She peered into the tissue that she'd balled up in her hands. 'I've been in Spain.'

He saw it then, the suffering she'd been put through on behalf of seaweeds. Just when you thought you were clear of them, they reappeared on the horizon like an endless range of mountains.

'Did you meet up with your ex, Nora?'

'I did.'

'And?'

She looked at him sharply. 'And nothing.'

'Well. The important thing is, you're here now. You're back.' The tone of his own voice annoyed him. He sounded like a father commending his daughter. 'What else have you been up to?'

'I saw the caves. They're going north, Manfred. The reds. Even a few greens. And browns, of course – lots of kelp. They're being identified all the way to the Arctic.'

'Changes to the sea-surface temperatures. Just like Mary-Margaret said.'

'There's something I want to tell you about. A research expedition's being launched. Near-shore and coastal surveys for renewable resources. They're going in June during summer solstice to hunt for any algae on the shorelines.'

He shifted on the sofa and turned in the direction of the sea. 'Who's in charge?'

'An international group, funded by a biofuel company – the Arctic, it's apparently the next place to harvest.' She squeezed his fingers. 'Mary-Margaret wants you to go, Manfred. To collect and preserve, bring back some specimens.'

'I got her letter. I almost didn't believe it.'

'If you discovered a new species . . .' Nora glanced behind them to where Gwen was inching nearer along the wall.

'I understand now,' she said, leaning in closer to whisper. Her lips were on his neck. 'What happened to you in Gweek . . .' She stared at the television, her face blank. There was a nature documentary starting. 'I think I've *heard* them, Manfred. When I dived down into the caves. And again in London.'

Manfred started to feel nauseous. He didn't think he could face lunch.

'I'm supposed to convince you to go,' she said. 'And to give you this.' Out of her rucksack she produced a wooden press and sheets of gossamer gauze. 'Collect your specimens at low tide. Rinse them in cold water, then dry them out – paper down first, seaweed on top.'

'I know all of that.'

She took a book out of her rucksack and placed it in his lap. 'It's her own copy. She said you should imagine yourself in its pages.'

He peered down at *The Future of British Seaweeds*. The bell for lunch sounded. The others started making their way to the cafeteria. On the television, some baboons were inside an enclosure building a ladder.

'I have something to tell you,' Nora said, placing her hands around her tummy. 'The reason I'm all over the place, emotion-ally.'

She was still talking, but Manfred couldn't quite hear. It was because John the former estate agent was standing in front of them, laughing. Gwen hurried over and took him away.

'*I* wanted to be chosen for this expedition,' Nora said, stand-ing up. She leaned down and kissed him on the lips. She placed her fingers along the bottom of his neck, where the Bullwhip had left its mark. 'If you go, come back safe.'

Manfred didn't have the strength to see her out. He stayed on the sofa and watched the documentary. The baboons had finished constructing their ladder. They emerged into a larger enclosure and were soon testing the strength of the perimeter walls. They climbed the trees. They stared straight into the cameras along the glass ceiling, and this time they were really trapped, with no other means of escape.

What counted for spring came and went. As the weeks passed he returned to the person he'd been before – a depressed middle-aged man.

Gwen deserved a great deal of credit for this improvement. By urging him to talk about his past, she brought out the source of his associations. There were cycles to nature, she led him to understand. The cosmos spins, space reflects the water, and the waters reflect the surface of the sky.

'I really think I like Gwen,' Manfred told the others over breakfast.

'Only a way station, this is,' Jacko replied, levelling his eyes at Manfred. 'I'm not sure she has our best interests in mind.' John giggled so hard he spilled his coffee. Miles the young mathematician ignored them as he buttered his toast. 'Her experience in academia may or may not be a benefit. She's been groomed – but she's also unafraid. She's been honing the most effective techniques in trauma reduction.'

The Arctic expedition release forms arrived. Manfred read them over. One form said he had to declare himself fit. Another asked about any issues with following orders of the captain and crew. The name of the ship was the *Farolita* – the lighthouse.

'Wait a little before deciding,' Gwen suggested. 'It's not unusual for people to stay on at Greenways longer than planned.'

He followed her advice and held onto the forms. He didn't remember purchasing any gear, but a new item began to arrive each day by delivery – snow boots, thermal underwear, a thick down jacket with a fur-lined hood. The staff carted everything to his room, and it started to pile up.

After two more weeks Manfred still hadn't decided. It had been a while since he'd held a seaweed, let alone spotted one from a distance. He had been hidden away in his inland nest, his eyes clouded over with a steady but manageable melancholy. What if his powers of identification had been depleted?

There was something else. It was that both Nora and Mary-Margaret seemed to believe he *hadn't* done it to himself in Gweek. The whole time at Greenways, the possibility of his mental illness had acted as a kind of therapeutic nurse. This nurse was there to explain and comfort, to tell him why: he suffered from delusions, he needed help. He hadn't agreed with this nurse, not fully, but the voice was *there* nonetheless.

Mary-Margaret trusted in his unique abilities. She wanted him to play a role in the future of phycology.

'Look,' he said, reading Gwen the bios of the passengers on board. 'This one manufactures Icelandic kelp flakes!'

'Sounds like someone's made up their mind.'

Summer approached. Even in Bodmin he could sense it. There was a great thaw across the moors, and people went outdoors without coats and hats. More expedition gear for Manfred kept arriving, and he had to store the deliveries in the lounge.

'So you're next?' Gary the lifer said. He sat alone with his hands folded in his lap.

'I'm heading up to the Arctic,' Manfred told him. He'd started to do sit-ups in preparation, and he swatted his tummy like a drum. 'Svalbard.'

'Like the others.'

'What others?'

'Part of the great revolving wheel.' The old man was trying to stand up. 'The great revolving wheel,' he said again, shaking his head.

'This is a research expedition for algae. I'm going to identify and collect.'

Gary kept trying to leave his chair. 'I knew you'd go there eventually,' he said, arms wobbling.

On the day of Manfred's departure, Gwen had him sign a few release forms. All the residents gathered outside her office to watch. 'Good luck,' she said, shaking his hand.

'So that's it? No more sessions?' He gave a nervous laugh. 'I'm cured?'

Gwen placed her clunky shoes side by side. 'It's a process, Manfred. You're always welcome here at Greenways, even if things change.'

Manfred hurried out. He didn't dare look until he was safely in the taxi. Everyone had crowded at the front window to wave goodbye. It took all he had not to run inside, put his suitcase back in his room and join them for lunch.

The flight to Longyearbyen, after their brief landing in Oslo, took place entirely in fog. As they descended, the black tundra of Longyearbyen rose up to meet the plane's wheels.

Manfred peered outside the window. They had flown over territories he couldn't discern, and now ice and snow covered every visible surface. The horizon held a disturbing wall of white mountains that stretched deep into the fog. The dark choppy waters near the runway didn't look capable of hosting any form of life.

Manfred had pretended, as a boy, that he lived on a ship. He'd stretched a bed sheet across the sofa and chairs in the family lounge, and he'd crawled underneath to sail among his imaginary crewmates. He hadn't needed to be a captain, or even a first mate. He had just enjoyed heading off on adventures and returning home to glory. Now while waiting at the arrivals gate for his luggage, he had gone back in time.

The expedition leader was there to meet him. Anna was Dutch. She took off her knitted cap, and her brown hair descended in ringlets. They stood silently beside each other, watching the luggage thud and clunk into the circling carousel. She kept glancing at Manfred with her ice-green eyes.

They set off from the airport in her car. Manfred rolled down his window and smelled the cold clean air. Svalbard felt like a refrigerated research lab. Yet the summer light had melted a great deal of snow. Derelict mineshafts hung precariously to the sides of the surrounding hills. Geodesic domes tilted in the mud. A network of gas and oil pipelines ran far above ground, raised high on thick metal struts. Bicycles had been chucked into the ditches. Snowmobiles waited abandoned in the tundra. Everybody walking the road carried rifles. In the sky were circling helicopters.

'What are they looking for?' Manfred asked.

'Polar bears.'

'Here in town?'

'They're hungry. Attracted to our rubbish. Nobody is allowed to lock their doors, nobody is allowed to lock their car. In case you need a place to escape.'

'And the global seed vault? Apart from the polar bears, it's the only thing I know about Svalbard.'

Anna winced. 'Recently the ground shifted unexpectedly. Some water came in.'

'It was supposed to be impregnable, I thought. Millions of seeds – to protect against the apocalypse?'

'What was supposed to be forever lasted ten years. They've taken the seeds away and haven't said where.'

She turned up a steep winding hill. Even the newer buildings in Longyearbyen were tilting. The whole archipelago seemed to be shifting from minute to minute. From high in the mountains came intermittent puffs of exploding snow, followed by tumbling rocks.

'A week ago there was an avalanche just here,' Anna said. 'Hundreds of people had to evacuate during breakfast.' She parked outside their lodge. They got out and stayed in the cold a moment, catching their breath in the thin air. Up in the highest mountains, the silence was frightening. It was a sound of nothing. It was where life could be brushed away like dust.

Suddenly there was a cacophony. From the ditch a clutch of barnacle geese came heading straight for Manfred with bobbing white faces. They flapped their wings excitedly, honking as if to raise the alarm. *Be careful of this one! Just released from Bodmin!*

Manfred shrank back. Anna looked into his frightened eyes, and in that moment she seemed to see him in his worst moments – standing on the chair, his head in the Bullwhip noose. As they came inside the lodge, the geese were still honking. The door closed and encased them in stifling heat. In the entryway stood racks of luggage and drying boots.

The other passengers had already arrived. They were congregated at the bar in their woollen socks.

'This is Manfred,' Anna announced. 'He comes recommended by Mary-Margaret. He's going to help identify and collect.'

One by one they introduced themselves. They were a mixture of men and women from the Western seats of power – the US, Britain, Canada, Europe – and had mutual connections within their various companies. While the London conference had had an academic focus, these were the stakeholders in agribusiness. One specialised in pet food. The next, biofuel. Here was a hair products rep, and over there, vitamin supplements. They were on the collective hunt for emerging habitats. If found, they were coming back with bigger boats, better equipment and exclusive harvesting rights.

Now that Manfred had arrived, their group moved to a large table where bread and cheese had been placed. He sat on the end and listened to them network and discover people in common. They all had such shiny hair and evenly spaced teeth. He couldn't help but think of Noah's Ark scenarios. What would happen if the continents submerged and these ten tossers were the only ones left? They were barking at each other with mouths full of cheese, firing up tablets and laptops.

'I have to say, it's not good in Newfoundland,' a Canadian man was saying. He had pristine outerwear, and his neck was neatly shaved. 'Fish stocks way down. And up here, puffins have dropped ninety per cent in the last decade. We're witnessing the emergence of new forms of biogeographical zonation, and an unleashing of new bacteria.'

'Plankton's our future,' a British woman suggested. She and the Canadian were having a little debate.

'Sure. But what happens when the *plankton's* gone? What will the fish eat?'

'You're concerned, then?'

'You must have seen the evidence, flying in. The remains of all those mining operations clinging to the cliffs. They've had industrial exploration here already. Whaling, coal, oil. I'm not trying to be an alarmist, but what will our seaweed farming leave behind?'

'The idea is to make it sustainable. We wouldn't be harvesting otherwise.'

'Sustainable, in a region with no soil? No trees, no insects? The impact of killing a single plant, it lingers for centuries.'

One of the older Europeans, listening to these two discuss the matter, winked at the others. 'This guy's got a conscience. He thinks seaweeds are the next dolphins.'

'Everyone knows China and Russia are the worst environmental offenders,' an American man said. 'With sustainable crops, why shouldn't we get an edge on the competition? Make things better?'

Manfred stayed on the periphery. He could feel Anna's eyes on him. The others began pulling up digital maps and unfolding charts, devising their plan of attack. It was all about who had what equipment, which fjord they explored, which bay had the most promising access, what tides to expect, which winds would help or hinder.

Anna stood up and put on her knitted cap. 'I'm heading up to bed. The shuttle to the wharf leaves at eight in the morning.'

'Who's our captain, then?' It was the British woman who asked.

'You'll meet the crew soon enough.' She shrugged. 'Some of you will know who the captain is, I'm sure.'

One of the larger charts slowly slipped from the table to the floor. A few of the older passengers held their drinks suspended in mid-air.

'Him? I wasn't told.'

'Isn't there someone else?'

'I didn't come here to be involved in *that* sort of thing again.'

Anna fixed them with her ice-green eyes. 'I can assure you, nobody reads these waters like he does. We simply can't reach the remotest islands without him. And remember – there are multiple experiments being carried out on this expedition.' She glanced at Manfred and looked away.

They were all studying him with concern. When Anna went up to bed, he was left alone as they returned to their conversations.

Finally he headed up to his room. It was a small rectangular box with heat blasting out of the vents. He unpacked his clothes for the morning. On his desk he placed *The Future of British Seaweeds* beside the wooden press with its gossamer paper and his parting gift from Nora – a tub of dulse she'd personally shredded.

It was too hot. He cracked the windows, but the curtains were too short, and the summer sun beamed straight into his room with no intention of letting up. With the window open, the room soon turned ice-cold. The sun seemed to enjoy watching him shiver, so Manfred got into bed and turned his back to its glare.

The next morning a minivan took them down to the wharf. Everyone collected their luggage and stood waiting to be allowed on board the *Farolita*. The boat bobbed gently at its mooring. It was sturdy and square – a twenty-four metre red and white survey vessel outfitted with a hydraulic crane. One of the passengers was supervising the transfer of stainless steel drills, evidently for extracting samples from the bedrock.

Manfred strolled off toward the other boats in the water. Most were small pleasure crafts, cruisers and tourist ferries. A short distance away, a grey Norwegian navy ship occupied its own pier.

A man on a bicycle was coming toward him. Manfred suddenly felt self-conscious, alone on the wharf. He looked down at the dirty brown kelp gathered under the cement pylons. More kelp openly bathed on the rocks and had slipped into the water near the boats' hulls. They were lurking in plain sight, probably waiting to hitchhike on vessels north.

The man on the bike stopped when he reached Manfred. Despite the cold he was wearing shorts and a thin tee shirt. He had long silver hair, and when he smiled he showed a few gold teeth. 'That your outfit?' He nodded at the *Farolita*, where the passengers had started to board. 'Where you off to?'

'As far north as we can. Depending on the pack ice.'

'Ah. Depending on the pack ice!' He smiled again. 'Is that all?'

Manfred didn't reply. It was hard to know if the man was being sarcastic. His feet were planted on either side of his bicycle as he reached into his shirt pocket for tobacco and rolling papers. 'A ship like that, it looks solid enough. Until it gets up into the waters of Friesland and Gustavland. Or Wildefjorden. Then there's no telling.'

'How do you know this?'

The man didn't reply. He finished rolling his smoke and licked the end to make a seal. 'Two ships lost this year already. And the summer's just begun. Tourist season!'

Manfred peered at the *Farolita*. A second minivan had pulled up along the quay. Two passengers were carrying equipment on board along a narrow metal gangway. More crates were being loaded into the hold.

'What are you up here for?' the man asked.

'Algae.'

'Ah, *life*. You won't find much of that, I'm afraid.'

Manfred pointed beneath the concrete pylons. 'There's bladderwrack.'

The man took a drag of his cigarette. 'Those dirty stragglers? They're not alive any longer.' He exhaled disdainfully. 'You don't look so good either.'

Manfred had gone cold, standing around. He made a motion to get by, but the man didn't budge.

'That *Farolita* captain. Best there is. But be warned, he always takes one more than he brings back.' He swung himself up on his bike and grinned. 'Let's hope it's not you!'

~

Manfred lay on his bunk and stared out of his porthole. The *Farolita's* engines roared as she entered a wide, flat fjord. There was no green anywhere. Icy water floated under a hard cold sun.

It was late, and he'd had a sleepless night. The captain hadn't emerged from his cabin to greet the passengers. The first mate Elke seemed in charge for now. She was a tall German with a wide forehead, and she only left the wheelhouse to come down to the mess room every few hours. There, her eyes averted, she refilled her thermos with black coffee.

Manfred had skipped both lunch and dinner. It was the prospect of engaging with the others. It was the silver-haired man on the wharf and his warning.

He quietly left his cabin to go for a walk on deck. He crept down the corridor past the other cabins and climbed the companionway toward the evening sun. He walked to the prow, the wind in his face, and clutched the railing. The captain seemed to be heading straight for the jagged mountains that filled the horizon. In the water were bobbing blue prisms of light. They'd entered the humanless void.

North Atlantic seaweeds would be migrating soon, according to Mary-Margaret. There would be a handful of kelp varieties – wakame, fork weed, feathery browns and sea fans. Maybe they'd come upon a red or two. It was doubtful they'd discover any freshwater greens. That said, a few spindly Mermaid's tresses might be rising that moment under the icy water. The brown kelp probably lay under the icy waves, entwining themselves, peering up at the ship's prow as it passed over.

191

Manfred became aware of someone nearby, watching him. It was the second mate Karl, a ginger German who was very tall and strongly built. He stood next to the anchor fastened to the prow as if guarding it. Anna had introduced him as they'd boarded – and later that morning, over coffee in the mess room, she'd discreetly asked the passengers to be especially tolerant toward this second mate, and to certain peculiar habits which they might find objectionable. She hadn't said exactly what these habits were – but she'd added that Karl was a valued member of the crew and had been a captain himself until recently.

Manfred noticed Karl staring, coming nearer. His broad shoulders were squared, and his wide mouth open. Just before reaching Manfred he gripped the railing, shook it like a child and screamed out at the waves. Manfred stayed motionless. The second mate continued screaming, even as the other passengers awoke and ran up from their cabins.

Anna made it on deck first. She stretched out her arms and came slowly toward the man. She managed to move him to the chairs under a canopy and sat with him there while stroking his head. Manfred stood back, shaken and embarrassed. The others kept glancing at him as if he'd done something wrong.

Later, over coffee, Anna reported that Karl was calmer, that he'd returned to normal.

'What's the matter with him?' Manfred asked.

'That massive tsunami in Thailand, a few years ago. Do you remember, over two hundred thousand dead? Karl was there on the beach. He was swept into the sea.'

'A miracle he survived.'

'He broke both legs in the initial wave. He managed to cling to the trunk of a palm tree, but for an entire day, in excruciating pain, he watched dozens rushing past on the way to their deaths, thrashing in the waves, screaming for help. Karl's an experienced sailor. He's trained in first aid and might have saved some of them – but he was powerless.'

Around the table, there was silence. 'Certain people,' Anna added, 'remind him of the faces he saw in the waves.' She looked at Manfred. 'I'm afraid it was you this time. If you could, try and avoid him for a while? Especially at night.'

Only white. Barren and colourless. Would they really find any seaweeds in the high Arctic? The passengers, on their second day in the fjords, asked this question with regularity.

Manfred had his hopes. It would be improbable, but not impossible to find something relatively rare like Bearded Twig Weed, a shy endophyte needing shelter. Mary-Margaret's field guide said it was only found with regularity on rocks and pebbles in Wales. But a net could catch a number of surprising things. A few flat reds might be spotted floating alone or in a small clutch of seashells. It also wasn't crazy to imagine something like a Grateloup's Fern Weed in the Arctic, bobbing along on its back like a swimmer conserving energy.

The expedition members started to form cliques. Certain passengers ate together, or shared cups of coffee in the evenings. Outwardly they were friendly enough to Manfred – smiling, greeting him politely – only to lower their voices to a whisper when he came near.

Two more days passed. They still hadn't encountered any other ships. Supposedly there were whole fleets in the Arctic, breaking through previously impenetrable ice sheets and returning with holds full of cod, mackerel and herring. Anna said scientific expeditions had set out from Longyearbyen searching for narwhal. Yet another ship was tracking the elusive Greenland whale. These ships were apparently sticking to more southerly waters. It seemed that searching for seaweeds required a further frontier. Manfred couldn't sleep in the constant sunlight. The prospect of new discoveries played with his mind.

Logistically, everyone on board was divided into two general groups. The crew and guides were in charge of navigation, safety and polar-bear protection – and the only ones allowed by the captain to be armed. Then there were the passengers, those paying for the operation but not technically in charge. The crew always ate after the passengers had finished. They also slept together, two or three to a room, in the forecabins. The passengers had individual cabins aft, each with a toilet and shower.

Meals were served buffet-style in the galley, where tables were arranged. It was a clean and functional space, with all chairs and tables fixed to the floor to prevent accidents. There was little room to move about whenever anyone wanted seconds or more coffee. Once, after Manfred had just taken a corner chair with his plate of spaghetti, he overheard the woman to his left talking to the man beside her.

'They said he was here for identifying and collecting.'

'That's just it. Obviously we can do that on our own.'

He had made an effort. He had showed them Mary-Margaret's guide over breakfast and pointed out the rarest browns and reds and greens. They didn't seem to care. Most of them had never even visited the London Herbarium. They had a determined ignorance that was designed to protect their stakeholders and funding bodies, their competing claims of governmental agreements, harvesting and distribution rights. It was obvious they were puppets, even if they didn't know it. Meanwhile Manfred had never felt more in control of his emotions, and his goals. He didn't *want* to stereotype, but he began to see in his fellow passengers, instead of the person behind the face, the kind of seaweed they hunted.

Anna had her own agenda, it seemed. She spent more time with the ship's dog Nemo than any human passengers. Yet she repeatedly said she didn't want any of her clients in the high Arctic to be ignorant of the surrounding environment.

Typically, most passengers went down to their cabins after breakfast, where they relaxed in privacy until the first search zone was announced – but by the fifth day Anna had called a meeting to suggest a detour. They gathered reluctantly around the table while she stood with her hair tied inside her knitted hat and her expression fixed. Before they started any expedition in earnest, she announced, it was important to appreciate certain glaciers. And they had an opportunity to land on one.

At the mention of the word *glacier*, the seaweed agents blanched. Their eyes became defensive – as if the very idea of glaciers had tormented them since childhood. They were executives, aquafarmers and merchants, not environmentalists. Anyway, glaciers were all over the Arctic. What was so special about them? Weren't they just lumps of old ice? Any landing site with little promise for seaweeds was out of the question. This glacier, Anna said, was very rare indeed. It was sixty metres high. It was a 'surge' glacier with unseen crevasses, newly formed valleys and spectacular ice bridges. It had been travelling for centuries and was now calving itself in the process.

'I think it's important to appreciate the beauty of where we are,' Anna explained. 'And the weather is accommodating us at the moment. Landing on a rare glacier like this – it's unlikely you'll get the chance again, ever in your lifetime.'

There was a vote. By a thin majority, the detour was agreed. Manfred was glad to be in the majority at last. From below, the captain ordered a due westward path. Maps and charts were consulted, the surge glacier marked.

Then, as luck would have it, the weather changed. They had barely reached the open ocean when a squall came rushing over the high jagged mountains. From below new orders came. Elke, up in the wheelhouse, was directed to the nearest fjord. There they dropped anchor to wait out the worst of the storm. It was just in time. That evening, protected by land on either side, the winds rushed into their harbour. There were low howls as from distant ghosts. The vote turned out to be propitious. If they hadn't chosen the detour, they would have been stuck in the ocean under the full force of the squall. That night, the general feeling on board was that the captain had averted disaster, that Anna should always be listened to.

Everyone stayed below except Manfred. He wanted to be out among the whipping spirits from the mountains. He didn't mind if he was wet and freezing cold. Then he saw Karl arrive on deck. He stood at a distance, clutching the railing and screaming at the very ocean they had barely escaped from. Manfred stood numb.

'Aren't you just thrilled?'

It was the Swedish woman. She was grinning at Manfred as the wind whipped the tassels on her hat. Out of politeness, Manfred nodded. There was nothing to see but waves and ice.

'Anna's right!' She came closer and gripped his arm. She looked green, possibly seasick. 'We should count ourselves lucky!'

He tried to shout back, 'Yes, we are lucky!' but his voice was swallowed in the wind.

They stayed in the fjord to wait out the weather the next day, and the day after that. It was almost summer solstice. By afternoon all the passengers stood on deck, restless to set out. The *Farolita* was scheduled in the seventy-ninth parallel with the sun at its peak. Many of them didn't have much experience at being patient and complained.

'It's time, surely.'

'I've got my board to report to.'

'Can't this ship handle a storm?'

Manfred felt secretly at ease. He had waited through worse. The passengers at the railings went suddenly quiet. The wind and rain had abated. Down in the water, maelstroms were forming.

The waters looked alive. Around the ship, swirling eddies formed – tunnels to territories below. It seemed a host of under-sea monsters were operating in concert, sucking the ship into the depths. All the maelstroms had the same counter-clockwise rotation, the same dark colour, as if they had been created by some further creature beneath, gazing into what was known from what wasn't. The second mate didn't make a sound. He just stood with his mouth open, staring down into the depths.

The skies cleared, the weather turned mild. The maelstroms disappeared with the last of the squall. Up in the wheelhouse Elke started the engines, and the *Farolita* left their fjord for the ocean once more. Manfred felt a tug inside like the activation of a homing instinct. Unseen forces had something special in store for him. He was being brought north for a singular purpose, lured by virtually unknown species.

For a few hours they streamed under the sun, quietly and completely alone. Then the surge glacier came into view. It rose up out of the sea like a white glistening cathedral with turrets and spires and partially submerged walkways, a floating Gothic castle that would trap them in the wake of its own destruction. Every few minutes, one of its corners tumbled off and fell into the ocean, sending ripples toward the ship.

Up in the wheelhouse, Elke got on the radio with the captain. She didn't want to bring the *Farolita* too close as the glacier calved, but he declared the waters calm enough to attempt a shore landing in Zodiacs. Nobody challenged this plan, even after two days lost in the fjord. It was as if they had become entranced by an edifice so massive and beautiful – and simultaneously dying.

The engine cut out, the iron anchor chain groaned as it dropped. Manfred felt himself turning colder. He had a bad feeling about setting foot on a structure that was sinking before their eyes.

'We have to see it,' Anna said, practically dragging everyone toward the life jackets. She took them off their hooks and handed them around. 'Let's go, put these on – it's our duty to see what it's like.'

The two guides had already set off in the first Zodiac to secure the landing spot. They took rifles, flares, holsters of bear spray and the ship's dog Nemo. The passengers watched as they motored off with Nemo in front, paws on the prow, toward the floating white castle dripping in the sun.

A little later, Anna's radio crackled. The guides had reached the shore and declared it safe. Karl lowered the second Zodiac from the hydraulic crane. He climbed in, fired up the engine and brought the craft beneath the ladder. One by one, the passengers boarded. Anna climbed in last – they all hung on as Karl headed off for the glacier.

It was their first time off the ship in four days. Karl proceeded slowly, navigating the bright blue icebergs that floated at them hissing and popping like fire crackers. There were shadows lurking beneath the blue. Suddenly a seal surfaced. People gasped and made hasty attempts at photographing their first sighting of life. A black nose, a grey dripping head, a shape twisting in the water – then gone. Meanwhile, the glacier loomed. Freshwater lapped at the hull of the Zodiac, and as soon as they arrived at the shore, the enormity of the structure rose high above their heads. It seemed they were landing on the edge of a continent. Karl nosed them into the glacier's long beach of black sand. It was fine and powdery and flecked with gold. The soil looked surprisingly dry, just metres from water. Then it was Manfred's turn to step ashore, and in seconds his footprints filled with melting ice. On every wall of the glacier, water was pouring off in fountains, rivers, multiple cascading streams. Hundreds of ice-cold spigots were bursting out of the patch of ground near his feet. He dipped his hand and drank this water that tasted like salty tears.

Nobody had anything sensible to say. They were all more or less ignorant of these edifices of ice and melting snow. They were now in nature, and they found nature to be unnatural. Nemo started to whine. He had found polar-bear prints in the snow, heading straight over the next hill, and his brown ears shook with excitement. These bear prints were *large*. Everyone gathered to look at them in silence.

The guides took the dog over the hill. A little later, the passengers were radioed over. Everyone stayed in a group and came cautiously over the top. The guides were waiting for them, standing around something in the snow – a huge circular bowl the size of a bathtub. Nemo was staring at it with his tongue out. Inside the bowl was an enormous pile of black goo, the white ice scorched with bright yellow piss.

Anna pointed to the next ridge. 'Technically,' she said, as they started off, 'a glacier is comprised of very old snow. It has more snow than can melt over the summer, and slowly compressed with ice. This one's relatively young, actually. It has occupied this general position for four to five thousand years.'

Manfred stayed close behind the guide and climbed. She was a Norwegian, and she had a rifle slung over her shoulder. Above them the ice cliffs gleamed in the sun. His boots sunk into spongy brown hillocks that squelched and spurted water. The dog was whining again, pulling at the lead as the guide pointed up the hill.

Half a dozen reindeer stood in the distance, nibbling at the mossy turf. They were small and soft-looking, like voles. They didn't seem to mind that humans were there.

'These have no natural predators,' Anna explained. 'Descended from the reindeers which once moved for long distances when sea levels were lower. Now they stay in one place, and not even the polar bears are bothered to eat them.'

They walked right past the lumpy little reindeer. They crossed a layer of rock which stood out in the ice by its dense blackness. Overhead were dark hollows, ice bridges and thick columns of compacted snow that leaned against others in columns the size of skyscrapers. Finally they emerged on a vast white plateau, where fields of ice extended far into the horizon.

'Those black rocks we passed,' Anna said, turning back to where they'd been, 'are actually boulders of ice, coated with dirt. This glacier has surged for centuries. It grinds over mountains, crushing and collapsing. It is the biggest organic ice structure in the world, and now it is coming apart.'

Higher and higher they climbed. In each wall of ice were dozens of caves. And high above these caves were the glacier's tallest, jagged peaks – ancestors of the caves beneath them. They passed gullies and ravines that had been left over after calving. Manfred tried to find a single place for his eyes to rest. Walking right on the glacier, it seemed he couldn't get close enough. And in being *too* close, he had no perspective. The glacier was a lost, lonely thing, now crawling with humans. It was crumbling back into the elements that formed it.

They stopped on the next ridge for a break. Facing each other in a great panting circle, many of the seaweed executives were smiling with exhilaration. They didn't know exactly what was going on inside them. Manfred did. He snuck glimpses of their cashmere scarves and hats, their new boots – outfits worn by so many seaweeds in disguise. One creature, living inside another. The laver and the dulse, the spirulina and the carrageenan – what better way to take over a species, when even the host was unaware? The top of life's pyramid had infiltrated the Arctic in woollen socks and digital cameras.

'Here we are on the boundary,' Anna said, pointing at the limestone. 'The interstice where sedimentary rock and meta-morphic rock collided.' The stone was etched with cross marks under their feet. The glacier had passed over the mountain and left a choreographic score.

Anna took off her hat and shook out her hair. It was long and multi-coloured, twisted into coils and ringlets. She tilted her head, let the strands open and breathe. Manfred watched along with the human seaweeds. With one hand, she ran through the tangles.

'Shall we keep on? It's going to get steep now.'

Manfred stayed beside her. They were traipsing straight into the clouds. They were climbing something alive, a creature that was shifting and sighing and venting trapped air. Soon they'd all stopped to rest again. The clouds thinned out, and they saw that they had made it directly above the beach. Below lay the mouth of the bay and their landing site. They could see the *Farolita* waiting on the flat sea.

'What in the world?' The American aimed his binoculars at the bay. 'The water's turning orange!'

'That's silt,' Anna said, 'carried down in the melt. It's not normally this much.'

Manfred took out his binoculars. The glacier was pouring itself into the blue water in bright orange spirals. They were watching a bay being created within a bay. Skua swooped among the rocks. He spotted movement in the water – bearded seals surfacing and diving, foraging for mussels. When the seals surfaced again, reddish clay dripped down their whiskers.

'Just imagine,' Anna said quietly, 'what it would be like with no stupid humans.'

He turned. She seemed to be winking at him with her ice-green eyes. Behind her was a long plateau, as far as he could see, with fields of unbroken snow.

The wind picked up. It carried rivers of unadulterated air. In the place where his thoughts had been, a new clarity came rushing in. This was the emptying out, the shedding. Down in the water, within the swirling silt, deeper currents were forming – new life forms created by the run-off. More algae were coming.

They were travelling north under the ice sheet, laying down roots.

The *Farolita* motored toward the mountains. Their destination, if the weather held, was the edge of the pack ice. To regain lost time, the captain had directed Elke through the long, treacherous Wildefjorden. The first mate stood tall in the wheelhouse, an unmoving dark figure behind the glass, as the sun arced from one horizon to the next. The Wildefjorden was a broad, dangerous fjord renowned for its unpredictable waves and icebergs hiding in u-shaped valleys. The lands to the east and west had no beaches or harbours – they were jaggedly cut. High in the cliffs were colonies of auk, guillemot, skua.

Through the intermittent fog, Manfred stayed on deck with his binoculars, watching the shorelines for seaweeds. If he had lived the majority of his life as an agnostic, or a person who dodged the major questions of life because of the blank emptiness he felt inside, he now tended toward a belief in a creator. The idea that all of what lay before him had been randomly and mechanistically created – the majesty of the towering mountains, the unmistakable breath of grace – was laughable. A person had only to open his eyes to see the hands of a designer. For too long he had been beset by melancholia. Now that his vision was unclouded, less subject to malign influences, he could look directly at nature unfolding. On Earth, the Great Seaweed Brain lay behind the gradual establishment of life. This life had nearly run its course. He had been placed on board the *Farolita* to make himself useful for the coming transition.

Because of favourable winds and the captain's navigation, they made it out of the Wildefjorden and into the ocean. From the side of the boat came a sound of grunts and growls. Islands appeared – low, rocky and *moving*. The passengers crowded on deck to see why.

They had come alongside a walrus colony. There was a great hulking pile of them, some basking in the sun, others fighting for the most exposed spot in the centre, yet all the while needing to be *near* one another to obtain it. The walrus on the apex had only one tusk, broken into a jagged shard. It bellowed constantly as it swung its bus-sized head back and forth, gouging any unfortunate that came near. It cast a quick glance at the *Farolita* and went back to its business.

The ship continued north and into the ocean. From the wheelhouse, Elke announced that they had reached the seventy-ninth parallel, a section of the seabed which apparently carried potential for two of the ship's passengers in particular. There had been no certainty about reaching these waters. The movement of pack ice was unpredictable, and there had been no returning ships to raise for information. What *was* known about the summer pack ice was that it was retreating, and by 2025 expected to disappear entirely – a trend that presented an opportunity for many of those on board.

Manfred was on deck when the ship's engines cut out. An instant silence followed, with only the sound of the wind and the waves against the hull. Karl came steadily across the deck, rolling in front of him a large, heavy object on wheels. He shouted in German to Elke and brought his delivery to the crane. Then he took the tarpaulin away, revealing two robotic arms protruding from a hull. It looked like a space capsule. He attached a winch, activated the crane and began hoisting the vessel above the deck.

'What is that thing?' Manfred asked the American next to him. This was Calvin, the kelp industrialist with silver hair and sensitive cow-like eyes.

'The latest UUV – unmanned underwater vessel. It's Katie and Dolph's baby. They're going to drag the bottom, collect some rock samples.'

'Katie and Dolph? I thought they were the spirulina reps.'

'They're moonlighting for an oil company. Funding this whole junket.'

The engines started up again. Karl kept up a steady chatter with Elke via walkie-talkies, and the ship rolled in the waves as the UUV hung suspended over the deck. Katie and Dolph directed the operation from satellite phones. They were small and compact and wore matching red boiler suits, making them difficult to distinguish from each other as they hurried about with their heads down. Some said they were siblings. Others insisted they were a couple.

Elke cut the engine again. For a few minutes they bobbed in the open sea. Karl hoisted the vessel higher until it cleared the railings, then swung it starboard over the waves. It was jet black and the size of a small car. Dolph and Katie shouted over each other while Karl made tiny adjustments.

Manfred stared into the water. He could feel something inside him shift and settle, like he was being slotted into place.

'Calvin, do you know anything about this rumour concerning the captain? That he always takes one more than he brings back?' He looked around, but the American had gone.

Katie and Dolph argued about the height of the waves until Karl lowered the vessel. He released the winch and the vessel dropped into the water. In seconds, it was submerged. A few guillemots and gulls plunged into the spot where it dropped, as if to follow it down to the depths. Then Katie and Dolph ran up the external stairs to the wheelhouse.

Manfred followed. He didn't ask permission. It was technically his job to observe any collections, even if they were done remotely.

It was his first time up in the wheelhouse. The cabin was warm and protected, with an array of mounted screens and monitors on either side of the wheel. Depth charts were laid flat on the table. Elke stood at the wheel itself, so tall her head almost hit the roof. She wore a black fleece jumper, her hair tied in a scarf, and drank black coffee all day from her thermos.

Katie and Dolph sat at the long table in the centre of the wheelhouse. They were operating the UUV like a drone, following its progress on a small black-and-white screen via an external camera mounted to the hull. Standing at the table, Manfred made a futile attempt to identify seaweeds. Down the vessel plunged through the shadows, into the icy black depths. An underwater world opened up – steep cliffs, billowing clouds, flashes of moving life. The picture was too dark and grainy, the vessel dropping too quickly into the primeval gyre. It was going where the maelstroms were made, where all the waves on the planet were born.

The UUV bumped on the seabed. Katie's computer made a series of beeps. 'We've landed,' Dolph said.

The external camera switched over, the picture sharpened, and they began to look through the vessel's eyes. The first thing they saw were swaying shapes.

'Kelp,' Manfred said. There was plenty of it. 'Hard to say what species. Midribs look thick. Unbranched tubes, wide waving blades.' Whatever kind it was, it had come, and it had established itself. 'Kelp,' he said again. 'But harvesting here in the middle of the sea, surely it's impossible.'

Katie and Dolph didn't seem to care. They just wanted soil. Katie took over the joystick on her keyboard. 'Now,' she said, 'we take a bite.'

Her lips parted as if anticipating the ocean's offerings – exclusive contracts, more dinners with energy ministers. The vessel inched along the seabed, churning up dirt and taking samples.

'Big waves coming,' Elke said at the wheel. She was tracking the tides with her monitor before they reached the ship.

'It shouldn't affect us, not this far down,' Katie said.

'Could mess up our calibration, though,' Dolph said. 'Get some samples, quick.'

'What do you think I've been doing?'

Suddenly there was no visibility on the screen – just darkness and swarming particles. It was as if something had raised a curtain around itself.

'I don't like what's coming,' Elke said. 'Hold on.'

The first wave hit. It pushed the ship over like a hand. Manfred was standing upright when he was thrown to the ground.

Another wave came, and another. He gripped the table legs and held on.

'We're moving away from contact,' Dolph said.

'Don't lose my vessel!' Katie screamed.

The ship bobbed and rolled. Manfred made it to his feet, just in time to see Dolph and Katie at the table, to see Elke holding fast to the wheel – when he fell again. For a moment he stayed down, clutching his little patch of the cabin floor. Finally, the waves subsided.

'Visual contact again.'

'Good. I'll just take a few more samples.'

Manfred crawled over to them on his hands and knees. Some books and framed photos had fallen onto the wheelhouse floor. One showed a group of women in front of a glacier in coats and hats – Elke, Anna and Mary-Margaret. There was one other face he recognised in the group. It was Gwen.

Elke took the photo away and placed it face-down on the shelf. Manfred stood up. His legs were weak and shaking, and he felt a hand on his shoulder.

Dolph had a fresh cut on his forehead. 'Why don't you go down to your cabin? It's not safe for you here.'

'Yes, get him below,' Katie said. 'He's bad luck.'

Dolph was already moving Manfred out onto the stairs. 'We're almost finished anyway. We find anything unusual, we'll let you know.'

The divisions on board soon become explicit. The crew looked after the ship and the safety of the passengers. The execs

concerned themselves with flow charts, algae zonal distribution surveys and financial forecasts. Manfred was the alien
Mary-Margaret had chosen, the patient Gwen had rehabili-
tated, the case study they both shared for their own research
purposes, the specialist nobody wanted at their table for meals.

The captain still had not appeared. He stayed in his cabin
under the prow, tucked away in the darkest, coldest chamber
of the ship with his porthole facing north. Apparently this
wasn't unusual. On most of the *Farolita*'s expeditions, Elke
was nominally in charge. Stories had circulated from previous
journeys – how nobody had ever laid eyes on the man, even as
they attested to his navigational skills, knowledge of pack
ice, and uncanny anticipation of the worst vicissitudes of the
Arctic Ocean.

In his quarters, it was said, were rare geological maps, nautical charts and personal logbooks from early explorers. He had
studied plate tectonics. He had become an expert in the ways
in which ocean basins had formed by the transference of heat.
He also tracked so-called Arctic vibrations – a little understood
phenomenon caused by ripples and fluctuations of ice sheets,
possibly caused by regular twelve- to fourteen-year cycles in
climate and water temperature, roughly corresponding to the
moon's intersection with the Earth's orbit around the sun.

Each night, Karl was seen taking the captain his dinner along
with a freshly caught fish in a bucket. The captain didn't eat the
fish. He opened its stomach and sifted through its last meals.
He made precise entries on what he found and mapped them
against the lunar cycle. A whale could be in Norwegian waters

one week and in Russian seas the next, only to surface off the coast of Canada a week later – and nobody, not even the most advanced marine biologists, knew why. This captain had his own theories, and was apparently steering the *Farolita* according to the stomach contents of randomly caught fish.

Some passengers openly called this quackery. Yet nobody denied that the captain consistently reached the northernmost islands of Svalbard, often on the very day he'd predicted. He had reached the shores of uncharted islands using these so-called vibrational techniques, and a number of beaches and harbours had been named after him. He'd previously attracted a shoal of ships in his periphery, like salmon following the feedings of a whale. Now the ecological window for harvesting seaweeds had arrived, and multiple expeditions were out staking claims.

The *Farolita*'s captain, it was said, used each expedition to fund his own secret research. Elke described supplementary logs of annual snowfall, bear trappers' diaries and fur-trading records going back to the eighteenth century. He was fascinated with how digestion worked during the last moments of life. The person left behind, so the rumour went, was always one of the passengers – not a species to be discovered, but a volunteer for solitary death. Scattered in various huts and caves were the remains of his former guinea pigs, each with their stomachs dissected later for examination of their final meals.

They continued north. While the others stayed in their cabins, Manfred stood on deck to keep a lookout for seaweeds. Occasionally he heard moans from below. At dinner, it had been announced that the depth finder had registered eighteen thousand feet, a piece of data that troubled those with vertigo. Down on the bottom of the globe, the Antarctic was a continent surrounded by oceans – but up here in the Arctic, he was crossing an ocean surrounded by continents. Jagged mountains rose in the distance, looming over vast stretches of snow. These mountains had been shaped by the slashing ocean waves and competed with each other for their resemblance to daggers. They might have been crossing over an inverted range of the Himalayas, where some aquatic avalanche could rise up and entomb them forever. They'd travelled further north than the heralded frost giants, Icelandic sea kings who first navigated Svalbard and waited out the deadly headwinds by listening to singing Norns flying overhead in swans' dresses.

Maybe it was being in motion, maybe it was the remoteness. Manfred had never felt more in tune with his own mind. He wanted more than ever to anticipate, to properly respond – and what he anticipated, perhaps for the first time, was a future with Nora. A job, a family. An allocation of happiness. She did love him, after all. Their relationship had grown because of their mutual love of seaweeds, and would last in spite of them.

While Dolph and Kate analysed the rock samples from the UUV, the captain announced his next destination. It was an island on the outer edge of their allowable search area. Based on his fish dissections, he concluded that this island had a high possibility for seaweeds. If found, it would be like discovering one of the guano islands of Ecuador – a concentrated source of nutrients from deep geological time, perfect for fertiliser, just waiting to be scraped off and sold for profit.

The passengers lined the railings, tracking the passing land through their binoculars. Some shorelines were indeed getting greener. They dropped buckets and collected straggling fronds or broken blades among the floating tangles of fish netting, plastic and driftwood. Out of the water an uncharted island appeared. It was brown above and reddish-green below. It came floating toward them like an egg perched on an underwater nest. There was even a small beach. With his binoculars, Manfred spotted blades along the rocks that might have been kelp.

Calvin the American didn't want to wait for the captain's destination. He asked Anna for a targeted shore landing immediately. The others agreed. Because it was low tide, timing was optimal for collection. Anna relayed a request to the captain through Elke, and from below, he soon sent up his approval. The guides took off in the Zodiac. It didn't take them long to establish the safety of the beach. A little later, they radioed back the all-clear.

Manfred went with the second landing party. He wore his Wellingtons. He took aboard his identification book, wooden press and collection bucket. Everyone huddled together as Karl sped off. The second mate seemed much better after they'd explored the glacier. Manfred hoped he wasn't the face of the tsunami's dead any longer, but he still avoided looking at Karl directly.

About halfway to the island, a few Dabberlocks appeared. These thick bobbing browns were hastening toward them between floating chunks of broken ice, as if precisely steering with their stipes and midribs. When they reached the Zodiac they seemed to stop and wave up at them with their wrinkly blades. Manfred didn't like the look of them. They were climbers. They would cling and grasp and take over in no time. He was glad when Karl made it safely to the beach. After he'd anchored, the landing party spread out and explored.

Manfred had already selected his survey area – a plot three-hundred metres long from the top of the shore to the sea. There wasn't a huge amount to discover. While the others took photos, he waded the icy shallows. He was after the ones still living, not washed up on the beach. He was hoping for Harpoon Weed, brown wireweed or wakame – the non-native hitchhikers Mary-Margaret had mentioned.

There was a bit of habitation on this unnamed rock. He found some serrated wracks. He'd also collected a few specimens that looked like sugar kelp when the first dark clouds arrived on the horizon. He dropped what he could into his bucket of seawater and kept searching in the shallows. Other translucent little ones had gathered, still alive and anchored to the rocks. They were thinly branched greens. Unbeknownst to the rest of the world, they were occupying the most pristine tide pools on the planet.

The weather turned quickly – fog and freezing rain rolled in, fast as thunder. The guides' walkie-talkies started crackling and everyone was ordered back into the Zodiacs. As they approached the *Farolita* at anchor, Manfred noticed the ship floated a bit lower in the water. He suspected the most intrepid Dabberlocks had already crawled on board.

~

214

Hunched over the sink in his cabin, he rinsed clean the specimens he'd collected. He laid them flat into the pages of his wooden press, waited for them to dry and checked them against Mary-Margaret's book.

The most prolific brown was *Saccharina latissima* – it had the wrinkled strap-like blades of sugar kelp. This find would please the others. Sugar kelp was a reliable source of nutrients, simple to harvest and quick to dry. It could be made into pasta or fertiliser. A pen of Arctic pigs would gobble it up by the bucketful.

The colony he'd found wasn't the goldmine they were after. They would need a survey area where seaweeds thrived in a large uninterrupted band, clumped in heaps along the shoreline – a place to serve as a future base. Still, it was something. He decided to make an announcement of his findings over dinner.

While Manfred was drying out his samples, Dolph knocked on his door. 'Here you are,' he said, holding out a thin plastic sleeve. 'I don't know if you'll find anything of value.'

'Thanks.' Manfred *thought* it was Dolph – but the two of them looked so alike, it could have been Katie. He held the sample up to the light. Inside the sleeve were just a few grains of black soil. It was no more than a teaspoon. 'That's it?'

'It's all we can spare.' He noticed the open press on Manfred's desk. 'You find much?'

'A little.' Manfred started to describe the specimens he'd collected in the tide pools, but Dolph wasn't really listening. He mumbled something and walked away.

'Hey,' Manfred called after him. He stepped out of his cabin and into the hall. 'Hey!'

Dolph turned. 'What is it?'

'How did your bedrock samples turn out?'

'Let's just say we found what we're looking for.'

As Dolph left, Manfred stood there staring at the thin green carpet. He could hear them in the mess hall, gathering for dinner. He could smell the food.

He returned to his cabin. He sat at his desk and shook the black soil onto a clean sheet of paper. In his kit he found his magnifying loupe. With a pair of tweezers, he separated the individual grains.

The soil was *very* black. It was hard to see anything other than the powders of ancient rock that had never seen the sun. It was a sample for geologists, not seaweed collectors. Then, as he sifted through each grain, something buried in the blackness caught his eye – a tiny red cluster gleaming up at him. He could easily have missed it. Even under magnification it seemed to come and go, as if crossing through some parallel universe.

He found a stronger loupe and sat back down. In the time he took to do this, the red cluster had disappeared again. He transferred the sample onto a fresh white page and slowly separated the grains again, one by one. Some of it kept binding together – as if to protect its own domain, its own secret inhabitants. Manfred teased the grains apart. And there, inside a thick black clump, tumbled out three intact specimens, each with miniature flower-like blades. It was algae. Looking at it made him tremble. It was Rosy Dew Drops, the very seaweed that had brought him to Svalbard.

For nearly an hour he gazed at the contours of the ruby blades, the miniature flowering stipes, the interweaving filaments. Similar star clusters were seen in deep-space photos of the heavens. In this one seaweed could be found the embedded architecture of the cosmos.

Manfred put down the loupe. He stood up, lightheaded. Leaving his desk, he stumbled to bed in a profound surge of warmth, a flush in his cheeks, a shortness of breath. In his seaweeds book he searched for the photo and description:

Porphyropsis coccinea, otherwise known as Rosy Dew Drops. Foliose. Ruffled crimson blades. At first a hollow vesicle, later flattened and leafy. A delicate species with a silky texture and a bright rose-red colour from which its name derives. Spores microscopic. Rare, but distributed in a wide geographical area. Drifts in the bubbles created by its tiny fronds. Details of asexual reproduction not known.

He put the book down. He wanted to be back together with Rosy Dew Drops right away. He leapt out of bed and checked the soil again to make sure there weren't other hidden clusters. Then he pressed the three specimens onto their own snowy-white page and left them under the gossamer sheet, beautiful, hidden and alone.

He went back to bed. He lay flat on his side and looked out the portal. Rosy Dew Drops in the Arctic! The little algae had probably hitchhiked on something equally rare, like one of the Cuvier's beaked whales swimming the darkest seas. Together they would have slept in underwater caves among the spiny crabs and slithering sea worms.

Just thinking of it made Manfred's face flush all over again. It was probably oxytocin. Pets and owners, mothers and babies – when they looked into each other's eyes, a hormone was activated. He couldn't control it. Before long, he sat straight up in bed and was staring fixedly at the press on his desk. He kept imagining Rosy there in its white paper bed under its gossamer. The three specimens were like tangerine seeds buried inside their husks, waiting for the right moment to break out. They were like dandelion seeds, anchoring themselves in someone's garden, waiting to sneeze their pollen at an unsuspecting carrier. They were like little triplets in a mother's womb.

His heart racing, he jumped out of bed once more. He rushed to his desk, seized the extra-strength loupe and peeled back the gossamer. There they were, even brighter and lovelier than he'd remembered.

The more he looked at Rosy, the more he was convinced that the Great Seaweed Brain had ordained their meeting. It explained his cheery disposition, his clarity of mind, his anticipation of a future – all from the moment he'd landed in Svalbard. It was as if he'd been chemically alerted, unconsciously primed for his eternal companion, his other half. It really appeared to be so. It *was* so. They might have been different species, but they shared the same spiritual composition. They had both been neglected all their lives. What was he, in the human world, but a few unnoticed atoms, a few buried pieces of matter in the vast black soil of the universe?

'It was me who found you,' he cried. 'That machine might have scooped you out of the soil, but I did the hard part.'

Rosy didn't reply.

'It's true,' Manfred said. 'Dolph and Katy didn't look closely enough at their own sample. I'm the one with a rare *sensitivity to seaweeds*. And you, my rare beauty, depended on me for your detection. Oh, I could look at you forever.'

The clusters seemed to converge, the little blades fold in on themselves. It was only natural. Rosy was shy and didn't belong to fixed society. It was a seaweed that had never been properly understood. Now, a strange man was hovering and fussing.

'I want to *be* you,' Manfred whispered.

Then it happened. The specimens, as if in concert, spread out slowly across the page, and the blades fluttered.

Manfred held the loupe as steadily as he could. What he hoped for scared him. He came a little closer. He could feel the seaweed's breath and radiant warmth. Another inch, and they'd be touching. He continued to stare through the loupe, half expecting a reply, but the echo of his voice rang through the cabin and nothing more.

'Tell me, Rosy – where do we go from here?'

It wasn't *enough* to look. He would need to use other sense organs. Poor little Rosy was out of its watery element. With the tweezers, he took one of the specimens and placed it flat in the middle of his palm. The oxytocin surged. The two of them were touching now. They were *holding hands*.

'My God!'

It was happening. The little red cluster turned this way and that with its petal-like blades. It was shaped like a heart. *Let me love you*, it seemed to say with its dancing motions. Then as if showing off, the specimen opened each of its multiple blades to make itself completely flat. It was deflowering itself.

'If I take you inside me, *we'll* be the future of British seaweeds. You, me and Nora. I'll go back home and introduce you to each other. I'll introduce you to the world. Help me do it, Rosy. Help me become your fronds, your bubbles, your drift.'

He leaned in closer. He would eat it. They would fill each other's vesicles. It had begun as soon as they'd met – their integration.

'Hello? Hey, Manfred – you there?'

The voice came from a person, not a seaweed. It was Calvin, the American.

'Manfred?'

'Just a minute, please . . .'

He peeled the specimen off his palm and placed it on his tongue. His mouth tingled as he swallowed. He licked his lips – it happened quickly, before he could think about it.

'Lasagne tonight, Manfred. Everyone's on seconds. If you don't come soon, it could be all gone.'

He put away the tweezers and the loupe. He closed the press and covered it with a towel. Everything was the same, nothing had changed. There were his clothes, his books, his collection kit.

Manfred went over to the mirror. There was a chorus of voices inside his head, a new gleam in his eye. For a moment he stood watching himself, as if from afar.

~

The captain, Anna announced, had a new destination in mind – the recently accessible northernmost corner of the archipelago. This remote area, with its swells and heavy fog, was normally the most dangerous part of Svalbard. However, based on his calculations of the dwindling ice pack, he strongly expected to encounter seaweeds. Shore landings would be difficult, but one island had a good emergency hut, built by the Norwegian government. It was the last habitation before the North Pole.

'Please finish and take your coffee,' she said, sending Manfred a quick glance. 'The crew haven't yet eaten.'

He was only halfway through his lasagne. He ate faster and tried to race the cheese as it melted onto his plate. The others were already passing the thermos of coffee along with a plate of chocolate-chip cookies. Someone muttered, 'This emergency hut could be an ideal place to leave one behind.'

Manfred looked up. Calvin stood up heavily and took his dirty plate into the galley.

The *Farolita* pitched in the waves. Above the dining table, the green glass lamps swung from their brass fittings. Manfred peered at the others in the shifting light. He had always *sensed* seaweeds, and now after eating a specimen of Rosy Dew Drops he was on the verge of fully *knowing* one. It was like inhabiting the ocean while still on land. He more acutely sensed the others' alignments with *their* seaweeds. He saw them clearly for what they were.

The British man harvested laver. Like anyone who worked in one industry over time, he'd started to resemble his product. The skin of his face was watery and thin, almost opaque, as if he'd been constructed out of cellophane. His particular laver formed the basis of Japanese nori, he wanted everyone to know. He always stayed out of the sun during shore landings and covered every inch of his exposed skin to protect his sickly, olive-green complexion. It was as if he worried about turning crispy and finding himself wrapped around raw tuna.

The Scandinavian woman dealt primarily with dulse – and the people of Iceland, Norway, and Sweden, she informed the group, had been eating this particular seaweed long before the Vikings. Her face was long, flat and reddish, as if she applied excessive amounts of blush to her cheeks.

'I've always been attracted to fertilisers,' she said, as the laver man lurked over her shoulder. Her fleshy earlobes wobbled. 'They're so wonderfully *rich*. If I can only find a specimen with a higher yield.'

Katie and Dolph snorted in unison. They looked smug and satisfied, possibly post-coital following their spirulina probe of the seabed. They were well-slept and lounged in high-performance athletic wear. At the same time, each of their arms and legs were coiled and compressed like clenched fists. It was still hard to tell who was Katie and who Dolph. Their genders were neutral, even flexible at a moment's notice – as if equipping them for optimal adaptation.

'Do you eat spirulina yourselves?' the dulse asked.

'Of course,' they chimed. 'They're not a fad, they're superfoods – the only nutritional supplements favoured by NASA.'

'Surely you didn't find any spirulina down there,' the dulse replied, wiggling her ear lobes. 'Isn't it mostly a tropical species?'

The two of them compressed their shoulders together and glared with their shiny blue-green eyes. 'Our company plans long-term.'

'I found a bit of sugar kelp today,' Manfred announced.

There was a short silence. It wasn't clear that anyone heard.

'Seaweed, it's all about multiple applications,' said the Canadian carrageenan rep. He had thick-set arms and a colourless, gelatine-like complexion. 'Makes no difference to me if I'm added to beer or shampoo. The less you specialise, the better. Smoothies, toothpaste – they all go down the same way! I've been to Spain, and I've been to Northern Ireland. Last month I was in Zanzibar, where our newest aquaculture farms are operating. We have staff working round the clock.'

'We've heard it already,' the laver said, a thin sigh slipping from his lips. He stretched out his pale arms, like two enormous membranes.

Manfred cleared his plate and left the mess room. In the companionway he found his boots, stocking cap and gloves. Outside, the sun sat low on the horizon. They were heading quickly north – on both sides of the ship bobbed larger chunks of blue ice. Calvin the American kelp was standing all the way down at the end of the prow. His coat hung open. He wasn't wearing a hat, and the wind came rushing through his shoulder-length hair.

'I see my past lives in these waters,' he said, as Manfred joined him. 'A kaleidoscope of mistakes, half beginnings, false starts. The sea has always been a projection of ourselves.'

Manfred nodded. 'Thanks for telling me about the lasagne.'

'A hearty dinner can be just the ticket.' He squared his shoulders at the wind. 'Get a *look* at all this ice. Mountains of it. Layers upon layers, covered with snow. There's a reason nobody lives here.' Calvin turned. Along his forehead were little nicks and buried scars. 'I was once in a bad spot myself, buddy. A place so low, I didn't even know it existed.'

'I'm actually doing okay.'

'It might *seem* that way. Until you find you've sunk lower than you thought you could. It's only when a man hits rock bottom that he finds the purpose to existence. Why we're here on Earth.'

'Okay,' Manfred said. 'Why are we here on Earth?'

'Kelp.' Calvin beamed with satisfaction. 'The mightiest of seaweeds. It carries an essential spirit.'

'I found sugar kelp today.'

'Of course you did.' He looked at Manfred steadily. 'Kelp is coming, no matter what. We saw it floating in the harbour. We passed it in the Zodiac. And today, you collected our first living proof down there in the tide pools.'

Manfred stared into the sea. Even as they spoke, the kelp seemed to be gathering under the waves. 'I didn't find a huge amount, to be fair.'

'Well, you aren't too familiar with kelp, are you?'

Manfred grunted. It was an involuntary sound – as if made by someone else. 'If only that were true.'

'I saw you, buddy. You don't know how to handle them. Tearing your specimens from the midribs, like they might bite.'

'I wanted to be careful, that's all. To allow them to regrow.'

Calvin laughed. 'They don't need help with *that*. Look here.' He held up his hand and touched off his fingers. 'Richest vitamins. Fastest growth rate. Most minerals. Highest protein content. Highest concentration of Omega-3 fatty acids. Got that? Kelp'll keep us alive long enough to survive the next major disaster.'

'You think kelp's altruistic? That it wants us to live? I think it would be quite happy if the human race ended.'

The American put his arm around Manfred's shoulders and turned him toward the water. 'I think it's like bear funk. Ever smell that? After a bear gets into your garbage and leaves behind a nasty stink?'

'I don't think I have.'

'Nasty, nasty shit. Wet dog meets skunk, meets urine. That's what I think of when I think of seaweeds. You think they've got personality, that you matter to them? Seaweeds aren't malevolent, and they're not altruistic either. They're like politicians. They're only concerned with power.' Calvin held him tighter. He had a pulsing, cord-like neck. Something hidden gathered in his forehead – memories, thoughts, long-buried feelings only the forehead knew. The forehead, and the kelp.

It was then that Manfred realised the other part of the equation. He'd been calculating things erroneously. Seaweeds had been in power for most of the planet's history. But now they also had to answer to humans. Once more, algae had to adjust. Rosy Dew Drops, growling in his belly, had allowed him to see this.

'But it's true what you say,' Calvin said. 'Seaweeds *are* special. My whole life turned around when I visited that start-up in

Brittany. In the back of a little boatyard, with fibreglass hulls all around us. What a facility. In that lab they were developing recipes for everything – linguine, soup stock, cheese. Facial creams. In the loading docks, tractors arriving with fresh bladderwrack. Quality stuff, grown in specially planted forests. A conveyer belt of kelp, all day long, on a little custom-made railroad track. I kid you not, buddy. I had goose bumps.'

'Why – the scale of it all?'

He patted Manfred's shoulder. 'The efficiency of the operation! The crate train moving to the shredding man, up on his stool, as he fed his kelp into those massive blades. That pungent, vegetal, briny smell. I was hooked. No, I was *reborn*. I'm on a mission, my friend. Demand has outpaced supply. We need more sources, more products. Pollens. Gelatins. Concentrated kelp pellets—'

'But aren't there big risks of industrial harvesting up here? Kelp grows so quickly. It might strangle the life out of more delicate species.'

Calvin released him. He seemed to regard Manfred from a new and distant perch. 'Like what? You find anything unusual today?'

Manfred looked away. 'No, not really.'

'You some sort of conservationist?'

'No more than anyone else.'

'So what are these *big risks*?' He sighed. 'Environmentalists must reckon with the embarrassment of their own failed prophecies. The future is food. The future is kelp.' Calvin stood on his tiptoes and looked high over the prow where the mountains beckoned. 'I know the vicissitudes of the human mind. I understand what you're going through. You don't *have* to do this, you know.'

Manfred shivered involuntarily in the wind. He searched the horizon for signs of life, and there were none. 'Do what?'

'Where we're going next, you don't have to go ashore—'

'So it's true?'

'—and be the one he doesn't bring back. Our captain,' Calvin said, lowering his voice, 'is one of those deep ecology extremists. It's all about population control. Sure, you volunteered after your *first* attempt. But you're not obliged to be their martyr, not if you don't want to.'

'I *don't* want to.'

'Why not consider a role for yourself in kelp? In the next twenty years we've got to feed forty per cent more people on this planet. Think about that. We don't need a few hundred shredders. We need *thousands*, day and night, turning seaweed into food.'

He gripped Manfred's shoulder again and craned his cordlike neck toward the sea. 'Just remember, our creator is watching us. Not only up in the sky, but down there, my friend. In all his tremendous ferocity.'

Back in his cabin, Manfred paced from wall to wall. He wanted to hide under his bunk. He wanted to slip into the shower drain and sink down into the bilge water. He thought he heard the last two specimens of Rosy Dew Drops crying out.

'You there, Rosy?'

He opened the press and seized the loupe. The clusters on the page looked forlorn and lifeless. Manfred felt no surge of emotions, no shortness of breath. The petals didn't open in invitation, they stayed closed and sunken. They seemed to be doubting Manfred's ability to do anything useful.

'Don't you understand? I *had* to keep you secret. You threaten their aquafarming. Can't you see how their species dominance is threatened by biodiversity?'

He couldn't take Rosy's silent treatment. He went back to pacing. It was not impossible that Dolph and Katie's undersea vessel had scooped up a *very* rare specimen here in the Arctic – not just the first, but the *only* arrival of the species. Rosy had wanted to be found, heading north.

Back and forth in the tiny cabin, four steps out and four steps back. Maybe he'd been wrong about a Great Seaweed Brain. Maybe there was no designer, and seaweeds were just so many weeds of the sea. The passengers on the *Farolita* were business people, that was all. He kept walking until he caught his reflection in the mirror. The gleam in his eyes had faded, the colour of his all-too human face fearful and pale.

'Go ahead and ask, Rosy. What's Gwen doing in that photo, if she isn't in on this whole thing? I know what you're thinking. They're feeding off me. Using me for a bit of collaborative research. One of them wants me for my brain, the other my body. But I'm not the first! Others have been sent up here, I bet. It has to do with that emergency hut . . .'

He went over to the porthole. The *Farolita* was barrelling through the frigid waters. The captain was on a mission against time, racing against the end of summer and the coming ice pack, forging his way to the last island in the archipelago before the North Pole.

'I have to be brave, Rosy. I have to resist the call to die.'

The ocean was turning darker. The sun on the horizon was already more distant. They had been in the Arctic ten days and hadn't encountered a soul.

NORA

She sat high on her stool in the middle of the cutting floor, feeding dulse into the Apex Comminuting Mill. The room was filled with the smell of brine. The dirty concrete walls of the derelict fish factory, still stained with blood and guts, enclosed her in the damp. At the far end of the room, a window looked out at the sea. To accommodate the extra orders, Pete had installed her in the largest floor of the factory where dozens of workers once processed the day's catch. Strip after strip of dried kelp, straight into the blades. Her boots were practically submerged in dust. There were patterns across the floor. The dust had fallen and formed little brown galaxies, blue-green star clusters, swirling red nebulae. For a moment, as the cutting blades whined, she stared blankly at what she'd created. It was like trying to read tea leaves.

It was too hot – she needed air. She turned off the machine, and the blades slowly stopped spinning as the engine whirred down. Then, in the new silence of the cavernous factory, her thoughts went sideways. It was an old building in an old abandoned corner of an old country. What was happening seemed to have taken place long ago, even before she was aware of her thoughts.

Nora made for the window. A part of her was still down in the caves. Strangely, she had felt this way before – taking that dive had just reinforced her urge for darkness and new depths, the urge to drop down and succumb. This instinct had always frightened her. And it was this she shared most with Manfred, the quality of being self-condemned.

She roamed the room, brushing off particles from her shoulders and shaking out her hair. She checked the fill of the bags and weighed them on the scale. At the wakame, she dipped her hand in and let the shredded fragments fall between her fingers. It was a good batch. She took a few strips and chewed. She was eating more of it than usual. The kelp was nutritious. Plus, it was free. Soon, she'd become a porpoise. A bloody manatee.

Pete should have installed a ceiling fan. The window was open all the way, and it didn't seem to matter – there was no wind. Far below her boots, through the open holes in the concrete, she could see the murky liquids pooling in the sand. It was the drain spout where the fish scales had gone, the blood and guts. It was low tide. Back along the beach, the mudflats teemed with dotted with oyster catchers. They were wading carefully, their white heads down and their beaks poised, making their way across the black hillocks of mud. Around them tilted the beached boats, their hulls and anchor lines dripping with seaweeds.

Nora ate more wakame. She could see Manfred's house. Nobody else had come to occupy it since he'd gone. The lights were off, the curtains drawn on the upstairs windows. The grass in his back garden had already risen to the gate. She ate more and still more, as if the seaweed had trained her jaws for just this function. It built up her bone mass, fortified her with calcium, strengthened her teeth. She was passing on the taste of it to her baby.

She hoped Manfred was all right. Weeks at sea, with corporate knob-ends for his fellow passengers? She'd wanted to contact him but there was no phone aboard, no Internet access. Only a hailing frequency on the radio reserved for emergencies. Mary-Margaret had sent him into the unknown. No matter, Nora decided, turning abruptly from the window – she had her orders to think about, more than she could possibly fill. The world wanted its sea vegetables. The crates of dried kelp stood stacked against the walls, waiting for the shredder. Across the floor, inside the galaxies she'd created, drifted industrial-strength white plastic bags ready for more wakame, more feather boa and sugar kelp for soups and salads. When she'd tried to quit, Pete had just raised her wages. Anyway, she needed the extra money now.

She made her way to the shredder with her hands across her stomach. She hoped the child was Manfred's. It wasn't because of love, not exactly. It was because she'd started to believe in him. To think like him. To plan for their future, as seaweeds might.

The blades whined, the dust clouds formed. The patterns on the ground evolved. They had multiple branches, deep spherical tunnels like black holes or planetary volcanos. She fancied there was something sophisticated going on – a kind of visitation from her ancestors. There were seaweeds on the ground, and seaweeds inside her. Each time she left the fish factory and walked home, she could see seaweeds in the night sky.

She filled bag after bag, order after order. Her boots were submerged in the rising ash. One day, her legs would be covered. Kelp dust would rise to her hips, her shirt, her neck. She would be like the girl in the fairy tale who turned into a frozen statue as she waited for her lover in the falling snow.

One morning, she heard a voice shouting over the engine.

'Hey! Nora! You ready?'

It was Pete. He was standing right next to her, his hands cupped around his mouth.

She reached down and cut the engine. 'What is it?'

'You ready to go?'

She took off her goggles and wiped the dust from her lenses. 'Where?'

'You nutter. You asked for a lift.' He stood back from her a little. 'Don't you still have that appointment in Truro?'

'Oh yes,' she said, lifting herself off the stool.

In the loo she washed her hands and face, changed her clothes. When she came back out, Pete was standing in exactly the same place and staring at the number of bags she'd filled.

'Later,' she said, 'if you want to help me finish these others . . .' Pete was already down the stairs, heading to his car.

They left Gweek and started up and down the hills and switchbacks. The farmers were driving tractors loaded with summer wheat. Further inland, the trees formed a darker canopy. Each time they emerged into open fields, the sun blasted the windscreen to make the world a blur. And Pete liked to drive fast.

Nora closed her eyes each time there was an oncoming car. Every week there was another major accident on these roads. The knowledge of this, along with the terrifying sensation of the oncoming vehicles, almost made her ill. Everybody in the world was always one swerve, one distraction from catastrophe – and now it seemed the hands of fate were deciding to take her life because she'd created a new one. The car came to a stop at last. She opened her eyes. Pete had pulled into the hospital car park.

'I can stay here if you'd like,' he said.

'Don't be silly.' She unbuckled her seat belt. She stayed where she was, staring at the hospital entrance. 'It's not as if anyone will think it's yours.'

'Thanks a lot.'

She swatted his chest. 'I only meant – you're far too stable.'

Together they walked into the waiting room and checked in. The next thing she knew, she was in green scrubs, lying on her back while the nurse was passing a wand over her stomach. She tried not to flinch. The ultrasound gel was cold. She wanted to be back in the fish factory where she was in control, where she had the place to herself, where all the galaxies were of her own creation.

'There. Look.' The nurse pointed at the screen with a gloved hand.

An image had materialised. It was a throbbing black-and-white mass of tissue. For a moment her baby had a stipe instead of a spine, branches instead of limbs. Then the picture cleared and settled. She saw the head, the arched shoulders, the tiny feet.

'Oh!' she cried out.

'You want to know the gender?'

'No,' Nora said 'Just the exact age, please. As close as you can predict.'

'You're at fifteen weeks.'

She closed her eyes. 'You're sure? I need to know.'

The nurse was kind enough not to ask why. 'Yes, I'm sure. I mean, give or take a few days. We can be more certain with blood tests, if that helps?'

'No,' Nora said, her elbow over her eyes. She felt tears coming. 'That's all I needed.'

'Things do look good,' the nurse said.

Nora flinched. The cold wand had moved again, right down her tummy.

'You can see a bit more, if you want. Even the heartbeat. Here, look.'

Nora wiped her eyes and blinked at the moving pixels on the screen. She couldn't pay attention because she felt even more scared than she'd been in the car. A creature was growing inside her with murky origins. On the screen were patterns on the cutting floor, solar systems in miniature.

A few days later, in the derelict fish factory, Nora sat motionless on the stool. Only one crate of unshredded kelp remained.

She hadn't yet turned on the Apex Comminuting Mill. Her ears were still ringing from her morning's work, big plastic bags overflowing with perfectly formed ribbons of kelp, waiting to be mixed into her posh salads. Under the lamp she sat staring at the three galaxies swirling in front of her – the branching brown sugar kelp at her feet, the red nebula cluster of dulse in the middle of the floor, and the blue-green spiral of sea lettuce over by the window.

Her hand drifted to her child. What kind of person would it be? Truthful or deceitful? Shy or bold? She had been created after an Indian takeaway and one too many ciders. This child was conceived from an equally uninspiring evening, as if she had been determined all her life to pass on some essential gene of reckless impulsivity. What if her offspring was a horrid little creature with murder in its heart? There was no telling. She told herself the date of conception probably didn't matter all that much, nor the biological father. When she looked at the galaxies in front of her, she only knew that seaweeds were in charge. They had built the bridges that connected her with Mary-Margaret. They had introduced her to Ben, her first true love. Then Manfred, her second. They hung like tapestries in the shadowy recesses of caves. Now they lay in front of her, shredded but somehow still alive, building pathways in her uterus between her and her child.

The hours passed. The sunlight faded against the damp cement walls of the fish factory. Instead of shredding the last crate at her side, she listened to the seaweeds. They were behind all her senses. They guided her eyes, her taste, her smell and touch. The surfer might have done it. But it was seaweeds before that, the proto-proteins and life-giving material for the world. The dust on the fish-factory floor told her that this was the way of the world – the world of oceans and everything that came out of the oceans to survive.

'That baby could use more nutrients.'

'Yeah, green ones.'

'Better feed it something brown.'

Nora tried to ignore their voices. She wanted to think about Manfred – it was a shame the child wasn't his. She had some decisions to make on that score. Then she heard herself ask, 'Do you think I should tell him it's not?' A little later, the seaweeds spoke up.

'He wants feeding.'

'Maybe it's not a boy.'

'Girls prefer red dulse.'

Nora stayed frozen on her stool. The voices ricocheted off the walls. The dust galaxies expanded in the dwindling light. Glancing quickly at the door, she stood up. Pete would be pleased to see these orders finished. But the seaweeds – what was it *they* wanted?

She crept between the three celestial patterns on the floor. Red dulse, brown sugar kelp, flat, crinkly green sheets of sea lettuce. Each galaxy had its own plastic bag. 'Tell me,' she said, 'what it is you *want*.'

Nora stood among them, trying to decide. 'Too many mouths to feed,' she said, lifting the bag of dulse. It was heavy. It took a lot of lifting to turn it upside down. It took some time to get it all out. She made a big thick circle on the floor, like one of Saturn's rings. The sugar kelp was jealous.

She was one step ahead of it. She was one step ahead of all of them. 'There you go,' she said, dragging the sugar kelp over to the window. With a grunt she lifted the bag from the bottom and shook out all of it, every last shred, into the hole for the blood and guts.

The greens were next. Her boots were soon covered in them. Down to the sea, back to where they came from. Thousands in sales, down the drain. What was the difference in the long run? A woman giveth life, a woman taketh away. She laughed in the billowing dust and whirled like an angel with no intention of coming back to Earth.

The cutting floor was clean. Along the wall, the crates of kelp were empty. The white industrial bags lay limply on their sides. After sweeping and mopping up the remains Nora had returned to her own planet. She'd destroyed all the galaxies in the process. There was still a bluish green smear by the window, traces of a reddish half-spiral and a dirty brown splotch at her feet. It was as if someone had failed to clean up after a murder.

For a long while she stared into the waiting blades of the Apex Comminuting Mill. Nora once had half-baked dreams of helping to save the planet. She had wanted to be a seaweed researcher, she had wanted to have a child with the man she loved. It was pointless, the seaweeds told her, a colossal waste of time to care.

No matter how many times she swept and mopped, the dried fragments kept talking. Nora turned on the machine. It sent up a great glorious whine. At least it never stopped, and was always hungry for more. She untied her hair and shook it out. It wasn't enough for the seaweeds to sit about. They had to find their way into everything. Eventually, all that they touched wound up dead. The blades were whirring. Nora sunk lower, and she bent her head toward them. The ends of her hair dangled over the shredder.

She had only to sink a bit more, to feed herself in. It was what she'd always wanted, to be entangled and eaten by the machine. She must have fallen asleep, just for a moment, because she woke to the sound of her own scream.

Pete volunteered to drive her to Bodmin. Along the way, he kept on saying that he blamed himself.

'Don't be silly,' she said. 'I needed time off, that's all.'

They left the moor and came into the centre of town. The terrace houses were built so closely together, they seemed to be hiding something. The office buildings covered their own secrets beneath the ground. The town was a raised bowl, a hollow on the hills, an elevated sinkhole crawling with recovering meth addicts and suicides. There were traffic lights. There were supermarkets along the ring road. And there was no smell of the sea.

'I *made* myself spent,' she said. 'No sleep, hormones out of whack. Anyway, you were the one who warned me I worked too hard.'

'What I don't understand is, why you rushed to fill those orders in the first place?'

Nora tugged at her woollen hat. They were waiting for the light, and even with the window down there was no place to breathe. It was a warm afternoon, but she needed her hat as protection from the sun.

At least Pete hadn't asked what happened to the full bags of kelp she'd shredded. She was grateful for that. He was a rare breed of employer, letting his staff go off to Spain and collecting them from hospital without questions. The surgery had been a success. Some of the skin on her scalp had ripped open, but she'd been lucky not to have lost an ear. The surgeon had cut all her hair off except for a thin fringe along her forehead. It had been a different doctor who advised a stay at Greenways.

Pete parked in front. He turned off the ignition, placed his forehead in the palm of his hand and peered up at the clinic through the windscreen. 'Here we are, I guess.'

They had been told to park at the entrance to the women's wing. Some of them had already gathered at the window, and they were staring at her in the passenger seat. The last time she'd been here seemed ages ago. Along the road, the neighbouring houses all had the colour of wet cement. She gave Pete an encouraging smile. She was the one who'd had surgery. She was the one with the fresh scar over her ear, and *he* needed empathy?

'I know what you're thinking,' she said. 'Rossman and his agrarian impulse theory.'

'I wasn't.'

'You think I did it to myself, that I became overwhelmed by the need to feed all the hungry people of the world.'

Pete looked at her sharply. Nora sat with her hands at her sides, unable to explain it. She didn't really have a memory of what had happened. They said if Pete hadn't run up from his office, there was no telling.

For a while she sat there, unable to move from her seat. She flipped the visor to check her reflection and was startled by the colour of her eyes. It was the sunlight this far inland – they had faded from blue to sickly green.

'Hey,' Pete said. 'Come straight back, all right?'

'For what?'

'For your friends. For Gweek. You'll always have your job back if you want it.'

Nora nodded gratefully, but she knew the truth. Pete was a well-meaning man, but he'd looked away to say it.

On the wall opposite her bed, there was a picture of a sailboat. If she stared at it long enough, she could imagine being on the water. This eased the burning sensation on her scalp, just behind her ear.

It was a narrow little bed. She turned toward the window and listened to the rain. The curtains were drawn, but she could hear the drops plop-plopping on the sill. She wondered how many women over the years had occupied this bed. How many had noticed the carrageenan in the shampoo? Or the agar in their meds?

The doctors had kept on asking if she'd planned it. No, she had never seriously considered hurting herself. Maybe the whole thing had started with that creepy image on the ultrasound. Inside of her was a small dark creature nibbling at the edges of its shell. Soon it would break out and creep across the room on its belly. It would be placed inside of manufactured clothes. It would occupy a chair.

The staff at Greenways were all very nice. But it did bother Nora that Gwen also suggested she'd intentionally done it to herself.

'Why would I do that?' Nora replied, during her first session.

'You told me, Nora. When we checked you in. Don't you remember?'

'Oh yes,' Nora said, even though she didn't remember that at all. Surely she was the same person who arrived two days before. The idea that a person could fall asleep and wake up more or less the same made no sense to her – but that's what had happened, as far as she could tell. The meds they gave her, they helped with the pain of that.

'What I *do* remember,' she told Gwen, 'was a battle for my child.' She placed her hands around her stomach. She could sense the seaweeds still preying on her from afar. She couldn't exactly hear their voices any longer, but it didn't take any effort to picture them along the seashore.

Gwen nodded. 'A lot of expectant mothers, they feel under attack.'

Nora laughed. 'Right.'

'Is something funny?'

'No. You seem like an intelligent person, but you have no idea about seaweeds. The battle goes on forever. After it's inside, you don't know who you are any longer.'

'You mean – you feel that your baby has changed you?'

'I mean *they* have. They wait until you're vulnerable. They lie in the mud, or on the shorelines, until you're fragile.'

Gwen raised her eyebrows. 'Tell me more about that.' She reached into her desk and took out a different notebook.

'You probably think I'm *really* nuts now.' Nora was relieved she could be honest about the whole thing. It was then that their therapy began in earnest.

From the lounge, you could look through a side window into a courtyard and beyond to the men's wing. You could see a few of them in there, dark shapes in robes watching television and playing board games. Nora remembered sitting on that very sofa, right where the men were playing backgammon.

One evening, all the women took a walk under the warm moonlight. It was summer, and it was wet. They went at night because there was less traffic on the motorway. Everyone put on high-vis jackets and stayed behind Gwen into the darkness of the moor. They trudged across fields of squishy grass until they reached Dozmary Pool. All the others knew about this place. It was known for being so deep that horses had fallen in and disappeared.

They gathered around to stare at the water, white and cloudy, with vapours that smelled of phosphorous. Every now and then, a burst of rising steam shone in the moonlight. They were standing before the very source, the primordial soup.

'I bet a comet made that hole,' one of the women said.

Nobody replied. They were sweating from the walk. Many of them had taken off their reflector jackets and stood around the pool in dark columns. Greenways was known to take people with incurable depression. One woman told Nora that she liked visiting Dozmary Pool *because* it was where the horses disappeared. She had a square face and dark streaks under her eyes. Most of the time she sat in the lounge without any change in her expression – but now, talking about the horses, she grinned.

'Have you noticed the algae in our shampoo?' Nora asked her. 'For years, we washed our hair without it. Then suddenly it was just *there*.'

'I think the horses were thirsty. This is the portal to all the rivers running underneath the earth.'

'I'm telling you,' Nora said, 'seaweeds just *know*. They can't go it alone, not if they want to increase their odds of survival. So they found their way into our everyday products, our toiletries.'

The woman wasn't paying attention. Low on the horizon, the moon was full. Nora walked toward the water. If this was the source of life, she wanted to look into its dark eye. As she neared the edge of the pool, her shoes filled with warm muck. She could sense Gwen watching.

The vapours were spiralling like the hot fumaroles she'd seen in the ocean vents off Tarifa. There was a sound of crackling fire. Tiny red particles rose and scattered. Higher up, they formed a bright tunnel, a beacon in the sky. Surely any spaceship travelling the Milky Way would see this beacon, look down at Earth and notice what was left of human life. Surely they would notice and take pity. In the stardust, images formed. Nora waited for them to settle into shapes. There was a man lying frozen on the Arctic tundra, face down in a bed of ice. Polar bear tracks surrounded the body. They had come to eat but hadn't taken a bite. A hand reached down and turned the man over. The clouds shifted, his face met the sun. It was Manfred.

Nora gasped. Manfred was pale, his face drained of blood. Where his eyes had been were bright red circles. Where his intestines had been were small sacs, and inside these sacs were tiny red algae like seeds in a pod. They were frozen, just before the point of flowering. They were hitchhikers in the icy innards of his guts. They were using him as a bridge from sea to sky.

Behind her, there were shouts along the road. Nora turned, and beyond their circle of women were figures running and leaping over the hillocks. The full moon had brought out the horror-chasers, dressed as ghosts and chasing each other across the moor.

'Come on back, Nora,' Gwen called. 'Time to go.'

Nora glanced once more at the pool. The stardust had dissipated, the images gone. But one of them stayed in her mind's eye, all the way back to Greenways. It was the hand turning Manfred over as he lay frozen in the tundra. She had recognised that hand because it was her own.

The next day, she still couldn't sort it. Her vision had been sent straight out of Dozmary Pool, through the medium of its bewitching vapours. The question was, who sent it?

In the past, long before the profession had been derided,

people consulted astrologers about messages written in the sky. These days they consulted professionals like Gwen.

'Tell me the most pressing thing on your mind,' Gwen asked at their next appointment.

'Lots of things.' Nora didn't know where to begin. 'Mostly the baby, I suppose. And more recently it's Manfred.'

'Tell me about that.'

'This is my first time in therapy.'

'I understand. Take your time.' Gwen folded her hands in her lap. She glanced at her wristwatch.

Nora decided she wouldn't talk about the present. She wouldn't talk about the future, either. That left the past – Gwen was supposed to help with that.

'It's strange,' she said, tugging the hat below her ears. 'All my life, I was almost morally opposed to having kids. You know, the environment. What kind of world they'd be born into, that sort of thing. Then I turned thirty.'

Gwen was probably listening, but it was hard to tell. 'Do you have kids?' Nora asked.

'No.'

This time Nora watched Gwen shift in her chair. Finally she gave Nora a small smile. 'You know, this isn't the way this is supposed to work. I ask the questions. You talk.'

'What was your question?'

'You were talking about your change of mind. When it comes to having kids. What happened, do you think? I mean, apart from turning thirty.'

'Manfred.' She looked out the window onto the road. 'Manfred happened.' The traffic light changed, and a series of cars passed by. Each of them had one person inside.

'Go on.'

'I guess he set off something in me, that had been forming for some time.'

Nora closed her eyes. Theirs had been a different kind of making love – as if nothing would ever be wasted. He had lain beside her without speaking. They never needed to be anything other than two people with legs entwined.

'What changed, then?'

Nora opened her eyes. Gwen had that notebook out again. 'What do you mean?'

'I mean, do you still feel the same way about him? Now that you're having a child together?'

'Yes.' She repeated this answer in her mind. It seemed they *were* having a child together, even if it wasn't technically his. 'Yes, I do. But . . . I haven't had good luck in the past. With men, I mean. So it's hard for me to judge.'

'Tell me about that.'

Now it was Nora who was shifting uncomfortably. She could see herself, as if from above, the emotionally disturbed woman expecting her first child. She tried to place this second person beside her and be kind.

'I think I realised I was being too much of a mother to men.' She laughed. 'Funny, now that I'm about to be one.'

'But you said you've changed?'

247

'Yes. When I met Manfred, I didn't want to be *his* mother. I wanted to be *a* mother.'

'And now?'

Nora sighed. 'I didn't want to talk about now, right now.' She looked up. 'You think I'm making a mistake?'

'I didn't say that.'

Time sped up into a single point. Nora stood up. It was as if she'd risen all the way to the ceiling, and she could hear the woman below, shouting. 'And now I'm deluded, right? Because I want to contribute to the human race, with my selfish thirty-something need for progeny?'

'Nora,' Gwen said, calmly. 'Lower your voice, please. Sit down.'

For a moment Nora could only stand trembling in Gwen's office, her chest rising and falling. 'I'm sorry.' She sat down and hugged herself and looked out at the empty road. 'I'm sorry,' she said again.

'It's all right. Listen. You're not trapped. You still have options, Nora.'

'Like what?'

Gwen gave her pen a click and placed it flat on her notebook. In that click, it seemed, she pronounced the child expendable. 'You met Manfred in Gweek, I think? In what context was that?'

'The context? Well, it was seaweeds. Speaking of which, I saw something unusual yesterday. At Dozmary Pool.'

'Oh?' Gwen looked at her watch. 'We've gone a bit over, I'm afraid. Perhaps we can talk about it next time.'

'Right. Next time.' Nora made her hand into a fist and dug it into her thigh. 'It was probably nothing anyway.'

'Do you remember our promise? Before we finish each session, you tell me the truth. Have you had any of those thoughts?'

'Of harming myself?' Nora looked down at her fist. 'Not really. I can't be bothered, to be honest.'

'Good. Keep that promise, so we can talk about the present during our next session.' Gwen stood up and opened the door. 'It *is* nice to have options, Nora. When we start to think clearly, everything in life is a bonus.'

Nora wandered the wing. The others in the lounge were watching TV, napping, or working on a jigsaw puzzle. There was a bookcase in the far corner with an armchair in front of it. There weren't any windows. It was a quiet reading nook, and it seemed hardly anyone had ever bothered sitting there.

Nora stood scanning the titles. She had to move things out of the way to do so, knick-knacks placed in front of books to gather dust – a ceramic seagull, a plastic lighthouse, two miniatures of sailboats in laminated wooden frames, an assortment of seashells.

She held a large conch to her ear. They were supposed to hold the voices of the departed, but she couldn't hear anything. A book caught her eye. It had been there behind the conch – *The Future of British Seaweeds*. She took it down, and found the copy well-thumbed.

With the book and the conch, Nora sat down heavily in the chair. So many chapters in the book were dedicated to reproduction. Some seaweeds released spores. Others germinated in plant matter. There were seaweeds that swarmed seasonally in tide pools. Others bored into shells and mysteriously survived for years, only to duplicate themselves without warning in long barrel-shaped chains.

This thing germinating inside her, was it a borer? Or maybe, after it was released, a swarmer? The greens seemed particularly British. They were even *called* British – mostly freshwater seaweeds in estuaries and harbours, salt marshes and mudflats. There were fewer of the greens than browns or reds, but there were a dazzling array of classes, orders, families. How persistent it was, this human need for naming, for taxonomy. She hadn't once thought of what she would name her own.

Nora flicked back to the reds. These were the oldest, the most prolific. Mary-Margaret had used abstract terms like 'fragmentation' and 'proliferation' to describe their methods of reproduction, but she knew these entries were speculative. They were just terms that stood in for real knowledge. Writing about seaweed behaviour without understanding their function was only half the story. It was like analysing the movements of an infantry without caring about the commanding officers.

She brought her knees to her chest. *She* felt under attack. This thing inside her, it wouldn't only be attacking for a few months, it would continue, in one way or another, all her life. Options, Gwen had said. What, a late-term abortion? Adoption? She'd imagined she would probably raise the child alone. Or, see if Manfred would co-parent. One day she would have to locate that surfer to tell him he was a father, wherever he was.

Nora leaned back in the chair, stuck out her legs and decided not to do anything for now. The big obstacles would be sorted. It was pointless to pretend she was in control.

She flipped to the Introduction.

For the intrepid explorer of our seashores, armed only with a bucket, many exciting discoveries are possible. Thanks to the developments of modern research, the algae found in our oceans, streams and estuaries are only now revealing to us their secrets. What we are finding is equal in importance to the astronomers and astronauts opening up the heavens.

Discovering new seaweeds may not seem as monumental as planets. But if we have learned anything from the history of geology, it is to understand the interconnections between everything we find and observe. In Brighton a seaweed collector now finds a brown Pom-Pom weed originating on the shores of Japan. Combing the beaches of Blackpool, one finds a brown Velvet Thread Weed which may be descended from an ancient spore, possibly delivered to Earth by a comet from a distant galaxy. For Britain, these considerations have environmental importance. The future of one country's shorelines depends on the behaviours of those in other countries, across oceans, perhaps even in planetary systems billions of miles away . . .

Something slipped out of the book. Nora stretched it flat in her hand. The texture was translucent, silky and smooth like plastic. It was a piece of dried purple laver. She stared at the specimen in her hand. It could have come from the bedrock or the tide pools. Or plucked out of a cluster of barnacles.

She placed the conch on the arm of the chair with its hollow side facing out, and she slid the purple seaweed inside. Soon, they seemed to be getting along. The roaming purple laver had finally found its permanent home – and the lonely shell had some company at last.

Nora took the seaweed back out and placed it on the arm of the chair. The laver was being naughty. It didn't want to go back inside the shell at all. It lay limp and flat, as if sulking. She picked up the shell and held it to her ear. There was nothing. Then she realised it was her bad ear listening, the one that almost got mangled in the shredder. Her other ear worked better. This time, she could hear the waves.

'Silly,' she said, putting the shell down. 'It's just my own heart.' The laver turned its little head toward her. It had a tiny peevish voice. It wanted to know why it would ever want to go inside a shell that was dead.

'Is that why they're choosing Manfred?' she asked the laver. 'Because they need a living vessel?'

There were new voices around the corner. These were from women, not seaweeds. They were her carers, and they didn't know Nora was listening.

'Away with the fairies.'

'And pregnant, too.'

'What happened to her hair?'

'Go on,' Nora whispered to the purple laver. 'Back inside the shell now. Things might seem dead from a distance, but they're not, always.'

Nora closed her eyes. In her mind she waited for the wave to come, stretched out flat on her board and paddling with her hands. Her carers could talk about her all they wanted. She was in the sea now, surfing off Tarifa. She was floating in the early evening light, the long stretch before the sun faded, flat on her stomach with her legs in the water. The swells were rising, and there was no separation between ocean and shore.

She felt a shift and a roll, far underneath. It was as if something had risen from the bottom of the sea. It had its origins in the caves. She had often felt seaweeds watching her from below. They had long had her in mind. The thick brown Dabberlocks, the purple pestle weeds, the green bootlace weeds that slithered up from the depths and somehow found their way into her wetsuit – they'd been clocking her all along.

It was too late. The seaweed had made its move. It could have been hitchhiking on that surfer.

Nora tucked the purple laver back into the book and placed it on the shelf. That surfer, he wasn't an idiot, he'd had his designs. She didn't know what country he came from. She didn't even remember his name. None of it mattered. Everyone knew the future of British seaweeds lay elsewhere. It came from a territory called *Random Proliferation*. When her child asked after its father, she would only sigh and say, 'One too many ciders,' as her mum had done.

~

Nora kept attending her therapy sessions. She even started looking forward to them. The meds helped blanket her emotions, and her worst thoughts subsided. After just a few weeks, her hair grew back around her ears.

'Are you ready now,' Gwen asked, 'to talk about the present? Maybe the future?'

Nora nodded. The thing growing inside her, it didn't have much interest in any other subject of discussion. 'I think I'm doing better. At some point, of course, I'll have to leave this place. Then—'

'If you keep your promise, that is.'

'Yes. If I keep my promise, I'll leave this place.'

She looked out the window at the road. She thought of the baby – and how it would take over. It already seemed to be doing just that. There wasn't just one person occupying her chair. 'I don't know if I want to go back to Gweek. I could, I think. But I still want to do something more substantial with my life. To make a new role for myself in my field.'

'Okay. Good.'

'But how do I do that? I mean, if I have to think of someone else's needs first?'

'The plight of mothers everywhere. Will you have support, early on?'

'I'm not going *home*, if that's what you mean.' She made a face – it was the face for home. 'I'll spare you all the reasons why. Anyway, we're not talking about the past today.'

'Fine. So you're not going home to have the baby. And you're against going back to Gweek . . .'

'Right.' She looked at Gwen evenly. 'And I'm not giving it up for adoption.'

Gwen took out her notebook. When she was finished writing, she looked at Nora with a triumphant expression, as if declaring checkmate. 'What about other forms of support? Help from the father?'

'Well, I'm hoping to see Manfred soon. I think he'll make a good dad, don't you?'

'I can't discuss him, Nora. Patient confidentiality. I can talk about your options as a parent more broadly.'

'That's what I *am* talking about. I think Manfred – the father, I mean – will help support me. He loves me.'

'Then wouldn't it be wise to contact him?'

'I can't, where he is. You *know* I can't.'

Gwen studied her. 'But why not? In your own words, what's in the way?'

Nora placed her hand over her stomach. 'Something he's working on.'

'Be specific please, if you can.'

'Seaweeds.'

Gwen nodded. 'That's right. Seaweeds. This comes up a lot, doesn't it? Whatever you are thinking about, among all the options in front of you – going back to Gweek, finding a new role in your field, contacting the father – we keep coming back to the same thing. Seaweeds are always there.'

Nora bit the insides of her cheeks. Gwen was writing in the notebook. 'Do you want to talk about seaweeds today, Nora? In relation to your future?'

'Okay.'

'Is it true that you still feel trapped? That each time you struggle to get free, you only ensnare yourself more tightly?'

Nora nodded. 'How did you know that?'

'I'm afraid,' Gwen said, flipping back in her notebook, 'this is something you said when you arrived: *I wish I could break free of the very thing that lies in front of me.* Remember that? Have you made any progress?'

'I suppose I haven't. In relation to seaweeds, that is.'

'But if seaweeds are of vital importance to your progression in every area of your life, sorting out your relationship to them is fundamental, don't you think?' Gwen stood up. She closed her notebook, leaned against her desk and stared over the rims of her spectacles. 'There are others who feel the way you do, Nora. It might be a comfort to know that.'

'Others?'

'Yes. This is a research area of mine. People who develop compulsions to do with seaweeds. Well, this includes someone we both know rather well.'

Gwen looked out the window and ran her hand through her hair. 'What do you think about a special visitor tomorrow? Someone who could be an ideal consultant for your future. She's on her way down from London. And she's been asking after you.'

When Mary-Margaret came through the door, arms outstretched, Nora could only stand there frozen. The others cleared the lounge so they could chat in private. She almost wished they hadn't. Right away she felt like a specimen under a microscope.

'You've started to show, love,' Mary-Margaret said, staring at her stomach. 'Do you know if it's a boy or a girl?'

Nora shook her head. 'I'm not that interested, to be honest.'

Mary-Margaret opened her bag. She found her lip balm and traced it along the curves of her lips. 'Plenty of time to worry about that later, I suppose.'

'Seaweeds don't.'

'Seaweeds?'

'They don't care about names, either.'

Mary-Margaret put her hand on Nora's shoulder. Nora could feel her mentor's eyes tracing the scar around her ear. 'Tell me what happened, love. Tell me what's going on.'

'Okay. But I don't want to sit down or my back plays up. It helps to keep moving.'

It was raining outside, so Nora suggested a few turns around the wing. 'It's the illusion of momentum,' she said as they started off, side by side. 'It makes me feel as if I have somewhere to be.'

'But you *do*.'

'If only I could convince myself of that.'

'Is that what was bothering you? The day you . . .'

'I don't remember. I just *don't*. But it was as if they were speaking to me. Telling me how pointless it all is.'

'Go on.'

'The kelp I was shredding. Dulse, sea lettuce, kombu. Day in, day out. It got to the point where I couldn't hear my own voice from theirs.'

257

They were passing the other patients' rooms. Some women had their doors open, and occasionally Mary-Margaret stopped and glanced inside like a nurse doing the rounds.

'How long do you think you'll stay, Nora?'

They reached the end of the corridor, where they turned and ended up back in the lounge. Some of the others – noticing the empty sofa – had already retaken their places in front of the television. 'Do I really want to go back to Gweek? I do have a bit of time to decide. I'll need money, eventually.'

'Do you like it here?'

'I'm learning quite a few things.'

'Like what?'

'Like how some seaweeds would prefer it if humans died off.'

Nora turned. She was no longer walking alongside Mary-Margaret. She had reached Gwen's office, and the door was closed. For a moment she stood outside.

Mary-Margaret kept coming toward her. Then she grasped Nora's shoulders with both hands. 'What a fool I am, not to have thought of it before. How would *you* like to volunteer?'

'Me? For what?'

'A new study in the Arctic. They're looking for women. Specifically, pregnant women. And they'll pay.'

The door to Gwen's office opened, and she peered out. She had been in there the whole time, as if waiting for them to arrive. Mary-Margaret started off again. Nora had to hurry to catch up.

'What did you say they're studying?'

'Gut bacteria. How certain algae help build up immunity against infectious diseases. And if that immunity is passed on to the foetus.'

'In the Arctic?'

They passed the lounge again, and they kept walking in a circle. 'The cold makes it a perfect laboratory. Researchers provide a consistent diet, study the effects of ingestion and control for other factors. All specimens can be preserved. Like in the seed vault. You'd be contributing to science, no question.'

'Without harming my baby?'

They had come back down the corridor again. Mary-Margaret was walking faster now, peering in at all the patients. 'It's not exactly *my* experiment, love. I've just been asked to interpret the data.'

From inside one of the rooms, a woman came creeping out. Mary-Margaret moved further down the corridor, as if to put herself at some distance. This woman was one of the older ones. She was still in bare feet and dressed in her nightgown. She nudged Nora with her elbow and peered at Mary-Margaret knowingly.

'What,' Nora said, 'you know her, then?'

'What, you know her, then?' the woman repeated. Giggling, she lifted up the bottom of her nightgown with both hands and ran back into her room.

Nora stared. The woman had turned off her lights, but her white nightgown in the doorway was still visible. She kept repeating, 'What, you know her then?'

It seemed to Nora that she was looking at herself. This idea so unnerved her that she hurried away to catch

Mary-Margaret. 'I can't put my baby at risk. Anyway, I'm waiting for Manfred.'

Mary-Margaret looked at her. 'I have to tell you, Nora, I've just had a message from the *Farolita*. Manfred's decided to stay on a bit longer.'

Nora couldn't reply for a moment. Her future was shifting in front of her. Finally, she said, 'Tell me more.'

'I'm not allowed to tell you all the details. If the weather stays clear, they'll reach an island that's normally inaccessible. Well – as it happens, it's the same island where *your* experiment would be.'

They stood on the front steps of Greenways as the last of the rain dripped down from the overhanging trees. Water pooled in the flowerpots. Across the grass, the grounds swelled with fallen rain. Nora shivered at the prospect of going anywhere near it.

'Come on,' Mary-Margaret said. 'Just a bit of damp. We can walk a bit more, then perch ourselves on that bench under the awning. I brought lunch.'

'You're right, as always,' Nora said, starting down the steps. 'I need to walk more.'

There was a decent footpath around the grounds. The trees were still dripping, but it was a wide path, and they were able to walk beside each other. They made wider circles than they had indoors, as if ejected into a new orbit.

'I want to know something,' Nora said, as they traipsed over the wet paving stones. 'Where did you come up with the idea of the Great Seaweed Brain?'

Mary-Margaret smiled. 'That's just a phrase I put in the book. A metaphor.'

'Only a metaphor, then.'

'Phycology's an obscure field. The idea of the Brain, it increased readership. An origin myth, like the Greek island of Ionia that supposedly birthed the cosmos.' They stopped at an overturned flowerpot, where slugs were crossing the footpath toward the soil. 'When I was young, my parents told me I'd be a leader one day, a woman who made a difference. And I believed them. Do you know, it's my earliest memory? We were walking the coastal path in Sussex. There were all these seaweeds drifting in the shallows on the shoreline, and I could have sworn they were listening to me – that *they* put the idea into my parents' head.'

Nora gulped. 'And you don't believe this now?'

'Spirit, life, seaweeds, what's the difference? The best answers are only better questions – or better metaphors. In the Upanishads, they call it Brahman.'

They stopped in the front of the clinic. Mary-Margaret waved her hand across the sodden grass. 'Brahman below, above, before, behind, to the right and to the left. Out of Brahman arise space, heat, memory. Water, appearance and disappearance, food and hunger. Strength and weakness, meditation, will, speech, mind, names, verses . . . in the Upanishads, this primal entity procreated the world. In later versions, Brahman is the *same* as the world. So it is with seaweeds. They may have come first, but it's all one now.'

She looked at Nora under the heavy wet branches. 'It's an intelligent monism. Out of the gases and microbial elements, out of the earliest bacteria, seaweeds emerged. They were the first organisms to show any coherent strategy, over a billion years ago. We were created by algae.' She laughed. 'And how do we thank them? By creating the conditions for their destruction.'

'Do you know, I thought all you cared about was discovering new species.'

Mary-Margaret's eyes flashed. 'Nobody bothered with seaweeds until I came along. There were only a few hundred known kinds, and nobody had any idea about their variety of habitats. They *all* deserve protection, Nora, not just the ones to be turned into food or fuel. What I don't care about,' she snapped, 'are all the bloody amateurs. The ones who can't be fucked to sacrifice their time.'

'Time? How much time?'

'All there is.'

'That woman in the clinic,' Nora said. 'In the nightdress. How does she know you?'

Mary-Margaret drew in a breath. 'Don't look at me like that, Nora. Every scientist needs subjects. Gwen has her research, too. Everyone is *asked* to participate. They volunteer.'

'In what, exactly?'

'It varies.' She lifted the picnic basket. 'Come on, let's eat.'

They walked over to the benches under the awning and sat down. Mary-Margaret unpacked the food. One moment, Nora thought, she looked like a slithering Gut Weed, the next a Sea Oak or a beautiful Black Siphon. There were alternating colours in her face and multiple hosting mechanisms – boring into people, floating out, jumping off. Nora worried she too was being used, that her whole armature was only a shell.

'It's always a symbiotic relationship,' Mary-Margaret was saying, as she set out the bread, salad greens and cheese. 'Maybe you just had a hormonal reaction to the smell of all that kelp. Pre-partum psychosis and algae? Who knows. One thing's for certain – visionaries, they've always been called mad.'

Nora listened, but Mary-Margaret was making her especially nervous. Whenever she talked about symbiosis, it usually meant the opposite. Eventually everybody was utilised for her advancement.

'I think what you have is an indication of something special, love. Something *important*.'

Nora faced the road. In the nearby trees, goldfinches flew in and out of the branches. They moved as one, as if guided by unseen forces. 'I've seen you do this before, you know – build up the people you later need.'

'Don't be silly. I came to help. Anyway, I hope you're hungry.'

Nora found a fork and started on the salad. She was, in fact, hungry. The salad had seaweeds in it – fresh, crunchy, delicious. 'If you really want to help, you'll tell me about this Arctic experiment. Talk to me as a friend, not a potential subject.'

'All right.' Mary-Margaret patted her arm. 'We're finding that certain algae are moving toward ultra-cold temperatures. Certain humans will follow. It's a mutual anticipation and response if you like, among species and between them. With climate change, we're all like wildflowers after a forest fire, desperately seeking new habitats. That's what's going on in Svalbard, territory disputes.'

'And Manfred?'

'He's volunteered to see which algae sustains him, which provide immunity from diseases. If the planet is sick, and humans *are* the virus, then we'll be nearly extinct before we can even think of getting healthy. And we need to model the recovery now.'

'Related to that NASA work, then.'

'We've got lots of metadata and genomics research. Now we need to study metabolic systems, life-cycle phenotypes. For future ecosystems, we need to track how humans digest certain algae over time.'

Nora glanced at the container of dulse. It was almost empty. She put down her fork, looked at the bright green tentacles on her plate and pushed the salad away. 'Sorry,' she said, 'I didn't mean to be such a pig.'

'You finish it. I've heard the food in there is not very nice.'

Nora picked up her fork. One by one she sent the seaweeds meekly down her throat, as if she were in charge. 'And what would I be doing in this experiment?'

'I'm glad you're considering it. I mean, you *could* stay here, and be gobbled up by boring people. Or, you could go on an adventure. You'd stay on the island, follow the diet. We'll take regular samples of your gut bacteria and control for other factors. Collection is essential – preserving what you find, especially anything rare. We have a rough idea of the species up there, and you'd be testing them out. Instead of just

Manfred, we'd study all of you. One nuclear family, subsisting on algae.'

'I see,' Nora said, nodding mechanically.

'Gwen will show you the consent forms. It's an opportunity to contribute, and it pays well. You'll be modelling the future, Nora. You and Manfred, and your child.'

The sky darkened. Across the road, from the direction of the moor, clouds came slowly toward them. 'There's something you should know about this baby,' Nora said. 'If you're planning to study us genetically.'

Mary-Margaret unwrapped her sandwich. 'Go on.'

Nora grimaced. It was the smell of the wet grass. One day, the rains would come up from under the lawn, and waves would erode what was left of the cliffs. The ocean would spill out over Bodmin, over all of Cornwall, and nothing would be considered inland. It was time, with Manfred, to begin the next stage.

'A history of alcoholism and heart disease, I'm afraid. On both sides.'

'Oh, that's all right,' Mary-Margaret said. 'We don't insist on the healthiest of subjects. Add a bit of mental illness, and you'll be the prototypical British family.'

MANFRED

'What's that smell?'

'Smeerenburg!'

'Portside!'

Shouts from the wheelhouse brought everyone up on deck. Down in his cabin, Manfred put on his coat as a thunder of boots ran overhead.

He came up the ladder. Right away he smelled something different. The *Farolita* motored beside a long dark shoreline. The air was warmer, and the shore radiated gaseous fumes. The sky was filled with birds – skua, tern, guillemot – swooping over the boat, screeching and fighting, feasting on something unseen.

The map in the Swedish dulse rep's hands flapped in the wind. 'Last year there were just a few birds. Nothing like this.'

'Gather round, please!' Standing before the passengers, Anna clapped her hands. 'We're at ninety degrees latitude now. Smeerenberg means *city of grease*. It's because Henry Hudson discovered whales here in 1607. Six years later, the first whaling boats had arrived, and the King of Denmark claimed sovereignty.

By 1650, there would be twenty thousand men here, hunting whales. Then the naval battles began . . .'

Elke steered the *Farolita* closer to the shore. Remnants of blubber smelting pits were still out there, lumped in the tundra. Tall piles of rocks looked like tombs. As they neared land, the birds screeched and banked from the shore. Long black ribbons hung from their beaks.

Manfred took out his binoculars. All around him, the passengers crowded the railings. A single word was being repeated.

'Kelp!'

He could see it clearly from the boat. Down the entire shoreline, heaps of thick brown seaweeds clung to the rocks. More kelp drifted toward them in floating islands. Smeerenberg was teeming with seaweeds. It was going to be difficult to land.

Elke motored slowly up the shore. More kelp rolled out of the water, spreading their long thick blades like welcome mats. At the railings, the others were shouting and pointing at them. Soon the seaweeds had encircled the ship and knocked against the hull. They used the waves to lap up onto the deck before sliding back into the sea.

Under so many birds, everyone had to dodge the continuous white hail of guano. Manfred stayed back against the wheelhouse steps. He'd started to feel ill. All that kelp hadn't even needed to establish a root system – it had simply drifted there like Sargassum using nutrients of the sea.

The motor groaned. The propeller kept getting jammed in the thick webs of underwater kelp. Karl paced the deck above the captain's berth. He was on his walkie-talkie to Elke, relaying orders in German. The others were taking photos and videos. The shoreline was swarming with kelp. The dripping rocks looked alive.

Manfred stayed at the bottom of the wheelhouse. The ship's propellers kept blasting out particles. It was as if the seaweeds were beckoning *and* prohibiting. The birds, no longer wary, started flying lower. They were feasting from the mounds, and carrying what they could to their inland nests.

The smell worsened as they came closer ashore. A few minutes before, the air had complete, unmolested purity. Here on Smeerenberg, it resembled Gweek. The ship sputtered forward. To make a survey, they needed some sort of beach. They had almost gone the length of the island before Anna pointed over the water with her binoculars. 'There,' she said. 'Straight ahead!'

Set back from the waves, a narrow beach lay in the cove. It was a landing site between enormous boulders, all covered with kelp.

The captain ordered the anchor lowered. Elke cut the motor and the passengers hurried into lifejackets. They were arguing, pushing for the rights to the first Zodiac. They had to be reminded that the polar-bear guides needed to set off first. The first Zodiac hit the floating seaweeds with a thud. Karl had to row the guides ashore. The sound of his oars slapped against the kelp. His ginger hair made a bright flame over the thick brown water.

Manfred could tell what it was through his binoculars. It was a rich band of Dabberlocks. They were glistening, and troublingly alive. He even spotted a few reds that had settled in. Some straggly greenish blades clumped in the shelter of the low-lying rocks. From a distance, it looked like dulse. The larger rocks and boulders were covered by encrusting browns.

The guides radioed back the all-clear and stayed on. Dripping with sweat, Karl rowed the Zodiac back along the *Farolita*. As soon as he'd reached the ladder, six passengers climbed aboard, including Manfred with his collection bucket.

The bay was filled with kelp. Manfred put his hand in the water, and it was instantly entangled. 'A sign from God,' Calvin said, as Karl rowed in.

Manfred came ashore first. He climbed up the slippery rocks and began collecting specimens. It was so warm, he could take off his coat. There wasn't a huge variety within the Dabberlocks. Their numbers could have been linked to the Dutch whalers who unwittingly served as seed carriers. If so, the ancestors of these seaweeds had hitchhiked on the bottoms of seventeenth century boats and lain there, dormant, until the waters had warmed. Even as he entertained this idea, Manfred knew it couldn't fully account for what he was finding – an unsettling explosion of life in a place where no life should have been.

He cut one at the midribs and stared at it wriggling in his hands. After a few more, he set down his bucket. He was standing in a carpet of seaweeds. He scraped off some of the encrusting browns from the rocks and put each sample inside plastic sleeves. Then he kept moving toward the blubber smelting pots. It wasn't an easy climb. The birds swooped and dive-bombed his head. Their nests had to be nearby. Up on the hill, he could see the tallest mound of rocks with an iron cross on top. This was the collective tomb of the original Dutch whalers, the ones who didn't survive their first winter. The clouds parted. Up in the sky, a blinding sun appeared. The others, down by the water, had taken off their outer layers. They yelped with joy as they took measurements of water and air. Manfred kept collecting along the higher rocks. It was only more kelp. He was reluctant to press any more next to poor little Rosy Dew Drops. The microscopic algae would shrink at its new cabin mates, and know how badly it was doomed.

He went down to the sand and took the Zodiac back out of the cove. Karl stared glumly at the Dabberlocks as he rowed. His oars kept getting entangled.

The passengers' dinner plates were splattered with grease, the air thick with their passing gas. That night, after their feast of reindeer burgers, the members of the expedition stayed gathered at the dining table. They leaned straight at each other with their hands encircling hot mugs of coffee. One by one, they announced their findings.

'Half a degree warmer than last year.'

'Twenty per cent less ice.'

'Air temperature – two degrees higher.'

'No seals, no whales.'

'No polar bears, either.'

'Good for harvesting.'

'Shall we itemise what we collected? Besides all that Dabberlock?'

'Kombu, bladderwrack.'

'Some dulse as well.'

At this, everyone sat up straight. They had found the hardy browns, the ones with the highest growth rates that fetched the most for food products, iodine, medicine, cosmetics and fertiliser. Calvin was the first to say what they were all thinking. With his silver hair and gravelly voice, he might have been a televangelist. He lifted his hands and said, 'Arctic kelp – from the purest waters.'

They started talking over each other. 'Arctic sea salt!'

'Svalbard shampoo.'

'We can get up here year round.'

'Kombu and bladderwrack both.'

'The key is centralized production.'

'Harvest, factory, seaport – all in close proximity. A joint Finnish, Norwegian, Canadian and American operation.'

'Shared costs.'

'In time, a town. A mayor.'

At the end of the table, Manfred stayed quiet. They didn't ask what *he'd* collected. They didn't care what he thought about their ideas. Their entire operation was being launched over coffee – a factory town, with farmers drying the harvest onsite. A line of integrated products to be shipped down the North Sea to Europe.

'This will mean biofuels.' It was the spirulina twins, Katie and Dolph. They hadn't bothered to go ashore. They were there at the table, mingling without their former air of pretension.

'Using today's data, I'll have an idea of the potential yield,' Calvin said, typing into his laptop. 'We harvest sustainably, rotating our farms around the archipelago. Our yearly return could be . . .' He typed, and he waited. Then he grinned. 'We're

271

looking at two million tons of kelp in northern Svalbard alone. Maybe more.'

'Holy shit.'

'That's not even taking into consideration the southern islands!'

Their shouts of joy rang out like bells. People stood up so quickly, they knocked each other to the ground. The dulse woman broke out brandy. The Canadian produced a bottle of whisky.

'And if the sea freezes – we'll just bring in the ice breaker!'

'Open up the Eurasian market from Murmansk.'

'Keep our operations in Europe.'

'Service St Petersburg from Helsinki.'

They carved out their niches, their stakes. They all pledged to come back soon with engineers and bigger ships. The Scandinavian dulse lost all trace of stoicism. The Canadian abandoned his earlier environmental apprehensions. Even Anna claimed a piece as shipping agent. The spirulina twins put on music and danced together.

Manfred just watched them. He kept thinking of the whalers' graves. So many nations, so many wars over who could kill whales the fastest. In Longyearbyen alone, the abandoned coal mines had never been cleared away. Mary-Margaret had sent him to search for the very species nobody cared about. Back in Britain, he would raise the alarm about maintaining Arctic diversity, but would anything really change?

It was what the Bullwhip had been trying to tell him. Why try, when it was futile? Darker thoughts crept into his consciousness, and he slinked away. It seemed best to remove himself from the world's proceedings.

In his cabin, Manfred let the Dabberlocks slop about in the bucket. He sat at his desk, opened the press and held up his loupe. The last two specimens of Rosy Dew Drops looked even smaller than before. They were enclosed in on themselves, as if gearing up for a long hibernation.

'They're harvesting the Arctic,' Manfred said. 'Soon there'll be no outer range for you at all. I don't know what she was thinking, sending me here.' He leaned in closer. 'Hey. Are you awake?'

He rested his head in his hands. Rosy wasn't going to speak to a failure. He needed guidance. He reached for *The Future of British Seaweeds* and went straight to the Afterword.

The future of British seaweeds? To some extent, the answer lies with us. If you have turned every page in this book, you will have seen only a tiny sample of the estimated 7,000 reds, 2,000 browns and 1,800 greens – each with its unique impact on our waters and shores.

Many of these species can be seen by eye. Other more fragile varieties cannot be identified without a hand lens or microscope. Just as we are beginning to understand the startling range of lesser-known algae, we must face the possibility of their extinction. Fast-growing Golden Kelp and Forest Kelp are harvested for their increasing demand in global markets.

Darwin said, 'Isolation breeds diversity.' Let us vow to preserve it. Human beings have a role to play in the survival of our biosphere. For those of you working closely with algae, including our most ardent amateur volunteers, seaweeds speak to you. Identifying, collecting and preserving carries its own rewards. Some people donate money. Others, time. If we think of ourselves as containers, we can start to see beyond our own lifespans. This book is dedicated to those pioneers who make the ultimate donation of their gut biomes for long-term study, thereby advancing our understanding of the rich tapestry of algae and their effects on humankind.

Manfred held the loupe for Rosy Dew Drops. He picked up the tweezers, took a specimen off the page, and stretched out his tongue. A new fear gripped him – he'd be permanently changed.

'Be brave,' a tiny voice said.

And plop, just like that, he had dropped the second specimen into his mouth. Before he could change his mind, he swallowed. The oxytocin surged all the way to his eyeballs.

Manfred looked around. His mouth twitched, his eyelids fluttered. Everything else was more or less the same. He went over to the porthole. 'Morphology, habitat, life cycle. I bet I'll know we're officially together when I won't need to ask. When our voices are one.'

He lay flat on the bunk as the midnight sun shone into his cabin. He could be a father at last. A mother, too. 'I like to think,' he said to Rosy, 'that you finally spoke to me because we have certain things in common. Ethical, aesthetic, even moral views . . .'

It seemed important to reassure the shy little seaweed, whose reproductive patterns were largely unknown. 'You mustn't worry. I too rejected children in the normal sense. You might say I saved myself for this moment,' he added.

He sat up and peered over at the press – the cabin had turned brighter. He could feel Rosy throughout his body. There was a new chauffeur at the wheel. Soon, his arms and legs would be its cells, his brain its nerve centre. When the Arctic becomes a rainforest surrounded by boiling waters, it would hold Rosy Dew Drops.

The ship shifted. The porthole swung lower. They were still anchored off Smeerenburg, and Manfred could hear the kelp lapping at the ship's hull. It was an ominous sound created by the ghosts of the unborn.

He went back to the desk for the tweezers. A tiny voice stopped him, pointed and sharp.

'You weren't the only one to yearn for parenthood, Manfred.'

He wanted so badly to have more of Rosy inside. To feel the double brunt, to submit his body as a vessel and let Rosy take charge.

The ship tilted suddenly. He fell off his chair and onto the floor.

'Such a fragile egg,' Rosy said, looking down at Manfred from the tweezers in his outstretched hand. 'Of course, your ancestors are infants compared to mine. Your shell needs to harden.'

Manfred scrambled to his feet. He would do exactly as he was told. With his tweezers he escorted Rosy back to the desk. Outside, he could hear more kelp slapping at the hull.

'That's it. Back in my press for now. Tuck me into the gossamer, please.'

'There,' Manfred said. 'But you're all alone now.'

'Like all orphans and exiles.'

'Tell me more,' Manfred said, leaning over the page with the magnifying loupe pressed to his eye. 'Tell me how you came here – on the back of a Cuvier's beaked whale?'

'Plenty of time to share our stories. Go and have a nap. You'll need strength to face the captain.'

He woke in the middle of the night. He hadn't slept long, but one night's dreams spanned over a billion years. It was because he had inside of him the condensed time of the entire universe.

Turning over in bed, he checked the porthole. The waters were calm, the sun partly obscured by clouds. He had taken Mary-Margaret's book to bed.

> *Porphyropsis coccinea* . . . a sac when young . . . expanding and splitting when mature into a foliose, red ruffled blade, one cell layer thick, 4 mm wide and 4 cm long. Details of sexual reproduction not known . . .

Manfred went straight to the press. He opened to Rosy. He had skipped dinner – his stomach was empty, his metabolism fired and ready. He held the loupe to his eye.

'Are you awake?'

With the tweezers, he collected the last red cluster. Quickly he stuck out his tongue. He felt a throb throughout his body, holding the specimen over his flesh – a warm sensation from the little dewy blades opening toward his skin, from its cells to his tummy and down to his toes. The oxytocin surged.

'I'm going to do it,' he warned.

He stuck out his tongue again. Rosy was silent. Maybe it was testing him. What if this *was* the only specimen in the whole of the Arctic Ocean? It took all of his will power to put it back, where it slept safe and sound under its gossamer sheet.

Manfred put on his coat. He opened his cabin door and slipped into the corridor. The ship was quiet – the others were in their cabins, passed out after their celebrations. He climbed up the stairs and headed for the deck.

The night was still, the air warm. Karl stood like a sentry at the stairs that led down to the crew's quarters. He had his hat off. His long ginger hair was tied in a bun. When he saw Manfred coming, he opened his mouth as if to scream. Manfred held up his hands to show that he meant no harm. There was a strange screech. Together they looked up as a gull swooped over to the ship from the direction of the cove.

'Where are we?'

Manfred searched for the beach. It didn't exist any longer. Where they had landed the day before was covered with seaweeds. The kelp had found its way down from the surrounding rocks, as if to conceal any trace of the passengers' visit.

In the water, more floating islands had appeared. Beds of kelp surrounded the *Farolita* and clung to her hull. Under the sea, dark shadows formed – it was hard to know where water ended and seaweeds began. Manfred could tell from where he stood what species they were: Hookweed, Wireweed, fast-growth Spiral wrack with its thick spiny midribs. The kelp looked prepared to climb onto the deck, shoot into the cabins and spread out. They urged him to help.

'Take over the wheelhouse, Manfred.'

'Run the ship aground, let us make a nest.'

'The polar bears will feast on raw meat.'

These seaweeds meant business. They were like the mosquitoes in Alaska – aggressive, bloodthirsty, determined. Soon the ship wouldn't be able to budge. What a sound the *Farolita* would make as they were sucked into the sea. It would be a crisp inhalation, like a fly caught by a toad. The seabed would take them eventually. And the seaweeds would lie over their ship like moss, the passengers forever entombed.

Karl was still watching him. 'My mission here,' Manfred told him, 'is to collect, identify and preserve.' He had to shout to be heard over all the seaweeds surrounding the boat.

He didn't care if kelp harassed him. He was spoken for now. One day, there would be millions of Rosy's red petals glowing in the sea.

Karl stumbled as the ship rocked. Under the water, the anchor groaned at its footing. The shadows were shifting, and it was hard to say if the waves or the seaweeds were taking them.

'I inhabit your blades,' Manfred muttered. 'I become the fronds, the bubbles, the drift.'

It was important to be quick. Otherwise, he would be joining *them* – another victim for the kelp and their fetid soup. Big Karl stood like a wall in front of him. He was solid and towering, his arms crossed.

'What was it like during that tsunami?' Manfred asked him. 'Both of your legs broken. Hanging desperately onto a tree, all those people drifting past you on the way to their deaths. Must have been agonising.'

Karl's eyes screwed into little red beams. 'Back,' he said.

Manfred came closer. 'I bet you still see their faces. I bet you hear them screaming.'

Karl's lips trembled. Then a rolling roar of pain came out of his mouth. It was louder than before. He stopped to take a breath, then kept going. He had too much grief, too much witnessed pain. His voice was breaking apart.

Elke came out of the wheelhouse. She stood on the top deck, staring down at them. Karl's shoulders were shaking as he screamed. He looked about to jump. From the crew's quarters below, Anna hurried up the stairs. She saw Manfred and stopped.

'It wasn't my fault,' he said. 'I don't know what happened.'

Anna took Karl into her arms. Right away, like a dead flower, his huge head fell onto her shoulders, and he sobbed. She led him over to the chairs under the canopy.

The ship groaned and tilted, the anchor dragged. Elke hurried back into the wheelhouse. Unguarded, Manfred crept down the stairway and along the dark corridor. It was colder in the prow among the fore cabins. The guides slept here, and Anna too, next to the first and second mates. Their narrow doors looked like sealed hatches on spacecrafts.

There was a dim glow from the end of the prow. Manfred kept on, as quietly as he could. He had almost reached the entrance when something sprang at him. It was a creature, hissing at his feet.

'Shh. It's okay, kitty.'

The cat made a low growl. Its eyes were shining up at Manfred from the shadows. Something stirred from within the captain's cabin. The light flickered behind an old brown blanket hung across a horizontal pole.

'So he's come to *me*, has he? Made his way to the phytoplankton diatom underlying life?'

Manfred froze. The captain had an English accent. Between the makeshift curtain and the wall, he could make out a huge shape with long curly hair, pacing, throwing out his hands. He came closer and peered inside. It was a large room with a wood furnace. On the table was a gutted fish on a block. On the floor, scales and blood lay scattered about.

'I'll bet you can feel the end of the world inside you.'

The captain picked up something on the block and chucked it on the ground. He did the same with the fish head. 'Cat. You there, Cat? Come and eat.'

Manfred neared the curtain. 'Hello?'

A face came to the gap, almost completely obscured by hair. Below the crumpled forehead, over the crack of a mouth and a short stumpy nose, two tortured eyes pivoted in their sockets. 'What is it you want?'

'Just to talk. May I come in?'

'Oh, I'd enjoy that. Too much. I could gut you as well.' The face disappeared. 'Where's Cat?'

Manfred looked down. The animal was still crouched at his feet, staring. 'He's here. Please – can you tell me where we're going?'

'Where? We're not going anywhere until the tide shifts. How many ships gone missing due to seaweeds? No exact records. No witnesses. In the thousands, you can depend on that. They foul the anchor. Punch through the portholes, bust the hull.'

'I did hear metal . . .'

'Of course you did! An anchor must drop clear of its chain with no twist or turn of cable. It still gets caught. Corrupted. Bound and dragged by all manner of things.' The captain started to pace again, his hands flying. 'You think you're secure at anchor. You went to sleep at night content, with a false sense of your well-being – but in fact you're in the most perilous of positions.'

Manfred stayed outside. The captain wasn't wearing shoes. His bare feet kept crunching over the fish guts and scales. 'If I'm not mistaken,' Manfred suggested, 'a befouled anchor is typically entwined with kelp?'

'That's right. You've imagined it. You're supposed to be at sea, aren't you? But you're woken up at night by the frantic shouts from your crew. Out of nowhere you have *land* at starboard. You were so confident in your anchor that you slept well – only to wake up to everyone in a state of panic, running about to keep the keel from scraping a reef or getting stranded on the rocks.

You ask yourself, is something else at work here? Some malicious force? Your equipment works. Your charts are updated, and yet they're wrong.'

'Wrong? How?'

'What, you think you're not in danger of losing your ship? The cold doubt, the terror, the fog separating from your porthole at the sight of land. You order the anchor raised, and you see *one* thing as you lift, one thing only. The same culprit, each bloody time. They've captured the lifeline, haven't they? They hang there twisted and wet. They've squeezed the strength out of the very iron. They take away your confidence. I've decided, once and for all, to have nothing more to do with them.'

The captain stopped pacing. He stood with his head hanging to the side, as if staring through the bottom of the ship.

Manfred cleared his throat. 'Excuse me? May I come in, please?'

'No, you may not!' The captain lurched toward the curtain. The face returned, the eyes roamed. 'I don't have any self-control, don't you understand? Stay there if you want to chat.'

Suddenly the engine roared. Doors opened and banged shut. The ship was moving again. Along the corridor, members of the crew came out of the cabins and ran up to the deck.

'Where are we going, sir?'

'What, you think I've got all the answers? When we get to the island, it'll become clear.' An arm came through the curtain, hesitated a moment and withdrew. 'You must prepare. Months without direct sunlight. The procession of the equinoxes, extreme solar radiation. Sunspot oscillations, volcanic eruptions, comets with trace minerals and dust clouds. An aquatic planet we're on, just a thin core of rock. That's *where we are going, sir.* To the oceanic planets. Until the others arrive.'

'Others?'

'What, you think you're unique?' The captain gave a snort. He wiped his nose and launched a glob at Manfred's feet. 'I don't know who they are any longer. I don't ask questions. I'm just delivering you as agreed.'

'But what's our destination?'

'Phippsoya. Once there, I'll release you like a fish. That is, if I don't break my promise and take you apart.' His eyes passed over Manfred's stomach. 'Agony and hatred . . . I am so sick of people. Especially you seaweed people. Sick with waves of disgust. My strongest desire is to carve you open.'

The captain stuck out his hairy arm once more. A hand hovered there between the two men, with blood-stained fingers and long sharp nails. 'Get going, you. Back to your cabin. Hurry, before I can't control myself!'

Manfred moved off so quickly, he almost tripped over the cat. He heard footsteps chasing him up the stairs and realised they were his own. He banged his head on the passageway and emerged on deck. The captain cried out from below.

'He comes back again, I swear I'll gut him!'

Over the railing, Manfred saw the waves breaking at last. The tide had come. Great surging channels of the sea splashed the seaweeds clinging to the hull and swept them down into the water. Smeerenberg lay behind them – they'd broken free.

They headed into deeper waters. The coastline soon disappeared behind the ship, and only the kelp islands remained. They seemed to have decided to save their main meal for later. They gathered into themselves, into a single concentrated mass, and they bobbed in the *Farolita*'s wake as she picked up speed.

Maybe it was seeing the captain's fish on the block. Maybe it was the prospect of being gutted. Manfred thought of Nora with each step down the corridor to his cabin. He had missed her, of course. But he hadn't *really* missed her until now. The *Farolita* kept sailing north, and he wanted off. He wanted to be home.

Passing one of the cabins, he heard voices. They were all in there. He heard each of them distinctly – the British laver and the Swedish dulse, the Norwegian spirulina twins and the Canadian carrageenan. The American kelp.

'So you're saying it's like last time?'

'Yes, Anna's just keeping quiet about it.

'The captain always has one suicide aboard.'

Manfred held his breath. He looked up at the ceiling lights where dust had collected in the corners of the brass fixtures.

'The crew agree to this?'

'They're deep ecologists. Fewer people. Biodiversity.'

'It dovetails with Mary-Margaret's metabolic vessel research.'

'And if the passenger changes his mind?'

'They're always volunteers. Recommended by some psychologist.'

'Suicides make the best volunteers, don't they – very determined!'

'So it's all set?'

'Phippsoya. The emergency hut.'

Manfred placed his hands flat against the door. Inside the cabin there was a long silence, as if everyone seemed to be digesting this.

'God help him.'

'Don't think about it. Just don't. Someone doesn't want to live, why stop them?'

'We just have to get ourselves back home.'

'But we're complicit now.'

'Can't someone talk to him? Double check? He doesn't look terminal or anything.'

'What's he going to say? He's mental.'

'It's always the plan. The volunteers come up here, and go even more mad.'

'They see the reindeer, the snow.'

'Get mesmerised by the summer solstice.'

'This *really* doesn't seem right. Not at all.'

'Listen, I've *had* a conversation with this guy. I think he's actually hiding something.' Manfred leaned in – this was Calvin talking. 'I checked him out, and he doesn't represent a scientific institution. No algae company, nothing. I'm worried he's a saboteur.'

'You think there was something in that sample we gave him?'

'He could go back and create problems for us.'

'Or, do something to the ship.'

The door swung open. Manfred tumbled head first into the cabin. Heaped together, dripping with sweat and decaying stink, they quickly overcame him. He shielded his head as they pulled him inside and poked all over.

'Who are you, anyway?'

'Tell us what you were doing out there.'

'How much did you hear?'

The American kelp's head bobbed. He looked like a Bullwhip bladder at the end of a long vegetal spine. 'I *told* you. He was eavesdropping out there.'

Manfred could feel their hands probing his underarms, searching his pockets. The spirulina twins were knuckling his back. The British laver spat and hissed. The Swedish dulse slithered damp fingers under his shirt.

'You some environmentalist?'

'You anti-seaweed?'

'Not denying it, is he?'

'Let's get this over with. Chuck him overboard.'

Manfred cried out. Their hands were curling up under his arms, and lifting him toward the door. 'Please wait,' he said, 'let me prove myself.'

'Hold on,' said the Bullwhip. 'Let him go.'

Manfred blinked away his tears. Calvin leered at him. His neck seemed to lengthen, as if about to stretch and coil into a noose. 'He's right, let him go back to his cabin. He's volunteered, right? We'll soon find out what his intentions are.'

Svalbard's jagged peaks pointed north. The pitching waves made Manfred repeatedly sick. Flat on his bunk staring out of the porthole, he didn't see anything alive. The bobbing ice was a deathly blue. There were no whales in the water, no birds in the air, nothing moving in the distant mountains.

For five days he'd been placed on a diet of boiled seaweeds. Their impact had been forceful. This had been in his contract – eating a variety of kelp to determine which ones took. Each day, Anna brought him a big plate, watched him eat and collected his stool for analysis.

He didn't remember agreeing, exactly, to this humiliation. He didn't know who or what to trust. The last specimen of Rosy Dew Drops had gone eerily quiet. He dreamed of the rolling hills of Cornwall and longed for Nora like a boy his mother.

Nearing Phippsoya, the weather turned for the worse. The captain ordered the *Farolita* to lie at anchor off a small dark glacier, protected by the winds, to wait for the waves to subside. Manfred stayed in his cabin. He stared out of his porthole into the glacier's caves and watched the sun lower against the whiteness. People said the Arctic was changing so quickly, it would soon be unrecognisable. Ten thousand tonnes of sea ice were lost each second.

On the sixth day of his new diet, the weather cleared. Anna entered his cabin, closed the door behind her and placed his plate of steaming kelp on his desk. 'I assume you're getting ready?'

'Ready for what?'

'Come on. Eat up.'

'I'll try,' Manfred said, climbing off his bunk. His stomach was doubled over with cramps as he made his way to the desk.

Anna watched him pick up his fork. He'd grown weaker, but he chewed and swallowed the fibrous blades, one after the other.

'Any stool sample?' she asked, after he'd finished.

'Not today.'

'I hope you haven't changed your mind. Or – you've become confused?'

He wiped his mouth and looked at her. Of all the things he'd been accused of, mental illness galled him the most. 'My mind is clear.'

'You had us worried there, sneaking down to the captain. Eavesdropping.'

'I was never going to harm anyone. I wouldn't sabotage this ship.'

'The others thought you might.'

'What does the captain think?'

'He's mostly interested in what's in our guts. He wants to save us, you know – all of us. And he's very impressed by the sacrifice *you're* making.' She wandered over to his bunk and glanced out of his porthole. 'That is, if you're still brave enough.'

'I don't know if I am, to be honest.'

Anna sighed. It was a long sigh, and it carried a great deal of disappointment. 'I hope you understand this is a collaborative research expedition. We don't often get volunteers for this. And you did sign that consent form.'

His stomach grumbled. 'I didn't appreciate the extent of it.'

'Of course you're free to change your mind, to back out – but it would certainly be a violation of the trust placed in you. The costs incurred, the investment made.'

Anna came over to the desk. She leaned over him in her crisp white shirt. He could smell her skin as she opened the press and traced her fingers along the gossamer sheet. Manfred held himself still. 'These are nice, these ones.'

'Thank you.'

'We've heard some interesting new seaweeds are washing ashore on Phippsoya. You might discover some – even eat them, one day.'

He looked at his press. He felt Rosy rising up, speaking through his mouth. 'I'd like that very much.'

'Think of it, Manfred. You'll keep a record of what specimens you find. A log of your thoughts and feelings for future scientists to understand. Astronauts don't chicken out, do they? You hear those engines? We're moving again, and Phippsoya isn't far. If the weather stays clear, we'll attempt a landing in the morning.'

'Anna. Can you tell me about the emergency hut?'

'The hut?' She picked up his empty plate and looked at it in her hands. 'It's got a bunk, a lamp, a furnace. There's a supply of wood. You can come ashore and see the whole thing before you decide. Nobody forces anyone.'

'Are you going ashore?'

'We'll all be. It's a very special place, Phippsoya. Especially this time of year. There's a beach, and a beautiful view of the bay. Survival by itself is worth surviving for – that's Darwin!' She frowned. 'That's why there's a hut, of course. The last one before the North Pole. Only a few have visited. Even fewer have decided to stay – the special ones, the heroes, the ones everyone remembers.'

After Anna left, Manfred climbed back into his bunk with *The Future of British Seaweeds*. The book read like a family album now, a blur of taxonomic incest. It held his ancient ancestors, distant relatives and recent cousins.

All his life Manfred had gone through the motions with a creeping sense of being created for a role he only dimly perceived. The idea of that tiny hut filled him with dread. He didn't *want* to die that way – alone and cold, bloated with kelp. Surely he had something else to offer. It seemed Mary-Margaret and Gwen had hexed him like witches in a coven, ensnaring human-algae hybrids with a mad captain at their command.

In her copy, Mary-Margaret had scribbled the names of her latest discoveries. Her second edition – was it really possible he could contribute? He turned to the Afterword.

It is our duty to imagine new places. Think of places like the South Pole and the Arctic. Think of Europa.

Our most ancient seaweeds carried plans for their future survival, and they are still our most effective anticipators and responders. We owe them our lives. They are part of our myths and legends – our Great Seaweed Brain. Of all of these, the ancient reds have travelled the furthest. It is a tragedy that they are threatened, because one day they may help seed algal forests within the sea ice – our last frontier on Earth. That is, if they can be preserved. And if we can help them create the ideal vessel.

Manfred crossed the deck as the ship rolled in the choppy waves. The way was clear, the stairs unguarded – as if the captain wanted him to return.

The cat crouched under the makeshift curtain with its menacing eyes. Manfred inched closer. When the cat hissed, the curtain parted, and the thick curly hair appeared, the crumpled forehead, the alien tortured eyes.

'What is it now?'

'I need to know how to prepare myself,' Manfred said.

The captain's eyes roamed inside their sockets. 'Come in, then, if you must. But I warn you, don't stay very long.'

The cat scampered in, and Manfred followed. There was a sharp smell of blood and more fish bones scattered across the floor. The cabin was warm – a wood fire blazed in the stove. There were blankets on the chairs, and on the table lay open books and nautical charts. Above the small kitchen, a single porthole looked straight over the prow into the icy waters.

'Sit down,' the captain said, pacing in his bare feet. He wore a pair of old trousers and his unbuttoned shirt hung open. Up close he was bearish – over six feet, with broad shoulders, narrow hips, and dark matted chest hair. He stabbed a knife into a wooden block. 'If I feel an urge, I'll try to control myself with tricks of the mind. Or I'll order the second mate to tie me up.'

Manfred took the chair by the stove. The cat came over and sat beside him, licking its mouth. On the shelves were sealed jars with captured things inside – spiders, beetles, flies, organs floating in formaldehyde.

'Karl caught a rare Mexican fish yesterday.' The captain fingered its dark remains lumped on the wooden block.

'A Mexican fish, up here?'

'Fifteen thousand feet above the snowline. In water from a volcanic spring! Very old, very rare.'

Manfred peered at what was left of its head. 'What was it doing in Svalbard?'

'He'd run out of his favourite beetle, hadn't he? The temperatures increased, so he had to move out of the mountains or starve to death. Those marine beetles in his stomach told me the story. And you? That kelp making you feel funny yet?'

'It is.' Manfred sat up. He could hear the sound of clinking chains. 'I was hoping you could tell me about the best vessels.'

'Oh? I don't know that I can help with that. I'm just hired to land you.'

'I'm interested in shapes. And sizes. Which are ideal for long journeys?'

'Ideal?' The captain scratched the top of his head with both hands. He was about to answer when a wave hit. The cat crouched and stared into the distance with widening eyes.

'I'll tell you a story,' the captain said, as the sound of chains grew louder. 'When I was young, much younger than you, I became afraid of myself. Afraid of what I'd do. So to get away, I joined the merchant navy. Eighteen months at sea. *That* ship was a long way from the ideal vessel.'

He stood at his porthole. Oncoming waves splashed the glass with ice. 'I'd become a father. Pushed into it by some unseen hand. I loved them both, those kids. But not long after they were born, I had a horrible desire. One night, I caught myself hovering over their crib.' He turned to Manfred, his eyes screwed into tight balls under a mass of hair. 'In my hand was a lump hammer. My wife, asleep in the next room. I'd even brought a towel to muffle their cries. Oh, I was frightened by myself. I left. I went to sea and never went back.'

'Why the sea?'

'I had never been on a ship. I needed a vast and heartless place, a place with no pity. Along the way I found other life forms to care for. Other things to kill. I can't stand people, mate. I satisfy my cravings in other ways.'

Manfred glanced at a jar above his head. The organ inside was purple-black, the jar still wet around the lid. 'Is it true you always take one more than you bring back?'

The captain nodded. 'Purifies the planet, at least for a second. Life! The withered underground root, the faint breath, the pulse beneath the veins. I do share that, I know. I nurture it in my heart and lungs, inside a body and brain that wants to *crush* it.'

Manfred stared at the captain's clenched fists. He seemed to be moving closer. 'And since you left, you haven't spent any time back home?'

'Still broken, when I returned. A woman put me back together. A different woman, not the mother of my kids. We went fishing and sailing. Studying jellyfish in the tide pools. She taught me a lot.'

The captain came right over to Manfred's char. He loomed over him with his dark hairy chest exposed. 'We heard you could spot the rare species, that you had the capacity to host them.'

He reached out for Manfred's hair and stroked it. '*You're* the ideal vessel for this one. The rebirth will come asexually. The ones with biflagellate gametes, look for them on the rocky ledges, in the subtidal zones. In the littoral pools.'

With his index finger, the captain poked at Manfred's stomach with his sharp nail. 'I looked into your stool. Full of kelp. Then I looked at your urine. You got something else in there, don't you? Something that makes new hormones.'

Manfred looked away. 'Maybe.' He could feel his stomach shifting. It was the smell of fish and blood, it was the pitching waves. 'Is that why I'm so cold?'

'You're carrying a zygote. Shivering, aren't you?'

Manfred nodded. His eyes fell to the open logbook on the table. On it was a list of names, each with a line drawn through. At the bottom there was his own.

'You want to avoid that, stay in the hut. Sit by the stove and wait. A plate of seaweeds, that'll produce all the gas you need.' The captain was drooling into his beard. 'Oh, I could gut you right now. Find exactly what you got in there.'

The captain wiped his mouth and went back into his kitchen. He reached for a hammer on the counter. The cat jumped on the shelf above Manfred's head. It sat forward on its paws, next to the wet jar.

'What are you doing?'

'Just sit there,' the captain said. 'Relax.'

Manfred checked the distance to the curtain. He tried to gauge how many steps it would take. They pitched again – and somewhere on the ship came smashing glass. On the other side of the wall, the chain kept clinking.

There were footsteps. Karl stuck his head inside the curtain. His face was red and weather beaten, his shirt soaked with sweat. He looked at Manfred and back to the captain. 'Anchor's sorted,' he said. 'Links got tangled.'

'Try to make bloody tea.' The stove in the kitchen had slid out of its slot, and the captain used the hammer to bang it back. 'Elke made mistakes in Smeerenberg. Never ask a woman to park a car, right?' He grinned and showed two rows of blackened teeth. 'I'll be making the anchorage decisions from now on.'

Karl disappeared, and the captain kept banging the stove into place. When he was finished he put a kettle on the hob. 'Milk and sugar?'

'Might warm me up,' Manfred said. The cat returned to the floor beside his feet.

When the water boiled, the captain dropped teabags into a couple of mugs. He added the milk and sugar while the bags continued to steep. He brought Manfred his mug and sat across from him. 'Why'd you volunteer, then?'

'I don't know. One day my mind is mine, the next it belongs to seaweeds.'

'Bloody ball ache. If it's not one thing it's another.'

Manfred sipped his tea. The captain kept staring at his stomach.

'You're building a good substrate,' he said. 'Microscopic hitchhikers have always thrived in intestinal linings. And Phippsoya, it's a perfect vault for you hybrids. Like the one for those seeds.'

'What kind of vault is it?'

The captain sucked the floating teabag out of his mug and spat it onto the floor. 'You'll see. Some volunteers still have algae inside. Like tiny crustaceans in ice cores.'

Manfred kept shivering as he stared into the stove. He wondered how long it took for the average man to become so lonely he *chose* to freeze.

'The first few days will be the hardest,' the captain said. 'The cold you feel, that's the algae using up heat in your stomach for incubation. Try to meditate, if you want to survive until the next ship comes. What I learned, back on land, is that meditation brings peace.'

Suddenly there was silence. The engines had cut out. Together they glanced out of the porthole. The weather had cleared, the waves flat. They were drifting nose forward into a small lump of grey rock, entirely surrounded by floating ice.

'What's that?' Manfred asked. On the near shore there was a dark figure by the water. It looked like a human being.

'That's the hut,' the captain said.

Manfred shuddered. It seemed to be standing there, waiting. 'Where was it you learned to meditate?'

'Bodmin.' The captain got on his feet. His head down, he paced once more in his bare feet, combing the fish scales across the worn floorboards. 'Same place you were, mate.'

Manfred nodded. 'You made it further than I did – I'm still afraid.'

'Of what?'

'Dying alone.'

The captain stopped pacing. 'You might not have to worry about that. This weather holds, I hear you'll be getting a companion.'

He was growing ever colder. The nausea rose and fell in waves. After taking his last stool sample, Anna returned with whisky. Breathlessly, she sat beside him in bed, her face flushed and her long hair down around her shoulders. She looked like she'd just had sex.

'It's amazing. Elke did it! And the guides, they just made their landing. Have you had a peek at the hut? Built in 1916, and still standing.'

Together they listened to the groan of the anchor seeking a purchase in the seabed for its long iron tooth.

'Cheers,' Anna said, as they drank their whisky. 'Look how lucky you are.' She opened her guidebook and showed him, on a map, how they'd made it all the way to the northernmost islands of Svalbard. 'Phippsoya – named after British explorer Constantine Phipps, who discovered the island in 1773 while searching for the North Pole. He had with him a fourteen-year-old named Horatio Nelson, who narrowly avoided being eaten by a polar bear . . .'

There were shouts up on deck. The anchor had found its rest.

'See you ashore,' Anna said. She gave him a kiss on the cheek and hurried off.

Manfred stayed in bed. He could hear the Zodiac being lowered and the guides setting out. The fog had returned. From his portal he couldn't make out a thing. One thing he knew, the floating islands of Smeerenberg had followed them all the way here. He could smell kelp.

He didn't know what to believe about a coming companion. He had a long hot shower, just in case. After getting dressed, he wiped the sweat from his forehead and collected his things. Then he went up on deck. It was much colder. The others were already in their life jackets. Manfred zipped up his coat and joined them. One by one, they descended the ladder to the Zodiac.

'No fresh water on Phippsoya,' Anna shouted to everyone, as Karl steered them across the bay. He had to navigate through bobbing ice. The fog briefly cleared and gave them a view of the approach. It was a rocky beach, and the rest was ice. There was the hut on the shore, and a few mounds behind it.

'No streams, no glaciers.'

'Total isolation.'

'Except for a few bodies, that is.'

'And the occasional polar bear.'

Karl landed on the beach. He shut off the engine, stepped into the water and dragged in the nose. Manfred came ashore with his belongings hugged tightly to his chest, including the bucket, the wooden press and the *Future of British Seaweeds*.

'You never know,' he explained to the others, 'what collections and identifications are needed.'

They stood there staring at him. Out in the unprotected sun, he could see more clearly their rubbery skin, patchy hair and fleshy necks. The laver, the dulse, the spirulina twins, the carrageenan and the Bullwhip were marching around, barking at everyone to hurry up before the weather turned.

'Well?' Anna peered at Manfred. 'Shall we go and see the hut?'

They trudged through the snow like elephants returning to their ancestral home. The hut was made of wood. It was even smaller up close, sunken there in its rocky moat. The roof was torn, the chimney crumpled, the window covered by a wooden hatch. Jaw bones of polar bears were placed neatly outside the door.

The hut was unlocked. Everyone took turns investigating the interior because it was too small for all of them to go in at once. Manfred hung back. He kept glancing from the empty shoreline to his bucket.

'I'll just go and collect the decomposition samples,' Anna said, heading off. She climbed the hill to the mounds behind the moat.

One by one, the others came out of the hut.

'Not much, is there?'

'A few paperbacks.'

'A person could *almost* get warm with that stove.'

'Until the wood ran out.'

'Anna still up there?'

'Paying her respects to the heroes' tomb,' someone said, and gave a nervous laugh.

For a little while they stood there and stamped their feet. Anna returned, holding a stainless-steel briefcase. 'Manfred may stay behind,' she said. 'Mary-Margaret Dennison's selected him for additional research.'

The others started for the boat. It was very cold, after all, and besides having a look at the emergency hut, what was there to do? Karl was already in the Zodiac, starting the engine.

Manfred walked with them down to the shore. As the passengers boarded, they didn't even bother to say goodbye. Dinner would be served soon – nobody wanted to miss it. Manfred felt a quick panic. He kept one of his boots in the shallow water. As long as he had it there, there was still time to leave. He looked around the barren island and felt his face go pale. Out in the bay, the *Farolita* pointed south.

'Almost forgot,' Anna said, reaching into the boat. She placed a bucket of kelp on the rocks along with a jug of drinking water. Then she handed him a stick with a black cloth tied on the end. 'The captain will wait exactly one hour. As you know, we give volunteers a final chance to withdraw – something the psychologists like to keep track of. I'll be watching with my binoculars. You change your mind, just step outside and wave, okay?'

Manfred stood at the window staring at the white. There was old snow, high on the rise to his left, breaking apart and crumbling under the sun. There was a dusting of bright new snow on the foothills. Down by the water, more snow swirled in gusts. Within each wave, more oncoming whiteness. It was the colour of death – the polar bear hidden in the snow, the hollow breath of the dying, the ice that lay everywhere from the distant terraces to the bobbing ice in the flat water of the bay.

The captain had kept his promise. In the bay, the *Farolita* waited with engines running. It was too cold for anyone to be out on that deck. The passengers were probably sipping coffee in their cabins, watching the hut through their portholes.

He gave the place a quick survey. It wasn't a hut to prevent an emergency, it was a hut to experience one. There was a stove and a stack of wood. The wooden bunk was covered with splinters, the blankets riddled with holes. A single shelf held books, rolls of toilet paper and an old can of motor oil. Someone had scrawled on the wall, *Prepare for the end!* There were drawings all over the hut, and names with various nationalities underneath. These were from long ago, from a past when the world's myths still reigned. He had come from the newest period of nothingness, an emptiness not even legends reached. It was a land of hollow sounds without echo, where gods experimented on old childless men to see how much they could stomach.

Visiting Stonehenge as a boy, he'd seen messages carved into the rocks – daggers and stars, cryptic names of the dead and dying. In the hut, there was a cauldron filled with peacock feathers. Another showed the moat collapsed, the hut submerged. Someone had drawn a picture of a human head on the stove, cut in half and boiling over. Inside the head were seaweeds. A faded Norwegian government poster had been hung on the wall as a warning about polar bears. The bear in the photo was standing up on its hind legs, nostrils twitching. It seemed to stare at Manfred through its limitless black eyes. Manfred stared back and wondered if this was the way it would happen.

He tried out the bunk. It wasn't *too* hard. The paraffin lamp on the stand worked fine. He scanned the books on the shelf – Lysenko's vernalisation studies of wheat seeds, cheap paperback novels in Dutch, English and German. Under the shelf, a dog-eared manual on hybridisation lay under a spade.

Manfred hugged his shoulders to stop himself from shivering. As the hour passed he closed his eyes and thought about the mounds behind the hut. When the next ship arrived, he'd be opened up and his intestines examined. Things long ago eaten: beef burgers, potatoes, chicken, bread, soybeans, pork belly, lettuce. Things more recently eaten: kelp.

Meditate, the captain said, be at peace. The entire question of existence: seaweeds. The totality of all human life: seaweeds. Seaweeds, and everything to do with seaweeds, including the consciousness of seaweeds. The double condition of an insignificance that doesn't *want* to be, not at all, and the collective problem of everyone's double consciousness, leading to multiple conditions of awareness, the awareness of awareness of awareness, not to mention dreams and drugs that change sense-perceptions, if only to exist without this awareness. To be intelligent, it seemed, meant a perpetual desire for ignorance in the face of one's destruction. He could see the civilisations passing before him in sheets of flame and hot gusts of death. Food committees, rations, gangs and warlords, air filled with smoke all day and night. Eventually, every human being dead – even the strongest. Underneath them all, seaweeds.

He opened his eyes. Where was that peace the captain mentioned? Didn't it require a purpose? He had felt summoned here to the Arctic. Being summoned, though – it required an active agent doing the summoning, and where in the snow and ice could this be? He took out his loupe and turned to Rosy. Under the gossamer sheet, the last specimen winked. Maybe the only solution was to take into your body a living soul, and thereby give birth to its future. Rosy didn't disagree. On the other hand, the algae looked too weak to say anything. Manfred wanted to eat it – but to do so meant deciding once and for all to stay, to offer up his body as a vessel and prepare for the end.

He stood at the window. He glanced compulsively from his flag in the corner to the ship in the bay. The light was fading. The hour was nearly up.

He could see even further into the future from where he stood on the windswept verge. The Earth, a red hot ball with nothing left of merit – just embers. He saw it. He smelled and tasted it. The Great Seaweed Brain would be the last to rise up out of the oceans, resurrected in colour like a reverse rainbow, a cascade from the depths below in which everything living was dark and denuded and covered with cinders. The last algae would survive until they had nothing left to eat. Then only bacteria would remain, searching for a new host.

He glanced at the press. He took out his loupe and tweezers and collected the last specimen of Rosy Dew Drops.

'Are you sure it's time?'

It sounded like Rosy's voice. It sounded like his own. This fact so unnerved him that he put the specimen back. He returned to the window, where his rapid breath made white clouds on the window pane. The islands were coming. At the entrance to the bay, from the direction of the ocean, dark shapes were advancing quickly. They encircled the *Farolita* like ghosts.

Cold air crept under the door. Manfred checked his watch – one minute left. In the corner of the hut he picked up the flag. He had to warn them. There would be some indignity in a last-second surrender. But wouldn't it be worse, far worse, to die in the hut alone? He opened the door. The wind had picked up. He stepped out into the rocky moat, and suddenly he couldn't see in the icy biting wind. Over the snow-covered mountains, a thick fog had come rolling in across the bay.

Manfred waved the flag and cried out. In no time, the hut was enveloped in the white. The ice particles stung his eyes. As he waved the flag high overhead, his arms seized. He had been in that cold hut for only an hour, and already he could feel his body starting to freeze. The flag fell from his hands. He scratched among the polar bear bones as it flew across the snow. He crawled back to the place the door had been, now lost in a field of white. In the lowest part of the moat, he doubled over as more wind gusted over the water. He cried out again, but this time his voice was nothing. He tried to breathe slowly, to conserve energy. Out in the bay, the ship's engines roared. He could hear the groan of the anchor, the clogged propellers fighting to break free, and at last, the engines sputtering out.

There was a short silence, followed by screams.

The clouds parted, and Manfred sat up in the moat. The ship wasn't moving. The islands of kelp were on her, the seaweeds gathering for a great feast. As the *Farolita* took on water the lifeboats were lowered – but these, too, were quickly overcome. He saw it all from the moat, the passengers waving and shouting to him for help. Their faint voices eventually disappeared as if they'd never been.

Soon the prow of the *Farolita* was pointing straight at the sky. The hull was completely covered by kelp, bursting into the portholes and sucking the ship down into a dark churning whirlpool. A moment later she was gone.

Manfred was panting so quickly he couldn't breathe. There was a stillness on the water, and he knew the real business lay below. He could imagine it happening, down within the cabins – the last drowning gasps, the mouths filling. The captain clutching his cat; Elke activating the emergency beacon in the flooding wheelhouse; Anna, Karl, and the guides twisting among the fronds.

Later, the vertical trunks of kelp would find holdfasts in the seabed. They would cover their buried prey in a death embrace, then rise fit and strong in thick columns.

For six days Manfred rationed the seaweeds in the bucket. He kept a record of what he ate, just as he'd agreed. Each morning he put on his boots, wrapped himself up and trudged down to check the shore. He kept a fire going in the stove. He melted snow for drinking. And he kept a close eye on his dwindling stack of wood.

The kelp islands waited offshore like enemy ships. They seemed to be debating whether or not he was worth it.

When the weather cleared, Manfred gathered his strength to climb the hill behind the moat. He reached a ridge where there was a row of rocky tombs, each with a round metal cap where they removed samples. There weren't any names. There wasn't even a plaque. It was just a place for extraction, like drilling into a glacier for ice cores. He climbed back down in a hurry. He went into the hut and curled up on his bunk. The hill of tombs had been depressing, of course, but it was only his ego that had been offended at the lack of proper recognition. He thought of the recently discovered oarweed that had lain dormant for sixteen thousand years, a refugee from the last ice age, only to surface in Scotland and recolonise.

He went to sleep and had a pleasant dream of the book launch for the second edition – Mary-Margaret at the podium, Nora in the front row with Rosy on her lap.

'This book is dedicated to a brave volunteer who lies in the high Arctic like an egg between two worlds. In his gut we recently found a microscopic algae called Rosy Dew Drops. This rare seaweed is fully metabolised and preserved in the kelp substrate of his stomach lining, a living ecosystem vital for modelling future colonisation.'

The next morning, he could see them coming from the window. They had arrived at the shore like memories from the past.

They were seaweeds. All of them were tough, hardy browns. They lapped in the waves and carried nutrients of the freshly dead.

Manfred made his way down to the shore. He bundled them in his arms and dragged them back to the hut. The Knotted Wrack fronds were leathery with hard round bladders. They looked like a cat-o'-nine-tails. He lay them out to dry beside the stove. Knotted Wrack for breakfast, lunch and dinner. How long could he survive on them? Six days, maybe seven?

That night, the weather worsened. Snow without pause, and pack ice approaching. He melted snow for drinking water. When the storm subsided, there was a much cleaner smell in the air. He left the hut to search the shore. The islands were gone, the horizon clear. Along the rocks he found a frozen pair of men's trousers with a piece of chewing gum in the pocket. In the water bobbed one of the captain's jars, still sealed, with a dead beetle inside. The seaweeds had taken what they wanted and sent him the rest. They had eaten their own – the captain and his crew, the agents of dulse, carrageenan, spirulina and kelp.

He took their gifts back to the hut. He ate the gum together with the beetle. It wouldn't be long before he found jellyfish in the shallow water. He would be so hungry, he'd scoop them into his hands and eat them whole. Then auks and skua dive-bombing – maybe he'd capture one, drink blood from its neck. A familiar story. A man lives a while, until the day something goes wrong.

He ran out of wood. The window froze shut, and the real cold came. All day he watched the shoreline for visitors, but there was nothing except rocks and ice.

He burned the wooden bunk. He burned *The Future of British Seaweeds* and all the paperbacks. Shivering, bent over with cramps, he considered the walls of the hut. Finally, he opened the press one last time. He had eaten all the others. He placed the last specimen on his tongue, felt a quick surge of heat down to his toes, and swallowed.

It was night when he went down to the edge of the moat. He could feel Rosy burrowing into the dying warmth of his innards. He was breathing fast and couldn't stop. It was because the heavens were so brightly arranged with constellations. It was because of the bridge across the sky. He walked toward the water. The seaweeds would find him soon enough, somewhere between the hut and the shallows. They would use him for a nest. They would float him out like a raft of plastic containers and crusty bottle caps.

It was all in Manfred's head like a vision. He must have fallen, he was too cold to get up from where he collapsed for good. He opened his eyes and saw a polar bear leaning over him, nostrils twitching.

Later, he heard an engine, and the sound of oars.

A hand grasped his shoulder and turned him around. When he looked up, he saw Nora. Behind her, a survey ship waited in the bay. 'I'm already gone,' he told her, his voice only a whisper.

He was so very cold. He had been prepared for his burial with rose petals placed over his eyes in the lengthening light.

Nora came closer. She opened her coat, took his hands and brought them to her round warm belly. Slowly, a fire entered his legs. He could see himself in the future, walking with their child in a garden of wildflowers, and he gathered the strength to stand.

ACKNOWLEDGEMENTS

This novel was greatly enhanced by encouragement and critical feedback from the following friends: Ian Breckon, Andy Brown, Juliet Brodie, Paul Bryers, Jen Dickinson, Richard Francis, Lee Froehlich, Jim Kelly, Ben Lyle, Kylie Fitzpatrick, Adrian Markle, Jill Schoolman, Eleanor Walsh and many seaweed enthusiasts I pestered over the years. Thank you, Aaron T. O'Connor of the Arctic Circle Residency and my shipmates on the *Antigua*. Deep thanks to the true believers: agent Chris Combemale, editor Moira Forsyth and the entire staff at Sandstone Press.

I am most grateful for the unparalleled vision of Leslie Maslow, who embraced this odd hybrid soon after its birth and lovingly nurtured it into watery maturity.

www.sandstonepress.com

Subscribe to our weekly newsletter for events information, author news, paperback and e-book deals, and the occasional photo of authors' pets!
bit.ly/SandstonePress

facebook.com/SandstonePress/

@SandstonePress